The Salt-Stained Book

b

Blet
)1908)

MK C
1908

wpc
908

"It really is a wonderful book. It's also a fantastic tribute to Arthur Ransome and I'm sure he would have loved it ... After your book I'm going back to reread his ... It's terrific."

Jan Needle

(author of *My Mate Shofiq and A Fine Boy For Killing*)

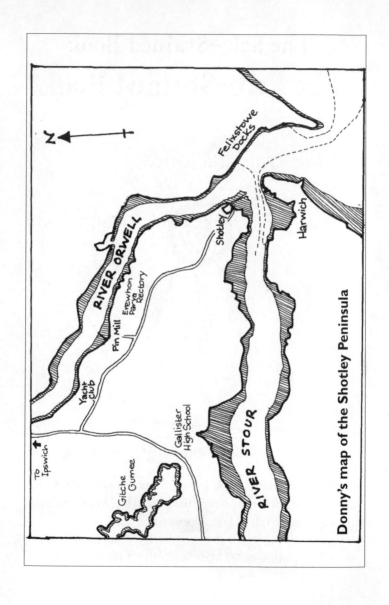

Donny's map of the Shotley Peninsula

The Salt-Stained Book

Julia Jones

VOLUME ONE
OF THE *Strong Winds* TRILOGY

GOLDEN DUCK

First published in 2011 by Golden Duck (UK) Ltd.,
Sokens,
Green Street,
Pleshey, near Chelmsford,
Essex.
CM3 1HT
http://www.golden-duck.co.uk

ISBN 978-1-899262-04-5

Design by Roger Davies
rogerdaviesdesign@btinternet.com

Printed and bound in the UK
by the MPG Books Group, Bodmin and King's Lynn.

Contents

This book is dedicated to Bertie, its first reader

and to all who sail in *Peter Duck*.

HMS Sparrow, the Barents Sea, February 17th 1945

The ship he was watching disintegrated before his eyes. He couldn't breathe. Refusing to believe what he saw. Then, seconds later, the explosion. Muffled. Horribly real. Gut-punching. A U-boat so close … a torpedo … how could … ?

Dark, thick, obliterating smoke.

"All hands!" he shouted. "To your stations! Starboard ninety degrees. Full ahead and man the boats!"

They raced to the spot but there was nothing. Nothing left of his brother's ship but a few pieces of driftwood and the reek of oil. His seaboats were launched within minutes. Their crews trained, intent, methodical. All eyes searching for survivors.

But there was little hope. No one could live long in these icy waters and the weather was worsening. Already the swell was increasing, lifting then hiding each boat. The wind was freshening fast. He could see the white streaks of driven foam that foretold a gale. He knew he should recall his men and move on. It was his duty.

He gave the order. Then he handed over command and left the bridge to meet the returning boats. They had brought no one with them alive. The storm spread like a bruise across the sky as the last of the seaboats was winched on deck. He stared at his men as if they had become strangers: his ship no longer his.

Then, receding into the emptiness behind them, he saw a white face between the tossing waves. An arm flung up.

"Ned!" he shouted. "Ned! Hang on, old chap, I'm coming!"

He was over the side before they could stop him. Forgetting, in that instant, everything except the younger brother who he loved.

He was lost at once in the churning wake of his own ship's propellers.

There was nothing they could salvage. Only the second lieutenant, standing by, noticed the slim blue book that fell from his captain's pocket as he made that suicidal plunge. It lay open on the deck for a moment, pages whipping in the arctic wind. A scattering of spray wet it like salt tears; then a bigger gout of water reared up over the metal bulwark and splashed heavily down on the abandoned volume. It was sodden now and lifeless. In another moment it would be washed out through the scuppers and follow its owner to the deep.

The second lieutenant stepped forward and put the soaking book safely in his duffle pocket. The captain must have next-of-kin. Perhaps not parents but he thought he'd heard him mention sisters…

Both brothers lost.

Poor girls. They would be desolate. What comfort could it be if he sent back a single, salt-stained, book? Perhaps he'd keep it as his own memento; put it in the club library if this war ever ended.

The ship steadied on her course. The throbbing rhythm of her engines was restored, her radar swept the bleak horizon, sonar plumbed the killer depths.

Greg Palmer had been a good captain. His book belonged to seafarers.

CHAPTER ONE

Book Stopped

Colchester, Essex, September, 2006

When Skye Walker thought that they were close to meeting Donny's Great Aunt Ellen, she did a very odd thing. She drove them to a town and bought a book.

In many families this would not have been unusual. Mothers of thirteen-year-olds quite often drive into towns and it's not unknown for them to visit bookshops together —as well as buying clothes, sports equipment and electronic games. But for Skye and Donny this was a first time and it looked likely to be their last.

Skye's instincts warned them that there could be trouble but she'd got it coming from the wrong direction.

"Great Aunt Ellen," she had signed. "From the land of the Dakotahs."

Donny had nodded. They both felt wary of this new relation.

"Why should we buy a book?" he signed back. They were stamping out the remains of their small campfire and concealing all traces of the night they'd spent down an empty farm track in the last stages of their journey south.

"Nokomis said that it would help you."

If that's what Granny had said, that was okay by him.

So far in Donny's life, he'd always lived with Skye and Granny. Their rented bungalow on the outskirts of Leeds had been their safe place, their private world. They had their own language – sign language – told their own stories, looked after each other. Donny went to school of course and did all the normal things – but normal at school and normal at home were different normals. They didn't usually mix.

The private world was mainly for Skye, his mum. She was the one who used the special names. In the normal world Granny's name was Edith, not Nokomis.

Edith Walker and Ellen Walker. Sisters. That should have been all right. Except Donny and Skye didn't know anything about Ellen. Hardly even that she existed until now.

Granny was dead. She had a stroke and lay helpless; then she had another and was gone. After that it was like the fence had fallen down. Social Services and Learning Services and Health Services and Welfare Rights Advisers and Mental Health Officers and Housing Officers and Disability Living Consultants began coming in one after another to make Assessments of him and Skye. Mostly Skye. They asked the same questions time and again and didn't seem to listen to the answers.

Quite often these unwanted visitors didn't even bring a signer when they came to Assess Skye. This bewildered Donny. Surely they must have known that his mother had been profoundly deaf from birth and was so dyslexic as to have almost no idea of written language. Else why had they come?

They had Concerns, they said.

Granny, who organised everything, hadn't quite organised

their survival without her. Death had been too quick.

The first thing that had happened was a man they didn't know came and searched Granny's room. He was a small man in a suit and a dark tie. He showed them some sort of ID but Donny wasn't really clear who he was. He said it was routine. To ascertain the Last Wishes. Maybe he was an undertaker or a lawyer or something. They didn't see him again so Donny couldn't ask him what he'd thought the Last Wishes were.

It was the small man who had found the letter in Granny's drawer. It was right on the top, very tidy and was addressed to her only surviving relative, her sister, Miss Ellen Walker, Shanghai, People's Republic of China. It could have been there for a while, Donny didn't know, but it was ready stamped and licked shut. The small man said he'd take it. He'd post it for them. No need to worry.

Donny was suddenly certain that he didn't want this man to have Granny's letter. He grabbed it back from him quite rudely and ran out of the house and down to the corner of the street where there was a post box. He shoved it in and as he turned to walk home again he saw the post van pulling up to make the afternoon collection.

The small man had left by the time he returned. Granny's address book and her most recent diary had left too.

"Who is Great Aunt Ellen?" he'd asked Skye later.

But Skye's signing had gone wobbly.

"Pirate," he thought she said. Or was it fighter? She'd started counting complicated patterns on her worry beads and rocking slightly. It had been a horrible day and they were both tired and sad. So Donny had put his arms around her and hugged her tight and soon she hugged him back.

Donny didn't ask any more questions about Great Aunt Ellen. He just made sure that he was up and ready for the postman every morning. Skye couldn't read but he could.

The letter must have taken ages getting to Shanghai because they'd had Granny's first and second funerals by the time Great Aunt Ellen's answer came. Maybe the stamps had been wrong.

The first funeral hadn't been much good. It was in the crematorium and there was only him and Skye and a couple of neighbours. And a social worker. Donny supposed one of them must have organised it. The man giving the talk didn't seem to know anything at all about Granny. He even said she'd 'taken on' Skye as if she was some heavy burden rather than a beloved daughter. Donny'd been signing the service to his mother but he skipped that bit.

Skye hadn't looked very interested anyway. In the first weeks after Granny died she'd spent a long time working on a piece of wood, which she'd said was called a grave-post. It was brightly coloured and carved in ways that were particular to Granny. Donny thought it was beautiful. He expected they would keep it for ever.

When Skye had finished she left the grave-post one last night and a day in Granny's room with all Granny's clothes and hairbrushes and things. Then she took it out into the garden and burned it.

As the sparks flew up into the twilight, Skye signed to him that they were letting Granny go and all her problems and her pain and they would keep their happy memories. What problems? What pain? Donny wondered briefly. Skye stretched her arms upward in farewell; the paint blistered and flared. The edges of the flame burned black.

Granny's clothes and shoes and brushes and bed-sheets went into a bin liner and Donny never saw them again.

It was a pity they couldn't get rid of the visitors so easily. Then they'd have got on okay. Donny thought so anyway. He went to school as usual and did the shopping while Skye washed and wove, baked flat bread and cooked aromatic meals. He tried asking if there was paperwork that they ought to do. He thought he needed to understand Skye's money and how they paid the rent and things. But of course the visitors told him not to worry which wasn't any help at all.

Then he very nearly missed getting Great Aunt Ellen's telegram because he hadn't expected it to come by messenger and he was so fed up answering the door to people with clipboards and zipped cases.

He read the telegram to Skye (or part of it) and they left. As soon as the school term ended Skye packed their food and clothes, and the few things they cared about, into the camper van that Granny had used for holidays.

"Going to wait for Aunt Ellen," she'd signed. "Better a Dakotah than these frowny-faces. You tell me where."

They could have walked it faster. It took them all of August to come south, travelling a few miles most days and stopping when they liked somewhere. They used country roads and stayed in woods and on the edges of fields. Skye drove (very slowly) and Donny navigated. People were usually surprised that Skye could drive at all. Granny had taught her years ago when they'd been staying on a big campsite for their summer holiday. Then she'd gone to some special tribunal to get her a licence. Granny had been like that: always ready to fight for Skye.

By the time they got near the end of their journey it was September and Donny should have been back at school. That was when Skye signed that they needed to go into a town. A town with big shops: a town where they could buy a book.

"You don't ask much, do you, mum," he didn't say. He could see from the road map that they were quite near a place called Colchester which looked big enough to have a bookshop but he hadn't got a town plan and there'd be pedestrian areas and one-way systems. How was he going to get them in there? He couldn't sign to Skye while she was driving because she had to watch the road. They'd get lost and she might panic.

In the end he decided that they should go into the first car park they found and walk the rest. Symbols were okay so he drew her a white P in a blue background and showed it to her before they left. It got them into the car park anyway. They might have used some sort of service entrance by mistake but they'd done it. They'd parked the van and bought their ticket and now they were in the bookshop.

"We'd like a book with children and an island please," Donny asked. "And a lake. And boats."

Skye seemed to know exactly what they'd come for. She wanted pirates and treasure as well. A green parrot. All of them, in one book. Quickly.

"No," he said, "I don't know what it's called. Or who wrote it."

Skye was getting excited and Donny was finding it increasingly hard to keep up with her and to interpret her sign language for the bookshop staff.

"No, we haven't seen it on TV. We haven't actually got a TV. And I don't think it can be a new book because my Granny told her about it. And she's dead."

This was embarrassing. A crowd was beginning to gather as if they thought this was performance art – like juggling in the street or pretending to be a statue. People did often stare at Skye. Mainly Donny didn't take any notice but today it was getting to him. Okay, Skye was … unusual-looking. She was tall and big with a coppery skin and long dark hair which she plaited with bright ribbons. She wore tie-die kaftans and beaded skirts, which she made herself, plus lace-up shoes, a man-size anorak and sensible woolly jerseys.

The anorak and jerseys were Granny's choice. Old Nokomis (a.k.a. Miss Edith Walker) had been a small neat woman obsessed with keeping people warm. When Donny was younger she'd regularly sent him to school wearing two vests and two jerseys and two pairs of socks. It was as if she couldn't quite believe that schools had central heating.

Dear Granny … Donny missed her every single day. But he did sometimes wish that she and Skye could have harmonised their taste in clothes.

"That's sick! I know what she wants!"

One of the shop assistants – a girl dressed as a Goth with a white face, black clothes and studs – gave a sudden, delighted smile and turned purposefully to the children's section.

"She wants *Swallows and Amazons*!"

The book she pulled out was a bulky beige and purple paperback, with some crudely drawn children on a turquoise sea. Skye looked uncertain. Then the girl opened the front cover and showed her more pictures and a map of a lake. There were drawings all through the book. Skye's face brightened. She seemed hugely relieved.

"Granny's secret book," she signed to Donny. "For you. Explains."

He paid the assistant gladly though it took almost all the rest of their money. That didn't matter: they'd still got lots of tinned food on the van and they wouldn't need to buy much more petrol now. Donny knew that he could always understand his mother when she was calm and they had time. She would tell him later what it was that Granny had wanted this *Swallows and Amazons* book to explain. What the secret was.

As it turned out there wasn't a later. They took a wrong turn in the car park and the camper van got stuck under a height bar. Then a queue built up and people began hooting and sticking their heads out of their windows and shouting. The car park manager was called and a breakdown van.

Skye couldn't hear the shouting but she knew they were trapped. Like a squall coming out of sunshine she had the worst panic attack she'd had for years. She clutched the steering wheel until her knuckles showed white and she screamed.

Then someone called the police and the police noticed that

the van's tax disc was out of date and Donny didn't know about its insurance or its MOT or where Skye kept her driving licence. He knew she had one but he wasn't sure that they believed him.

All the while Skye was screaming. And there was nothing he could do to help.

In the end he sat down in despair and cried as he hadn't cried for years for himself and for her and for dear dead Granny, who would certainly have checked the tax and insurance before they went on holiday and would have known where all the papers were. Granny would have seen in advance that the van wasn't going to make it out beneath the bar. He should have seen it. He was useless. How long before Great Aunt Ellen would get here and take over all this responsibility?

Plenty of people did get there. A fire engine arrived and an ambulance, then a second police vehicle. Two of the firemen took down the height bar; then a truck arrived and hooked up the camper van to winch it onto a low trailer.

"Where are you doing with our van?" Donny asked but they didn't answer him. "You can't just take it, it's got all our stuff in it!" he shouted.

"You'll have to speak to them about that," said the truck driver jerking his thumb towards the policemen who were talking into their radios. Then he swung himself up into his cab and towed the van away.

A paramedic in a fluorescent jacket tried to offer Skye a sedative. She let go the steering wheel and knocked it from his hand. She got out, looking wildly round for Donny. Quick as anything, as if they'd been waiting for the chance, they put some sort of jacket on her, strapped her to a stretcher and gave her an injection.

Then the stretcher was inside the ambulance and there was a policewoman standing next to Donny telling him not to worry and his mum would be all right now.

"Where are they taking her? I need to go with her."

"Not in the ambulance, dear. You're too young. They're taking her to the hospital and she'll have a nice sleep."

"I'm thirteen. I need to be there. For when she wakes up."

"No. Not just now. We'll take you home and find someone to look after you. Where's your dad today?"

"I don't have a dad." He'd never had a dad. He didn't know anything about his dad at all. Dads didn't feature. Skye hadn't had one either.

The policewoman didn't look especially surprised.

"Well, there must be somebody. Don't you have any other relations? Friends? A neighbour maybe who can keep an eye on you? Where do you live? We'll run you home and I'll stay while you get in touch with someone."

"No. We don't live near here at all. We've come from Leeds. We're planning to meet my Great Aunt Ellen. I really do need to be with Skye. She doesn't like hospitals. They frighten her."

"Skye?"

"My mum. It's difficult for her to understand people because she's deaf. I've learned signing. I can explain."

"They're used to deaf people in hospitals, dear. She's in the best place. It's you we've got to worry about. Where are you meeting Auntie? Can I give her a ring and tell her we're bringing you round to her house? What's Auntie's number?"

"No!" Donny was feeling desperate. "She's not here yet. We're meeting her at a place called Shotley. We were going to wait for her. I need to be with Skye."

"Never mind Mum. Let's just think about Auntie. Shotley's not too far away. I'm sure she won't mind coming a little early if we let her know that Mum's been taken ill. Does she have a mobile?"

"NO! She's coming from China. In a ship … I think …"

The policewoman was looking disapproving now. Oh why did Great Aunt Ellen have to be so awkward? Why couldn't she have been like Granny?

But it was no good thinking like that. He needed to sound confident, even if he wasn't. He looked at the policewoman and tried to smile.

"We'll be quite alright waiting in the van. Skye likes the van. We've had lots of holidays in it before."

"With proper tax and insurance I hope. No, young man, if your mother's ill and there's no one else in the area to look after you, I'm afraid you've going to have to come back to the station with me. We need to have a little chat with the Child Protection Unit."

CHAPTER TWO

Ambushed

Tuesday, September 12th

It was a good thing, thought Donny, that no one had asked to see the actual message they'd received from Great Aunt Ellen. He hadn't even told Skye exactly what it said:

> YOUR SIGNAL RECEIVED AND UNDERSTOOD. STRONG WINDS CRATED BUT NO BILL OF LADING YET. PLAN TO TRAVEL STEERAGE. EXPECT DESTINATION FELIXSTOWE. ETA LATE SEPTEMBER. RENDEZVOUS SHOTLEY. NO LANDLUBBERS. ELLEN.

It was all very well Great Aunt Ellen saying that she'd understood whatever Granny had written. But the only bits of her message that Donny had got his head round were that she was planning to arrive sometime late in September at some place called Felixstowe and would meet them at some other place called Shotley.

When he'd looked it up on the Great Britain road map, Shotley seemed like a pretty small town. It was down in the East of England across a river from Felixstowe, which was a port. So that part of the telegram was okay and that was what he'd read to his mother. The rest was not so obvious at all.

Once they'd started their long journey south, he had asked Skye, casually, whether she knew anything about this 'Strong

Winds' but she'd shaken her head and hadn't answered for a while.

Later she reminded him of the four winds in their favourite poem. Granny had had a small collection of Everyman classics which she had read and signed to him and Skye during their long peaceful evenings together. The collection was small because Granny hated clutter: if there was a book they didn't want to read again she got rid of it. If they liked it they read it again. Often. She used the library as well and Donny got books from school.

The book that had somehow slipped off Granny's shelf and into all their lives had been Henry Wadsworth Longfellow's *Hiawatha*. And that had started with winds.

The West Wind, mighty Mudjekeewis, had been Hiawatha's absent father. He was cunning and potentially treacherous as well as invincible, not the sort of dad who you'd want to take along to parents' evening or spend a Sunday watching cricket. The South Wind was fat and lazy and the East Wind was basically okay. The wind that Granny had really hated, in life more than in the story, was the strong North Wind, fierce Kabibonokka. How she had locked the windows and drawn thick curtains when wild gales from the north came howling over the Leeds housetops. She'd be tense and somehow far away. You couldn't talk to her then.

But you couldn't put winds in a crate. 'Strong Winds' sounded more like a thing – or things? Maybe it was a piece of art. Something valuable that she didn't want to leave behind. He'd find out eventually, he supposed. Strong Winds was (or were) the least of his worries. He didn't know what a 'bill of lading' was or an 'ETA', and the bit about 'no landlubbers' was scary. Donny had a bad feeling that he and Skye were definitely landlubbers – whatever that meant. Yet Great Aunt Ellen was their only hope if they were going to escape the welfare people.

If …

Once the ambulance had gone, the policewoman took him to the Colchester HQ and called a duty social worker. Her first suggestion was that Donny should be sent straight back home to Yorkshire. By taxi if necessary.

It turned out, however, that he didn't have a home in Yorkshire any more. Granny's death and their summer's travelling had put them behind with the rent. The landlord had repossessed the bungalow and had already let it to someone else.

"Great Aunt Ellen'll be here soon," said Donny. He needed to sound certain even if he wasn't.

Then there was talk of finding temporary bed-and-breakfast accommodation for the two of them, if Skye was well enough.

"That'd be good," Donny agreed, "except we haven't got much money. There's still plenty of food in the van. We'll be quite alright if we can just park it somewhere near Shotley and wait."

But the van had been seized – that was the technical term. It meant it had been taken off to some dump somewhere and they'd have to pay to get it back or it would be scrapped. And, as Skye's money had pretty well run out even before they'd bought that book …

The social worker phoned the hospital administrator who

put her through to a ward sister who said that Skye seemed muddled and unresponsive. She hadn't properly come round from the sedation.

"I ought to be there," said Donny. "She's my mum. She needs me."

But then, fatally, someone from Leeds phoned to say they had Concerns about Skye's ability to care for Donny. They quoted their Assessments.

And Donny wasn't going to be allowed to care for Skye because it wasn't long before the hospital phoned again to say they'd had a Conference and decided to transfer Skye to a mental ward in a different town where she could have tests and be given more sedatives. Four times a day if necessary.

Donny felt like he was in a nightmare. How could he make them understand?

And it got worse.

No mum, no granny, no address or phone number for Great Aunt Ellen. That meant Donny was officially At Risk. The policewoman told him that they'd applied for an emergency order so he could be Looked After. She seemed to think that she was doing something helpful.

"We need to know that you're quite safe until Auntie comes. Then we'll talk to her and find out what her plans are."

"But she told us to meet her at Shotley!"

Great Aunt Ellen hadn't sounded that enthusiastic about having them. Especially if they were landlubbers. If they weren't waiting at Shotley when she arrived she'd probably turn round and go straight back to China. Wasn't there anything he could say?

Two more people came into the room just then. They made everything feel squashed and smelly. The man was wearing a policeman's cap which he didn't take off: the woman had a hard face and a frilly blouse.

The policewoman and the social worker stood up and offered them their seats. No-one said why they were there. Or if they did, Donny didn't get it. This man should be in the Guinness world records. He'd had to turn sideways to get through the door.

"You can drop that story," said the man to Donny. "Port of Felixstowe's where your alleged great aunt claims that she's arriving. Shotley's a blind. There's no *legal* passenger traffic from Shanghai to Shotley – and very little to Port of Felixstowe. I've a Special Role in Port of Felixstowe – checking for *il*-legals. We'll be on the lookout for your alleged great aunt. There's no chance she'll slip past us."

Huh? Even though they'd been treating him like he was totally pathetic, the policewoman and the social worker had obviously been trying to sound nice. This man was rude and angry straightaway.

"My Great Aunt Ellen's not illegal," he said. "And she's not alleged either. Her name's Miss Ellen Walker. She's my granny's sister and the only reason I've never met her is that she's been living in Shanghai and we've been living in Leeds."

"That's quite enough from you." The policeman jabbed at the table with his pudgy forefinger. Donny couldn't help staring. What was his problem? "The duty officer ran a computer check on your alleged great aunt as soon as you came in. We don't spend public money having kids looked after if there's family available. He found no trace of your Miss Ellen Walker – as you call her …"

"That's because it's her name."

The policeman stood up again and moved very close. He smelled sweaty.

"Mind your manners, young man. We've done the checks. She hasn't shown up. Port of Felixstowe's for container traffic only – as I'm quite sure you know – and none of the shipping companies have any Miss Ellen Walker being registered to travel. Passenger or crew member." He leaned even closer blocking out the rest of the room. "She's got no UK passport, no tax records, no medical card. There's been no visa application and you've given us no contact details. Your next of kin are Miss Edith Walker, deceased and Ms Skye Walker … incapable. There's no father prepared to put his name to your birth certificate and, as far as I'm concerned, at this moment in time, your great aunt doesn't exist. Not *legally*."

He sat down again, buttocks ballooning over the edges of his chair. He planted both legs wide apart, put his hands on his massive thighs and leaned forward. He was watching Donny all the time out of piggy-sharp colourless eyes.

"I'm on your case as per procedure. Until we meet Miss Ellen Walker, and she satisfies us of her identity and her right of entry into this country, I'd like to formally advise you that I'll be keeping a very close watch indeed. On *you*."

No Great Aunt Ellen on a list? Perhaps she wasn't coming…

Donny took a deep breath and gulped down his panic. Great Aunt Ellen's message had been definite about that if nothing else. Rendezvous Shotley, she'd said.

Should he pull the paper out and show it to them? That would do it.

No. Not to this man. No way! Great Aunt Ellen was Granny's sister. There would be some good reason.

Then Skye's word 'pirate' popped into his mind.

"… and Aim going to make quaite sure you attend school while you're with us."

This was frilly blouse. Was she even weirder than the fat man? She was wearing a short leather skirt and the pointiest pair of shoes that Donny'd ever seen in his life. They were sort of snakeskin sandals with criss-cross thongs that went right up to her knees. After that there was so much bare leg that Donny had to look away.

The social worker had fetched her a cup of special herbal tea. No one else got one.

"Aim Denise Tune. Aim the Education Welfare Officer. Aim developing my role in a multi-authority context under the next government initiative."

Her waves of perfume came rolling in over the fat man's b.o. Donny started to feel a bit giddy. He wondered if he could ask someone to open a window. Probably not.

The way she said 'I'm' was amazing. It had a sort of special emphasis and came out as 'aim'. He guessed he was her target for today, getting riddled with government initiatives: Aim… FIRE!

"Aim talking to Suffolk even as we speak," she continued, drawing attention to her own remarkable powers. "Shotley's in Suffolk. We're in Essex. Health's going to keep the mother. But Aim sending him on as an example of co-operation. It shares the costs as well." She grinned toothily at the other adults. Then she turned to Donny and tried to look caring.

"You'll be available in Suffolk for your … Aunt to maike any appropriate application. You'll be kept very … Saife."

Donny could see that her smile was as phoney as the rest of her. "I think I should stay near my mum," he repeated.

"Your … mum's not well. You can have Contact when she's better. You're fortunate Ai've been able to find you a placement at such short notice. We don't have Yorkshire's budget!" Another smirk to the audience. "This is Sandra. She's your social worker. Ai'll be monitoring."

Wednesday, September 13th
That was probably Tuesday. Which meant that the next day was Wednesday and Donny was sitting on a school bus in Suffolk.

He'd been left in the room once the meeting was over, then put into a police car and driven to a tall, grey vicarage somewhere between Ipswich and Shotley. The vicar was called Wendy and she was his Primary Carer together with her husband who was called Gerald. They'd asked him whether he had any allergies or eating disorders and when he'd last been to the dentist. Then they'd given him some cold supper and shown him to his room.

To be fair it had been pretty late.

The room had been cold and empty. Donny hadn't brought anything with him. Except the book. He still had it – the ugly paperback that had caused all this trouble. He'd been holding it when they'd got stuck in the car park and unbelievably it had stuck with him all this time. Without him even noticing. He didn't feel that encouraged by it.

He'd helped Gerald to make up the narrow bed and Wendy had given him a pair of pyjamas that looked like they'd been left over from the parish jumble sale and some clean underwear for tomorrow. A glass of water and a toothbrush. The pjs were crumpled from being in a bin bag but the toothbrush was new: Gerald put its packet in a container marked 'plastics – misc'.

Then they'd said good night and left him on his own.

Donny was tired. Really tired. This had been the worst day of his life but he knew that there was no way he was going to manage to get to sleep. When he lay in the dark, even if he shut his eyes, he couldn't stop himself thinking of Skye. Would it be dark in the mental ward as well or were there dim lights and unfamiliar shadows and the huddled shapes of strangers?

He got out of bed and switched the light back on. Skye had said that this was Granny's book and it would explain. So far all it had done was get them in this mess. Some sort of secret? It sounded as if Granny had told Skye that she wanted him to have it. It must have been before she died. Why hadn't she got a copy of her own? That was pretty strange.

Swallows and Amazons? Skye loved swallows. She called them 'shaw-shaws'. She used to stand and watch them when they started gathering on the telephone lines before their long flight south. He needed to make sure she didn't miss them this year… So maybe he needed to give this book a try?

It wasn't at all what he'd expected. But then what had he

expected? How could a book which was obviously about kids a long time ago help him cope with this nightmare now? It was good though because the kids in the book had the same surname as him. They were called Walker too.

The kids in the book were on holiday. They had a father away in the navy somewhere and a mother who was so posh that she even had a nurse to look after her baby! The kids wanted to go sailing on a lake and camp on an island and the first chapters were all about them packing up to set off. Someone had lent them a boat. As if anyone would just lend a load of kids a boat!

The boat was called *Swallow*. Not a bird; a fourteen foot dinghy with a brown sail.

Donny caught his breath and shivered in the empty room. Not cold any more, tingly. Not lonely either. He could see that dinghy – *Swallow*. Even before he got to the picture. He ran his hand round her varnished gunwale. Smooth glossy wood and such a beautiful shape: generous and reassuring and yearning to set out on adventure.

He pummelled the thin pillow to make it a bit softer and snuggled down in the bed to read more. He felt an excitement he couldn't understand.

The older of the two boys in the book had his own name – John, John Walker – the name he'd been given when he was born. No one who knew Donny ever called him John. It had been 'Johnny' when he was a baby then, apparently, when he'd started talking, he couldn't say Js properly so he'd called himself 'Donny' and it had stuck. It was one of the words his mum could almost say, "Doh … doh."

Anyway … this John wasn't a bit like him. This John took things seriously. He was a real leader. His mum and dad trusted him to look after all the other children and their boat and everything.

Like no-one trusted Donny. How would Skye know that the fat policeman and the horrible woman were keeping him away from her? That he wanted to come. Wherever she was.

Donny got back into his story again quickly. He'd be hammering on the walls if not.

John-in-the-book was a really good sailor. So was his sister. It seemed like they all were. They stepped the mast and found cleats under thwarts. Then they pointed her bows into the wind and hauled away … boom, yard and sail; painter, forestay, sheets and halyards; blocks and sheaves; tiller and rudder. He didn't properly understand the words but the language was lovely. It was like words that he'd known before he knew any words at all. Magic words.

Donny found he was shaking slightly. Breathing a bit fast.

So he sat up in bed again. Looked round the bare room. There were no other books or pictures in here but the carers had left some plain scrap paper, a pencil and crayons.

Donny began to draw a diagram of how he thought John-in-the-book was fitting the dinghy equipment together. The words fell easily into their proper places. Then he read a bit more. They were ready to set sail.

Was that a baby crying? Donny lifted his head and listened for a moment. Yes, somewhere in the distance. In this bleak house. One of the carers had evidently got up to try and quiet it but the crying went on and on.

"Poor baby," thought Donny, as he and his crew slipped slowly out towards the mouth of the bay. Then they rounded the point and felt the steady light breeze behind them. Donny forgot the baby. He was asleep.

He'd like to have woken up in a boat. Or in a tent on an island. Or, best of all, back in the bungalow in Leeds with Skye and Granny and none of this happening at all.

But he didn't. He was in the same hard bed in the same bare room and the male carer, Gerald, was banging on the door telling him he had to get up and get ready for school. He'd supplied thin grey trousers and a white shirt that had obviously come out of the same bin bag as the pyjamas. At least Donny got to wear his own shoes.

Then there'd been breakfast and Wendy had dropped him at the school bus stop. She was hassling to go to some meeting and had a temporary bus pass he could use. Gerald gave him an old rucksack and a re-filled water bottle and asked whether he'd like a re-cycled tissue from the Greenworld box by the door. Donny hadn't bothered answering.

There'd been some other kids in the kitchen but they'd looked grumpy. Two boys, he thought, possibly a girl? That must have been the baby he'd heard in the night, sticky and a bit whiny in a plastic high chair.

There wasn't time to get to know any of them even if he'd wanted to. And none of the school kids said hi when he climbed on board the battered single-decker. He didn't care. Let them listen to their iPods or play games on their phones. He didn't want to say hi to them either.

It was actually a nice day – like it usually was when kids had to go back to school. These roads were quite narrow and the hedges were tall and leafy. Donny kept his face to the window as if he was doing a sponsored stare. There were trees and fields and not many houses. Not like home. It reminded him of all those little roads he and Skye had been driving down together.

Or the summer holidays that Granny used to take them on. The ones she said were adventures except he knew that she'd been planning them for weeks. Everything would be properly stowed and labelled and the van would be wax-polished and their tidy house left even tidier. And they'd be away to the hills or the moors or maybe a forest. She always hid the maps when they were travelling then brought them out once they'd arrived. It was a bit of a strange thing to do but he'd got used to it. It made a sort of space between their home life and the new world of their holiday.

Donny felt a sudden hotness around his eyes. He squeezed them tight shut for a moment and took deep breaths. Maybe he should have said yes to Gerald's tissue.

Nah. He could feel one corner of the *Swallows and Amazons* book in his rucksack digging into his back between his shirt and the seat. Granny's secret book. And he'd packed the crayons and pencil and the diagram he'd started, showing how the boat worked. They were his. They'd do.

CHAPTER THREE

By the Shores of Gitche Gumee

Wednesday, September 13th, morning

There were glimpses of water in the distance through the trees. Donny used his sleeve to rub the place where his breath had misted the window. It wasn't that clean but – so?

"You got a bus pass for that thing, Ribiero? Takes up way more space than a new Year Seven. They're such pathetic midgets."

Some boy was calling out from a few seats back. Probably at the person who'd sat down next to Donny. Someone lugging something big. He didn't bother looking round to see what they were like.

"Hey man," objected a warm, drawly voice – a girl's voice – "Will you give my cello some respect? The parentals commanded extra practice time or no trip to Weymouth this weekend."

"What's special about Weymouth, Ribiero – donkey rides?"

"I do so hate to disappoint. This weekend we have the *Laser* 4.7 championships at Weymouth. Are you impressed? No. But that's because you have no idea what I'm talking about. You probably think the *Laser* 4.7 championships means crawling around on your hands and knees in some redundant cinema playing paint ball with the lights out."

The boy didn't answer and there were a few uncertain

laughs. Donny didn't know what a *Laser* 4.7 was either but he wasn't going to ask. This girl next to him had attitude. Okay the boy had sounded hard but she was scary.

"Lighten up, Xanth. Loads of people here know that *Lasers* are sailing dinghies and there's different sail plans for the different categories. It's just no-one's as obsessed as you. Radials or 4.7s – they can get along without the knowledge."

This girl had the same warm voice but lighter. She sounded nice. He could feel the one next to him settle back in her seat.

"Little sis," he heard her say, "such people have sad, sad lives."

Donny carried on looking out of the window. He wondered how much longer this journey would take. Not that he wanted to get there. He felt tired, disorientated, incredibly nervous. He didn't need a new school. He needed to go see his mum.

The bus made an unexpected turn to the right. Donny's forehead bumped hard against the glass.

That was such an amazing sight! It was like the world had sunk. No more trees and hedges and lumpy fields; but wide, flat, shining water as far as Donny's eyes could see. For a few magical seconds it filled his view; blue-grey and glinting like a CD in the sun. Then, as the bus completed its turn and the horizon crowded back in, there was a pounding of wings, harsh cries and a skein of geese muscled their way upwards.

Those geese were 'wawa' – in Ojibwe language.

Forgetting everyone he stood up to watch them fly. Then, abruptly, he sat down again, twisting backwards to get a last glimpse of the lake or sea or whatever it was. He felt like he'd had a vision, straight from Skye's favourite poem.

"By the shores of Gitche Gumee!"

That was the first line. He was breathing a bit fast in his excitement. The book in the rucksack dug harder into his spine as he leaned back in his seat, squeezing his eyes shut for a moment to keep that image safe in his head.

Then he remembered where he was.

On a school bus. Behaving like a complete idiot.

He shrank down, praying no one had heard him.

"Gitche Gumee! In your dreams – !" said the girl with attitude next to him. "Gitche Gumee was one of the Great Lakes. We lived in Canada five years. You could drop the whole of this county into any one of them and it'd sink without a ripple. *That's* a reservoir. It stores water for people to flush their toilets and make cups of tea when it's half time in the footie. And if you can't sail properly you can rent some old *Topper* and blow about for a couple of hours on a Sunday afternoon."

Another rude person! Were they all hostile down here?

He turned to look at her. Reluctantly. She was tall, probably taller than him if they were standing up. Older too, he thought. Dark-skinned with a mass of springy black hair pulled into a short pony-tail. There was maybe a glint of amusement but Donny wasn't going to bet on it.

"Maggi and I think it's so totally *un*-cool."

She seemed to want him to take her on. But why?

He noticed that she had a cello in a scuffed wooden travelling case beside her and across the aisle sat another girl, very similar at first sight, except prettier. They both looked

35

stylish; their blazers were shapely, blouses snowy white and their school ties knotted fashionably low.

The second girl was looking across at him now.

Donny tried not to care that his grey trousers were a couple of inches too short and showed his shrunken fawn socks. He didn't have a tie or a blazer or PE kit yet. The social worker, Sandra, was going to meet him at school and see what else she could find in the lost property store.

"Xanth, I just cannot believe you sometimes! Do you not drink tea or go to the loo or even wash? I'm happy to say that I do. I *like* clean water. And people who live near lakes use them as reservoirs you know. Even in Canada."

They must be sisters. It looked as if the older one was about to speak but the pretty one carried on. "Your attitude totally sucks! Who persuaded Dad to buy us both wind-surfers last year so we could compete in the Tattingstone championships? And who was really gutted when she lost to that boy from Windermere? Do I see her sitting on this bus? I believe I do."

The older girl scowled. Then she laughed. "Oh okay. I admit. The reservoir does have its moments … about once in a thousand years. But wind-surfing's not sailing. I could have beaten him to a stranded jellyfish if we'd been down on the river in dinghies."

"Maybe he didn't need to go down the river. Maybe he was just really good at what he did. Maybe he loved his surfer like you love *Spray*."

Evidently this was going too far. "Take it down, little sis, a surfer is a plank. My *Spray* is a foam-flyer, a sea-arrow. She has beauty – she has soul!"

But the younger girl still hadn't finished setting her older sister straight. "And you were way out of order with this guy," she indicated Donny. "Dad told you to stop yelling at people the moment they say something you don't agree with. Who else in this bus has ever even heard of Gitche Gumee or read *Hiawatha*? Anyone at all?" She looked round but most of the other kids blanked her. "Of course they haven't, why should they? I think you should grovel."

The older girl looked at Donny as if she'd suddenly remembered he was human. "It's my big mouth again. I'm sorry for what I said, stranger."

She smiled and paused as if she was giving him room to speak. Her arrogant face softened into a beautiful smile, wide and warm and totally genuine. But he couldn't say anything. His brain was stunned. Too much had happened over the last twenty-four hours. It was like a knock-down and he was going to stay on the floor a while.

Anyway *Hiawatha* was for him and Skye. And Granny. The private world. It wasn't for sharing with some gabby girl on a Suffolk school bus.

"I shouldn't have spoken like that. It was mainly a wind-up but how could you know? It's your first day. You're just a dude. Don't let it get to you."

She paused again. Donny managed a sort of shrug. Then she held out her hand in a curiously formal manner, made awkward by the cramped seats of the bus.

"Hi," she said as if they were being introduced in some drawing-room. "I'm Xanthe Ribiero and this is my sister, Marguerite, usually known as Maggi. You might make the common mistake of thinking she's a bimbo but actually she's not. And I'm not as bad as I sound. Believe me. What's your name anyway?"

"Donny," he managed, and took her outstretched hand. It appeared he had no choice. "Donny Walker. Adults sometimes make jokes about some whisky called something like that but they're not particularly funny."

"Adults' jokes so often aren't," she agreed, shaking his hand firmly. "Welcome to Gallister High, Donny. If anyone else tries to give you grief tell them you're a friend of Xanthe's. Xanthe Ribiero, Year Eleven."

Her sister went back to chatting with her neighbour but Xanthe relapsed into silence until they arrived at the school. Then she got off the bus with him and showed him the way to the admin entrance.

"By the way," she said, "in case *Hiawatha's* some sort of family thing for you, I'll let you into one of ours. My family call this cello Long John – out of *Treasure Island*. You know? Partly because of it only having one leg but mainly because they say I'm like a wild parrot, squawking on its shoulder. You should hear me play – I am truly terrible!" She pulled a rueful face, then added, "You can blurt it on the bus if you want revenge but most of them won't get it. They don't usually do books. Not classics anyway."

*"By the shores of Gitche Gumee, by the shining Big Sea Water,
Stood the wigwam of Nokomis, daughter of the moon, Nokomis …"*

Donny was sitting in a sunny corner of the Gallister High School library. He'd got his bits of uniform, been given a swipe card for the catering system and allocated to a tutor group. Then apparently he needed to do some tests but there was nobody available to give him the papers.

The social worker, Sandra, had been okay but she was gone. The administrator was looking harassed. Her phone had been ringing all the time she had been filling in his forms for free school meals. Now it started again.

"Try the library," she said, "and ask someone to show you to the DT suite later. Your tutor's Mr McMullen. This is A block, by the way," she added, already reaching for the telephone. "Straight up those stairs. Ask the librarian for an induction session so you qualify for a resource card. Tell her you're new. Only temporary." She picked up the receiver and turned away from him, "Good morning, Gallister High School …"

He'd done the induction, got the card, then he'd found a place where he couldn't easily be seen and dozed off drawing 'wawa', a picture letter to send to Skye. If anyone would give him her address.

A colourless girl had approached while Donny slept. She picked up the drawing and studied it a while. Then she put it down and walked quietly away to use one of the computers. Her face showed nothing of her thoughts.

By the shores of Gitche Gumee … Donny shook himself properly awake. The dream had been good but he was hungry. He stood up to see whether there was a clock in the library.

Then he noticed what was out of the window.

It was real. Why shouldn't it be? The reservoir was maybe half a mile away across some fields. What a view!

Xanthe Ribiero had been right, though. Looked at from above it wasn't really big. Not like an inland sea. There was a concrete wall at the end nearest to him, with metal railings and a low square building that looked as if it might be a pumping station. And beyond the concrete wall, their coloured sails bright against the glitter of the water, he could see dinghies.

Sailing dinghies.

Sailing …

The pull was so strong that he stood up from his chair and was walking towards the door before he realised what he was doing. How could anyone ever settle to any work in here?

"If you've finished, you'll need your card to check out with," called the librarian. "We're monitoring student use-patterns this term."

"Oh … no … I haven't … quite …yet. I was … er … fetching something."

He crossed to the bag-park and took out *Swallows and Amazons*. Then he helped himself to some more paper from the recycling tray and went to sit down again. Obviously he couldn't simply walk out of the school, cross the fields and step into a boat. He had to think. He was on his own here, a castaway, marooned in un-charted waters.

Un-charted waters … okay … yes, Donny did know what he should do. What those kids in the book would have done. They'd get going on a map. He'd been looking at maps the whole summer as he navigated down from Leeds: why stop now? He needed to know where he was: where his mum was: where Great Aunt Ellen would arrive.

He got up again and asked the librarian for the school postcode and whether it was okay to print out a map of the local area from the Internet. She said it would be fine as long as he took only a single copy.

So he did that and then he began drawing a map of his own. He traced the outline from his Internet printout and promised himself that he'd add places as he discovered them. Even plotting the school bus route would make him feel less like a package.

There'd been distant glimpses of water before the reservoir. He'd keep a lookout, check if he could work out what they were. Plot them.

The printout showed that his school was in the middle of a triangle with rivers on two of its sides. They were the River Orwell and the River Stour and the point where they met was … Shotley!

So now he'd go navigate himself some lunch.

CHAPTER FOUR
An Aid to Buoyancy

Wednesday, September 13th, afternoon
The footpath led him to a little beach half-hidden in a bay. Trees ran almost to the water. He stood where grass met sand and he watched.

Bunking off from school had been ridiculously easy. With a good slab of lasagne inside him plus apple juice, muffins and custard he'd felt so mellow that he'd almost considered joining in some lessons for the afternoon. But his common sense told him that this was the time to go. When he was so new as to be practically invisible.

There'd been a bad moment when he thought he'd seen the snakey lady talking to the school administrator. Checking up on him? Donny didn't wait to find out. He dodged down a crowded corridor and discovered, by luck, that it took him to the DT block. So he had turned up to registration but his tutor, Mr McMullen, wasn't there. Some bored-looking woman was marking the register and she didn't have any tests for him to do. Or a timetable. She ticked his name on the bottom of her list and asked him if he knew where he was going next. "Yes I do, thank you," he'd said, not lying.

Donny took his shoes off. And those horrible fawn socks. Scrunched them up and shoved them in the rucksack. Felt the grass, slightly prickly and the sand, gritty between his toes. Rolled up the too-short trousers. Paddled, just a little way. Then stood still again, feeling the water, quite warm, lapping his bony ankles.

He'd never seen anything like this before. It was as if he'd walked into the book – *Swallows and Amazons*, Granny's book.

So it may have been. But Granny had never taken them anywhere like this. The longer Donny stood there, feeling the wind on his face, the ripples splashing more impatiently up towards his knees, the more certain he became that Granny had been holding out on them. On him and Skye. There had been no real water in their lives. Ever.

Okay, small streams in the forests where they'd parked their camper van and ornamental ponds in parks. Nothing like this. No lakes, no rivers, no seas. Nothing you could go sailing on.

If only you had a boat …

Donny was getting obsessed, watching the patterns that the wind made on the water. From in the library the surface had looked flat: close up, here, it was in constant motion. As the wavelets washed up against the sand, they were translucent, fringed with creamy foam; further out they seemed darker, more pointed. Then he saw cross-hatchings of smaller ripples, advancing in swifter lines, ruffling the shiny surface into greyer, more urgent textures. Cats-paws, he thought, unexpectedly finding a word he didn't know he knew.

It was like he was hypnotised. But stuff was coming up at him. From the depths of the water and the power of the wind.

Twice, people sailed into his tiny bay and beached their dinghies there. Donny watched intently. These dinghies were nothing like the *Swallow*. There were many more ropes, much thinner and more colourful; the boat was some sort of plastic, not wood, and all its fittings were smaller and more specialised. Yet he was sure that he understood them.

The second dinghy heeled sharply as it left the shelter of the bay. Instinctively Donny shifted his weight to balance her, gave a little on the sheet ... "I could sail!" he realised. "I don't have to read about it. I could do it!"

And in that moment he got a tang of salt, which couldn't have come from the reservoir, a buffet of a much fresher breeze, the exhilarating sensation of surging forward into a different element.

Donny stood at the reservoir edge for a long time. His feet got cold so he moved backwards and let the dry sand coat them. He knew he'd been given some sort of gift. Here, beside the water, his life had changed.

He forgot about school: about the foster home, the bullying policeman. He even, for a while, forgot about Skye. Slowly and painfully he began to understand what the stuff with the maps had meant when they went on holiday with Granny. She'd kept them hidden on the journeys so no-one could suggest a diversion. They would never take an unexpected turning to a beach or choose a route that ran along the coast.

Granny had hated water. He knew that now. Like she'd hated the North Wind, Kabibonokka. Maybe what they'd said at the funerals had been right: maybe Granny had had problems ... secrets, even.

Donny shivered. The sun had gone in and a stronger wind was whipping up the grey waves into dark excited crests.

There was only one dinghy near him now; a very small white dinghy with a fluorescent-striped sail. It appeared to be going nowhere – except backwards, sometimes, or sideways, quite often. The little boy on board had almost given up. He still had hold of the tiller and was pushing and pulling it randomly from side to side but he'd let go of his mainsheet, which was trailing in the water as the dinghy tossed and wobbled. His sail was shaking violently and the boom was crashing irritably across and back.

As the boat drifted towards Donny's beach, the child looked round, white-faced. The boom caught him a sharp clip on the side of his head and he fell into the bottom of the dinghy, crying.

Donny swung his rucksack on his back, heaved his trousers higher and waded in. If he'd had a conscious plan it was only to grab the dinghy and hold it steady, comforting the boy until someone else arrived. But as soon as he'd touched the hull he knew what he was really going to do.

"Want Mummy …"

"Do you know where she is?"

A shaky finger pointed to a distant landing.

Donny retrieved the dangling sheet, was over the side of the dinghy and in. "Then that's exactly where we're going."

The few hundred metres beat, in that tiny beginners' dinghy, was one of the great experiences of Donny's life. As he climbed in, he turned the dinghy's bows just a few degrees away from the wind's direction, pulled in the sheet, controlled the tiller and they were off.

He could do this. He knew he could.

The wind hit them as soon as they left the shelter of the bay and sent the dinghy scurrying. She was pulling like a puppy on a lead. Donny could feel the waves bumping the thin plastic underneath him.

"Stay still where you are and keep your head down," he told the boy. "We'll soon get back to your mum."

He wasn't worried. Not in the least. This was a very stable little boat, squarish and short – a bit like an animated margarine tub. Donny shifted his weight up onto the gunwale and grinned to himself with total delight.

Then he started thinking. He couldn't point the dinghy directly at the landing place. The wind was funnelling straight down from one end of the reservoir to the other. He could get there by tacking, zigzagging across the wind's direction. What he wasn't sure about in his head, because he couldn't believe he'd ever done it, was exactly how to make the turns at the point of each zigzag.

He'd watched other boats do it. Some made it look so easy, pivoting round in a single graceful manoeuvre, like a dance step, but he'd noticed others come to a total stop, sails flapping, unable to progress in either direction. He'd seen a couple of dinghies capsize, knocked right over.

Deep inside he knew he was going to be okay.

An orange rescue boat came close up-wind of them, the man and the woman inside shouting something that Donny couldn't hear. He supposed they were offering help. He freed his left hand by holding the sheet in his teeth for a moment and waved cheerily. Then he took hold of the sheet again and crouched down, staring ahead, making it obvious that he was carrying on.

The boy waved too and the powerboat veered away.

It didn't go far. Donny guessed that the occupants were sticking close to them, checking they were safe. That was good for his passenger's sake but it upped the pressure. He must make that turn soon. He must get it right.

"Ready about," he said, using a command that came without thinking. The boy ducked his head down further, though he didn't need to, and Donny pushed the tiller away so the boat swung eagerly into the wind. He waited just a second until he was certain she was coming right round, then he shifted his weight, swapped hands on the tiller and sheet – and they were away again.

He felt a surge of happiness.

"Okay?" he asked his passenger. The boy sniffed, nodded, sat up straighter and started looking ahead as intently as Donny himself.

Only three more tacks were needed to bring them to the landing place and they were all perfect.

A concrete slope ran out into the water so Donny aimed for that. He felt viscerally connected to this little tub. He knew without having to work it out that he could stop the dinghy's progress by turning her straight into the wind's eye and holding her there, but he mightn't have known exactly when to pull the daggerboard up if the child hadn't done it without being asked. Then, at the last moment, Donny realised that he could release one of the coloured strings and their rudder would bob up behind them.

Suddenly they were in smooth water and gliding onto the

concrete like a pair of pros.

"Thanks. You were great," said Donny to his crew.

The child probably didn't hear. He scrambled out over the side as soon as they grounded and stood holding the painter until someone came to push a trolley underneath the dinghy and wheel her up the slope and onto the land.

Donny climbed out after him. He stood to one side watching the boat being taken away, water dripping from her hull, her bright sail still flapping slightly.

He felt bereft. The solidness of the ground shocked him. His body felt heavy and strange.

The powerboat landed alongside and the child was being hugged by the woman passenger.

The powerboat driver came striding over. "Where the hell's your buoyancy aid?" he shouted. "Don't you know the single most important rule on this reservoir?"

Donny looked at him. He felt completely furious.

"There it is," he shouted back, pointing to the little white dinghy. "There's my buoyancy aid. I'd have said it was a pretty good one. You can keep your pumped-up sausage skins. Mine's a proper boat!"

Then he clenched his hands into fists and walked away. Past the man, and past the buildings, and along a gravelled track that soon turned into a road. He walked away from the water without once looking behind him.

CHAPTER FIVE

A Rescue Myth?

Wednesday, September 13th, evening
By the time Donny left the reservoir and turned onto the main road he was beginning to feel a bit shaky. He didn't normally speak like that to people – but people didn't normally speak like that to him. Except down here, now he was on his own, without Skye, without Granny.

His trousers had come unrolled when he climbed out of the dinghy so he stopped and wrung some of the water out of them. Then he put his shoes and socks back on and pulled out the Internet map. For a scary moment he couldn't remember where he was meant to be living. Then he calmed down and worked it out.

The map showed a four- or five-mile walk ahead. That wasn't so good. The school bus would have gone long ago. His watch had been left in the camper van with his other stuff but this felt more like early evening than late afternoon. He was going to get shouted at by Wendy and Gerald as well.

Afterwards, Donny realised that the only person who'd done any actual shouting was him. Again.

It had gone so well to start with. He'd not tramped even a mile when a car overtook him; slowed, stopped and reversed. The friendly faces of Xanthe and Maggi Ribiero appeared at the windows asking if he was okay and offering a lift.

"We don't do the school bus most afternoons because of clubs and training and stuff. So one of the parentals has to come and fetch us. This is Mum. Mum, this is Donny. He's new and he doesn't know anyone. But he does know *Hiawatha* so we've decided that he's cool. Can we give him a lift, please?"

Xanthe's mother smiled from the driving seat. She was smartly dressed in a vivid turquoise and orange suit, her glossy black hair swept up onto the top of her head and fixed with an elaborate comb. She was an exotic sight in a Suffolk country lane but she had the same warm smile as her daughters.

"Hi, Donny. I'm June. I'm pleased to meet you. Don't let my girls push you into doing anything you don't choose. If you're happy walking, you stay walking. If you'd like a lift we'll gladly give you one."

Would he?! "Er … thanks. I missed the school bus and I'm not sure what time it is. I suppose my carers might be worried … I've only been there one night. It's the vicarage at … " he looked at the map and spelled it out carefully, "Erewhon Parva."

"Okay, that's good. Would you like to use the car phone? Then we can check you have permission to take a lift with us."

"Yes … I would but I don't have their telephone number. They were too busy this morning. They have other children to look after."

"Then they surely can't complain that you haven't rung in."

His whole body sagged with relief. Mrs Ribiero seemed capable of taking care of everything. She even phoned the school to tell them where he was. The administrator was just leaving but it didn't sound as if there'd been any fuss. That was good too. It wouldn't have been like that if he'd been missing for so long at home.

Suddenly Donny felt immensely tired. And lonely   in spite of the Ribieros' kindness. Luckily he didn't think Xanthe or Maggi noticed. Or maybe they did.

Whatever. The moment he said he'd been to look at the reservoir they both started telling him again about last year's wind surfing championships and their own two *Laser* dinghies, *Kingfisher* and *Spray*. Both dinghies had been named after yachts that had sailed round the world. The sisters were beginning to list some of the other names they'd considered … *Gypsy Moth, Lively Lady* "but we'd used that", *Whirlpool, Aviva, Kitty IV, Golden Hind, Strong* … when June turned into the vicarage drive and they all saw the police car.

"Well, young man, truant on your first day. Not a good start. You'd better tell me what you were up to. Exactly what you were up to – and who you went to meet."

The fat policeman was completely blanking Mrs Ribiero, who had got out of her car and walked beside Donny, obviously intending to introduce herself.

Donny felt really awkward. "I didn't go to meet anyone. I left school after lunch to go and look at the boats because there wasn't anything for me to do and I hadn't seen boats before. Or a lake. I mean … a reservoir. Then I forgot how long I'd been. After that I realised I'd missed the school bus. So I was walking."

"Don't lie to me, young man. You've been absent all day."

"No, I haven't."

"Yes you have. My colleague, Ms Tune, has already spoken to your school. They confirmed that they'd no idea where you were."

"Excuse me, officer." Mrs Ribiero cut in. "But I happen to have spoken with the school administration as well. Until I rang them on my car phone, not ten minutes ago, they had no notion that he was missing. He wasn't on the bus driver's list and, once he'd left the school, he had no way of making contact. He doesn't have a mobile and no-one provided a contact number."

"We telephoned at once. As soon as the bus returned." This was Gerald.

"But who did you phone?"

"Maiself. As per procedure."

The Welfare Officer from the meeting was there too. Had she told the policeman a lie or was it the school's mistake? He'd used his swipe card to check out in the library and he'd registered with the tutor after lunch. He even thought he'd seen her in the school office.

The policeman was looking at Mrs Ribiero as if he knew in advance that she was going to waste his time.

"And who might you be, madam?"

"I'm June Ribiero. My daughters are at school with Donny. We saw him walking home so we called the school and offered him a lift."

"But, in fact, madam, you couldn't be sure where, exactly, he was walking from."

Mrs Ribiero stood very straight and raised her eyebrows.

"It was certainly from the direction of the reservoir. And if that's where he says he's been, why ever should we doubt it?"

"We've found, madam, that the things this boy says are not always supported by the facts. When one comes to check the facts. As we do." He reached into his top pocket for a palm pad and made a note. "I must warn you, madam, that you may find yourself liable to some official criticism for colluding with a deliberate truancy."

He turned his back on June and looked at Donny again. A hard look. Donny felt embarrassed and obscurely afraid but he was also angry.

"You can check everything I've said. You'll find it's true. I went to the reservoir. I missed the bus. I was walking back. I knew I shouldn't have gone to the reservoir but I went anyway. People saw me there. Okay?"

"Ai shouldn't have gone to the reservoir but Ai went anyway …" Denise Tune mimicked, shaking her head from side to side and looking doleful. Donny noticed that there were other children watching from behind them. He hoped they were enjoying the show.

The policeman blew himself up like a toad on heat.

"Now that you're so lippy, young man, perhaps you'd like to tell me more precisely where I'll find this alleged great aunt of yours?"

"My Great Aunt Ellen is *not* alleged!"

"So you keep saying. But you won't say when she's coming or how she's coming. We've checked passenger lists to Felixstowe and Harwich for the next three months but *Miss Ellen Walker*'s not on them. This gives me problems," The

Welfare Officer was nodding now. Like she was his backing group. "Because I have a decision to make. I have to decide whether we start searching the containers – as we do for all the other illegals from Shanghai."

Both Gerald and June stepped forward at this point but Donny didn't see them.

"MY GREAT AUNT ELLEN ISN'T AN ILLEGAL! You go search wherever you like. I want you to find her! Then I'll get my mum back and I'll never have to see any of you again! RE-SULT!"

He turned and ran into the vicarage. He slammed the front door behind him and charged up to his bedroom.

He slammed that door too and shoved a chair under the handle so it couldn't be opened. Then he threw himself onto his bed and stuffed his head under the covers. He didn't hear whether anyone followed him. Today had finally been too much. He wanted out of it.

When he woke his room was dark. He felt horrible but he couldn't remember why.

Then his own shouting started coming back to him.

The clock in the bedroom said half past ten. If Gerald and Wendy were still awake he owed them an apology. This situation wasn't their fault.

He was hungry too. Maybe they'd have something he could eat. Even milk and biscuits would be good.

The study light was on and he could hear voices. Donny paused outside. He felt uncomfortable, a bit like an intruder. He didn't know these people and this was their house. What if they were … being intimate or something? He listened properly. Maybe they were watching TV.

"Yes … it's an interesting case. Naturally one feels compassion. The trauma of losing his grandmother. Then he witnessed the mother's breakdown. Denise Tune says a rescue myth's not uncommon in these circumstances."

"A myth! So he doesn't have a great aunt at all?"

Donny recognised the voice. That wasn't TV. That was Gerald. And the other one had been Wendy.

But they couldn't be discussing …him?

"Well, technically he may have had one once. Leeds Social Services had been doing some fairly thorough research before the boy and his mother left. To see whether there was anyone else who could take responsibility. There was a consensus that the mother would break down sooner or later. As of course she has."

"But did they find an aunt? A great aunt, I mean. Or is she just his fantasy?"

Fantasy!

Donny had to grab onto the bottom of the banisters to stop himself from barging in and starting to shout all over again. They thought Granny's sister was his *fantasy*?

Inside the study, the voices carried on.

"Edith Walker, the boy's grandmother – if she really was his grandmother – was one of five. Three sisters and two brothers. Both the brothers were casualties and the files close on the middle sister sometime in the mid-fiftes. Not long after the mother was born … poor creature …"

"Hereditary problem?"

Donny's face was burning and his hands clammy with sweat. He couldn't believe that this was his family they were discussing. Probably over a nice hot cup of Horlicks.

Maybe it wasn't. Granny hadn't really had all those sisters and brothers. Had she?

"Hard to be certain … Leeds found Edith Walker very difficult to deal with. Paranoid secrecy about her family affairs. She made them take new names, you know."

There was a pause. For head shaking probably. Or swigging.

Donny was frozen to the spot. What did they mean about names? Did the Social Services know how they'd sometimes called each other 'Nokomis', 'Minnehaha', 'Hiawatha'? Donny couldn't believe Granny would have told them that. It was private! Anyway that was Skye, not Granny.

Rev. Wendy hadn't finished. "It was extraordinary that she managed to persuade them to let her keep the boy when that poor mother got pregnant … spent everything she had on lawyers, apparently."

"No father there either, I suppose?" Gerald asked as if he already knew the answer.

"No trace of one …" Her voice dropped and there was the sound of spoon on saucer. "I know you thought Inspector Flint was being a little harsh, dear, but one can't leave anything to chance in these difficult times. I understand, from Denise, that the Inspector plays a vital role in our protection."

Gerald mumbled something that Donny couldn't hear. It didn't sound like a protest. Then Wendy carried on as if she was catching him up on the first episode of a Sunday night serial.

"The only trace they've found, you know, is an inclusion in the Foreign Office Undesirable Aliens list."

"So, let me get this quite clear. Denise Tune's Assessment suggests that either the boy or the mother concocted this story when they realised that Leeds were about to section her? But … a story like that … in those circumstances … seems almost rational! All this talk of Shotley – and Shanghai?"

"Fantasists often provide a surprising level of detail, Denise Tune says. And she is the Professional. I believe she's leading a research project into children's rescue myths." Had Wendy needed convincing? "Or the grandmother – if that's what she was – may have planted the idea when she knew she couldn't look after them any more. Perhaps she thought they'd get an easier ride down here. The boy claims some arrangement has been made but there's simply no hard evidence …"

Donny was shaking with fury now. Hard evidence! He had Great Aunt Ellen's telegram upstairs. Granny had written a letter and Great Aunt Ellen had answered. That's why they'd come. Not to get an 'easy ride' … What a joke that was! Why couldn't these people just shut up and listen?

His hunger was gone. He turned and started pounding back upstairs to fetch his piece of paper so he could shove it in their faces.

Two at a time. He didn't care how much noise he made.

But as he reached the landing and climbed hastily over the safety-gate, the baby started its high abandoned wailing. The study door opened, spilling light into the hall. He could hear one of the carers coming up the stairs and the other one heading for the kitchen.

There was someone else at the end of the landing. A pale figure dodging out of view. Donny couldn't see properly. The only upstairs light was a floor-level low-wattage bulb glowing dimly beside the bathroom. He hurried into his own room and closed the door. Quietly.

Had he been watched all the time he'd been standing outside the study? Would the other person have heard what was being said?

He hoped it was another child. But they hadn't been coming from the bathroom. Maybe they'd been visiting each other. He didn't know where anyone slept. He wasn't even sure how many there were. Or whose side they would be on. He hadn't spoken to anyone yet.

Only shouted.

Donny sprawled awkwardly across his narrow bed. No chance of sleep. He could read *Swallows and Amazons*, he supposed, but what good would that do?

He'd put so much trust in Granny – childish, unthinking trust. After today he felt as if the person he thought he'd known was twisting away from him faster than the smoke from the burning grave-post. Sisters and brothers she'd never mentioned? Some sort of phobia about water that she'd never admitted? An old-fashioned story-book about kids and boats – with a secret?

Skye had said they needed to let Granny go. And that's what he'd tried to do.

Now he was beginning to wonder what was left? A few flakes of wood-ash in a garden that he'd never see again?

No return. The bungalow wasn't his home any more. That was a shocking thought. They'd lived there all his life and he'd left as casually as if he were going on a school day-trip.

Donny squeezed his eyes shut.

Skye had told him about walking in the mind. He'd see if he could get back home to the bungalow again, find if there was something he'd forgotten. Something helpful Granny might have left for them.

Their quiet road was empty and the garden gate was closed. No one saw Donny lift the latch and imagine himself onto the path. The new people hadn't arrived and the grass either side of the pebbles had grown stalky and dry in the summer sun. There were seed-pods too. He wished he could pick some and bring them back with him for Skye to use in her weaving. It was time to make new dream-catchers for the winter nights ahead.

He didn't hang about in the garden. He probably couldn't keep this up for long. He was glad to find the old blackened camping kettle in its place beside the door. (That meant he must be dreaming because he knew Skye had packed it safely in the camper van.)

But there it was, in his mind, with the house key safe inside. So he let himself in quickly and went straight to Granny's room.

The best way to find something missing was to retrace your steps, go back to where you last remembered having it and start your search from there. That's what Granny had said.

And it worked.

He went over to her desk and started pulling open drawers. It wasn't there.

The letter that proved that Granny had cared for them. Her Last Wishes. With Great Aunt Ellen's name and address written on it.

Donny had posted it but the small man had seen it first. Had picked it up. Wanted to take it.

Then, when he came back from the letterbox, the small man was gone and so was Granny's address book and diary.

Wouldn't he have checked the address book? Told other people in the Social Services? Granny would have written her sister's address. Donny was sure of that. She liked lists.

So why didn't Wendy and Gerald know that there was someone else who might take him off their hands? Why had they been told that Great Aunt Ellen was a Myth?

Social Service people kept copies of everything. They carried enough paper around. So what about the fat policemen and Denise Tune? Were they really as ignorant as they made out? They were so suspicious, so angry ...

And what was an Undesirable Aliens list? That sounded really weird. Did they think Granny's sister was from Mars?

CHAPTER SIX
Awful Anna

Thursday, September 14th

It was neither light nor dark in the vicarage bedroom. Not night any more but surely not yet time for another day? Donny tried to read the un-illuminated clock. He didn't want to be awake.

Half-five. Reluctantly he tiptoed along the cold wooden floor to the bathroom. He had a pee and then, because he'd woken up with Granny in his head, he brushed his teeth. She had always managed to make him feel guilty if he'd gone to bed without washing properly. She didn't even have to say anything. He hoped that Great Aunt Ellen wouldn't be quite so hot on tooth-brushing but it was probably too late. He'd never be able to kick that habit now.

The terrible thing about being called a fantasist – or a scrounger and a liar – thought Donny, climbing gloomily back into bed, was that you might have to spend a stupid amount of time proving that you weren't. Like having to sign a formal declaration every day to swear you'd really scrubbed for the full two minutes. And offering to take disclosing tablet tests.

Denise Tune would obviously have told Mrs Ribiero all her Professional theories about Great Aunt Ellen being Donny's 'rescue myth' or him and Skye having come here for an 'easy ride'. So that was the end of that friendship. Because he wasn't going to bother proving stuff. No disclosing tablets. Either they believed him or they didn't.

Donny sighed. He really needed to see Skye. He fetched his pencils and spent the next hour or so drawing more pages of her picture-letter. He still didn't know where she was but somebody must.

"We've asked Anna to be responsible for you on the bus," Wendy said at breakfast.

Anna, a small girl with mousy hair and a pale, pointy face, did not look up from her Weetabix.

"We're a little disappointed that she didn't show more initiative yesterday. But of course we forgive her. It's early days for her too. She's working through her resentment at her Maternal Rejection."

Including Donny there were five children round the vicarage breakfast table. They were all foster children – 'looked after' children, as Sandra called them. They didn't talk to each other much except for the two fair-haired boys, obviously brothers, who kicked and argued with each other constantly and glared menacingly at everyone else. Donny got the impression that the other four children were related in some way but he wasn't sure how. He imagined them wearing evacuee labels but with 'fantasist' or 'reject' written on them instead of names and addresses.

Rev. Wendy hardly had time to sit down. She was an older middle-aged woman with a round face and rosy cheeks. She looked as if she should naturally have been plump and jolly but instead she was thin and self-controlled. She was always gathering papers for some meeting or moving to the study to take phone calls. When she wasn't doing that she stood beside the table being Understanding. Donny noticed that she always seemed to pause for a moment before she spoke, as if thinking carefully how she should phrase some unpleasant truth. Unfortunately she only seemed to think about the phrasing.

Neither foster parent looked as if fun played a big part in their lives. Gerald was tall and lean and lined. He worked from home and did all the food preparation and baby care. Wendy explained to Donny that Gerald would always Be There for him.

Donny was glad he'd overheard their private conversation. Otherwise he might have wasted his time trying to like them.

"Were you on the bus yesterday?" he asked Anna, as they walked the half-mile of road to the pick-up point. It seemed mean that she'd had to be 'forgiven' when it was him who'd bunked off.

She nodded. "You didn't notice me. You were talking to those two girls."

"Not all the time," said Donny. "They weren't on the bus all the time. They got on later. Where were you at the beginning? As in now, for instance?"

"I was here. Wendy didn't offer to give me a lift so I went down early and waited on the other side of the shelter where you wouldn't see me. I don't like other people so I keep out of the way."

"But now you have to be looking out for me all the time or you're in trouble. I'm sorry."

She didn't smile back. Her face stayed expressionless and

pale under her scattering of freckles. She looked as if she had been sad for always.

"I saw you bunk off," she said. "But I didn't tell anyone. I never tell. Even at House Meetings."

"Thanks," said Donny.

They stood a few steps apart at the collection point.

"Er … what are House Meetings?"

"Wendy and Gerald have them at the end of every week. On Fridays. We all have to sit round the table and say things about each other. It's supposed to help us be more open about our feelings. I think Denise Tune told them to do it. Then they report back and tell her what we've said."

They waited in silence till the bus came.

"Do you mind if I sit beside you?" he asked her as they climbed on board.

"Suit yourself," she answered.

The seats around them had been filled by the time Xanthe and Maggi got on. "Hi, Donny," they called, amongst a flurry of other greetings, though not, he noticed, including Anna.

As soon as they reached the school Anna walked quickly inside. She didn't speak to anyone or look at them. Maggi was deep in conversation with three or four friends but Xanthe hung back.

"You go ahead," she told her sister, "I need to talk to this guy."

She lowered her voice as they walked the short distance from the turning circle to the school entrance. She looked worried and kind.

"Hey, Donny, what happened? We saw you shouting at that policeman but we couldn't hear. You looked well upset. Mum

was in such a moody when she came back. Said that the
policeman was completely out of order. Said she'd never seen
a situation handled so badly. Then she clammed. Are you
okay?"

Donny didn't know how to begin to answer. He'd stuffed his
second-hand school blazer into a locker before he'd bunked
off and he wasn't quite sure whether he'd find it again. He
couldn't be late for registration today.

"Yeah, I'm okay. Look, I've got to go. If I get in trouble they'll
blame Anna."

"Awful Anna? That grumpy-guts? What's it to do with her?"

"She's being made to be responsible for me. And she's not
awful. She's miserable. So would you be if you were her! You
don't get it. Not at all."

"Sorr-ee!"

But Donny had already gone.

Once he'd found his blazer and knew he was going to make
it to registration he wished he hadn't said all that. As if he
couldn't talk to anyone without snapping. Xanthe was only
being friendly. Anna had said she didn't like anybody so it
wasn't exactly surprising that no-one liked her.

She didn't give the impression that she liked him either. So
why risk falling out with the Ribieros? Their mum hadn't bad-
mouthed him after last night and there was something so
important that he wanted to ask them.

"Hmm, it's the Boy Who Missed the Bus is it?" said a snowy-
bearded teacher who had to be Donny's tutor, Mr McMullen.
"Well, you're not the first and I don't suppose you'll be the last.
Nevertheless a Higher Authority informs me that I've got to

keep you on report for the rest of the week. That means you're to call and see me at first break and before lunch and at the end of the day – as well as the normal registration periods at the beginning of every session. And you're to carry a card for staff to sign. You may feel that it's lucky for you that it's Thursday already. Alternatively you might decide that it'd be useful if we got to know each other better?"

He looked inquiringly at Donny then he shook his head. "Your choice."

The tutor seemed genial enough but being on report was a pain. Donny'd planned to spend all his spare time in the library. Not looking out of the window at the reservoir. Well, not all the time. He wanted to check out their local studies section for stuff about Shotley, in case it gave him any clues why Great Aunt Ellen wanted to meet there.

In other circs he'd probably have asked. But, however laid back Mr McMullen sounded, he was not currently to be trusted. He'd said he'd 'been told' to put Donny on report. So someone had got to him already. If Donny started asking Mr McMullen if he knew anything interesting about Shotley, they'd assume he was seeking more 'detail' for his 'fantasies'.

Mr McMullen didn't bother making Donny do tests: he'd rung his previous school and got all the levels from them. So Donny was straight off into lessons plus reporting back to the DT block at regular intervals to tell the tutor he was still on site. He didn't see Anna or Xanthe all day but did meet Maggi coming out of the dining hall as he was finally trailing in.

"Could you tell your sister I'm really sorry about this morning?"

Maggi looked a bit surprised but nodded cheerfully enough. "Yeah, sure, whatever ..."

He made it to the library as well. Eating was quick when you didn't have anyone to talk to. There was quite a lot of info about Shotley – mainly some old battle at a place called Bloody Point – but the bit that was good from Donny's point of view was that Shotley had once had a naval training base. He thought that Granny's brother might have been in the Navy.

Or was he getting muddled with *Swallows and Amazons*? That had Navy in it.

As he swiped his card in the library monitoring system and set off yet again for the DT block, Donny thought about Granny and about letting go. Skye had said that you mustn't weigh down your loved ones with your grief or they'd never reach the place of peace. Problem was that you couldn't let stuff go if you didn't know what you'd got in the first place. Maybe that was why Skye had broken down, so soon after they had bought their copy of Granny's secret book.

For the first time in his life Donny wondered if there was a reason why his mum was the way she was ...?

"Your social worker's coming to see you this evening, John," Gerald told Donny as soon as he got in. "She needs to check that you're settling into your placement and she'll want to catch up with the paperwork."

Did she *have* to? He'd planned to go straight out again. Take his map. Check around. Try and work out how far it was to Shotley. See if the foster-carers had a bike he could, er, borrow.

"There's a glass of water and some fruit on the table." Gerald was scrubbing organic vegetables for supper and sounded harassed. The baby was in a pen. It had a wipe-able book and a couple of bright plastic toys but they had been thrown down. It was pulling itself up on the bars as if it was trying to get to Donny.

Donny took a deep breath. Mustn't shout. He walked across to have a look. "I don't know much about babies. Is this one a boy or a girl?" He reached through the bars as he spoke. The baby grabbed his finger and started biting it with a warm wet mouth. It had grey eyes and red hair. It didn't seem to have many teeth.

"She's female. Her name's Vicky. Those are her brothers – half-brothers to be exact." Gerald gestured towards the plain glass window. The two little boys were pounding each other on the grass whilst a football lay disregarded beside them.

Then he noticed what the baby was doing to Donny's finger.

"Oh no, *no*! I don't suppose you've washed your hands since coming in. She's still in the oral phase. I can't risk infection. Why don't you go and make some social contact with Luke and Liam?"

Donny looked again at scene outside. One of the boys had rolled on top of the ball while the other was punching him in the ribs. "Um, actually I've got homework."

He got to his feet and moved towards the door. The baby let out a wail of protest, stretching her small hand over the top of the pen.

"Over-stimulation," muttered Gerald, wiping his hands dry and moving to disengage the baby from the rails. "Off you go, John. I'll tell Sandra where to find you … We have supper at half past six," he called after him as the baby began to howl again. Sighing, he extracted a stick of raw carrot from the fridge and pressed it into her spitty palm.

Donny heard the telephone in the study ringing disregarded as he stomped upstairs. Wendy must be out. It would have been so easy to get away if he hadn't had to wait for Sandra.

Unless she was going to give him Skye's address? That would be worth the wait.

He supposed Anna was already in her room. He wondered what she did there? Homework, maybe. Or reading. They weren't allowed any electronic equipment. Inappropriate, apparently. Or a safety hazard. He couldn't remember which.

Much later that night, when he was certain everyone else was either in bed or, in Gerald's case, trying to soothe the baby, Donny crept downstairs and checked the lock system on both front and back doors and the downstairs windows. All securely bolted.

His heart sank when he found a keypad beside the front door. The vicarage had an alarm system.

You wouldn't have expected that an old place like this would have something so modern. Donny didn't for a moment think that these security arrangements were to keep people out – vandals or burglars – as they would be in a normal house. These locks were to keep people in.

Even at this moment a ship might be pushing her way through the waters of an unknown sea bringing Great Aunt Ellen closer. How was he going to reach her? Donny stared at the LED winking green on the keypad. He supposed these things could be disabled but he didn't have a clue how. Would all the windows be connected as well as the doors? Maybe he should try. He could always say he'd made a mistake.

The rest of the house was in darkness, except for a couple more of the low wattage night-lights strategically placed by the study and the kitchen doors. Donny had been creeping round letting his eyes get accustomed to the near-blackness, doing everything by touch. The study door wasn't quite closed. It moved as he pushed it. Donny stepped back, oddly startled.

He stopped a moment. Had something, near him, rustled? This house didn't feel safe. The night-lights made the dark bits darker. Donny took a few deep breaths to steady himself. He'd got to have a go. Which window should he try?

He was in the living room and fumbling to find the window catch in the darkness when a voice hissed behind him,

"Are you completely dense? Can't you see the alarm's on?"

It was Anna.

"What are you doing down here then?" he hissed back once he'd got over the shock.

"My own business. Now get back to bed without them seeing you – or I'll … call the police!"

"I thought you said you never told," he whispered weakly as he turned away.

"This would be an exception."

CHAPTER SEVEN
Allies

Friday, September 15th, morning
Donny had a terrible dream that night. It was the worst dream he could ever remember having. Though in that peculiar way of dreams, while he was having it, he felt as if he'd had it before. That he knew what was going to happen next but he was powerless to stop it.

He was somewhere cold, very cold and he was on a ship. It was a destroyer and he was at war. At that moment when the dream began he was relaxed. The part of him that was in the dream was gazing almost idly at the collection of ships around him. They were headed due north. To Russia, he thought. Their mission was to protect a convoy of merchantmen carrying supplies.

His ship was fast and fine. He was in command. He had done a good job. So, for a moment, he was allowing himself to linger, forgetting his duties, watching another warship in the escort group, a junior ship, who carried someone very special to him.

"Don't look," shouted Donny to himself in the dream. "Look away, now. You don't want the next bit …"

The man in the dream couldn't hear him. He carried on watching the other ship rolling gently about half a mile away on their starboard beam. He was remembering the happy days of childhood. He pushed his mittened hands into his duffle pocket to touch the slim blue book that he always carried. It made him feel like a boy again.

His brother might be looking across. Might be thinking of him.

"DON'T LOOK!" Donny screamed, unheard.

The explosion … the searching … that white face with its desperate appeal … Down, breathless, down into darkness, crushed by the weight of the icy sea —

He shouldn't have been touching the book.

Donny was panting and sweating as he woke. Someone had switched on his light. He pulled himself up onto his elbow and stared around the empty walls, trying to remember why he was here.

Anna was just inside the door. Her pyjamas were so pale because the pattern had been washed right out of them.

"I heard you shouting," she whispered, closing the door with extreme carefulness behind her.

"I was having a bad dream." He still felt disorientated. She sat, unexpectedly and warily, on the far end of his bed.

"I've always had bad dreams, ever since I can remember," she stated quietly. "But I don't think I shout out any more."

Donny sat up properly now and bunched the blanket and thin quilt against his chest. Her attitude confused him.

"Did your mother used to come to you? Does … did …does she mind about dreams?" He too was whispering – the thought of Gerald or Wendy coming in was unbearable.

"She did to start with. Come in, I mean. After my dad was

killed. I think my stepfather stopped her. He used to get drunk and once he hit her. The dreams were always worse when he was home. I don't mind about dreams – I think they're a symptom."

Her quiet voice was unemotional.

"My mother thinks they're real. That they matter. She'd come. Except she can't hear me because she's deaf. So she makes dream-catchers. They have a web to catch the bad dreams. You decorate them in special ways." He paused, thinking how Skye might be at this moment. "She used to make them for herself as well."

"It was a pity you didn't have one tonight then."

"I don't suppose she's got one either. She's in hospital."

"In Ipswich?"

"Where's that?"

"Nearest town."

"I don't think so. I think it's further away. Where we were captured. That was Colchester but then they moved her. I asked the social worker but she wouldn't tell me. They think I'll run away if I know where to go."

"Would you?"

"Might do. Depends."

"You were trying to get out earlier. You were going to set off the alarm."

"I also need to meet my great aunt. That's at Shotley – that's quite near, I think. But why were you so angry? You're nice now."

"You were on my patch."

"Oh."

"You need to remember that you're not the only one here with problems."

"Do you … er … want to talk about them?"

"No."

Neither of them said anything for a bit. Donny leaned forward and hitched up the far end of his quilt and Anna put her cold feet underneath.

"Do you know how to make these dream-catchers?" she asked, after a while.

"Probably, if I could get the stuff."

Skye hadn't always used seedpods and dried grasses. There'd been strips of leather and horsehair, willow, painted beads and once they'd combed and twisted long strands of sheep's wool that they'd found tangled in a wire fence.

"I could help you if you liked. I'm good at making things." She looked alarmed at what she'd said. "Only I don't usually tell people."

"We can keep it secret. I'll make a dream-catcher for you if I can find some good bits, and you make one for me. It's better if they're gifts. I'll make one for Skye too."

"Skye?"

"My mum. They must let me see her eventually. Wherever she is."

"It's a lovely name." Her voice carried some emotion now. Wistfulness.

"Thanks. She's a lovely person."

He didn't ask about her mother. He didn't think she'd tell him.

Anna's eyelids drooped. She sat up, startled.

"I'm going back to bed now if you're okay. My room's opposite."

"I'm okay. Um ... sleep well."

She tiptoed to the door and slipped out more silently than he could have believed possible, closing it without the faintest click. There was no sound from the landing floorboards and nothing from her door either.

Donny wasn't ready to risk going to sleep again so he kept the light on and read *Swallows and Amazons* for a bit. Those kids did him good. They were so normal. He could almost smell their campfire.

What would one of them have done, stuck up here? His room was on the top floor. About as high as a lookout pine? Donny drifted off to sleep again, his mind full of confused ideas about ropes and knots and signals.

And boats. He would definitely need a boat.

"Hi, Donny! Er, hi … Anna."

Maggi and Xanthe had piled into the seat in front of them. Maggi was twisting round immediately to chat through the gap.

Anna looked away without answering.

"Hi!" said Donny. Why did Anna have to be like this? Okay, so she was tired but it wasn't that hard to be friendly. Was it?

Then he remembered how he'd snapped at Xanthe yesterday. She wasn't saying too much this morning.

"Um. I'm sorry about yesterday, Xanthe. I did try to find you but I've been put on report."

She turned round.

"In your first week? That's victimisation. Who's your tutor?"

"Mr McMullen."

"What's got into him? He's normally well cool."

Donny didn't want to answer. Not on the bus.

"We were wondering if you wanted to come round ours?" said Maggi. "Mum tried ringing you but there wasn't any answer at first. Then it was engaged for ages. We thought you were maybe surfing? Do they not have broadband?"

"No chance! There's a really old computer in the living room but all that's got is educational games. Times table practice. No access. They've got one in their study that's enabled but apparently we're only allowed to use that for special homework projects. And we have to be supervised …"

"What a boot camp!" Xanthe was outraged.

Half the bus was listening now. He felt Anna shift even further into the corner of her seat as if she was creating a personal exclusion zone.

"'T's alright really," he mumbled, trying to sound casual. "There's other kids there – and a baby."

Once again Maggi was more perceptive than her sister. "Shut it, Xanth. You're so embarrassing sometimes."

Then she gave Donny one of her lovely smiles.

"Mum was going to ask whether you'd come and have supper with us tonight? It won't be late because we've got a training session on the river tomorrow. But we'd collect you and take you back afterwards…"

She glanced over to Anna who didn't meet her eyes. "Maybe you could come too, Anna? I could use some help with this week's homework …?"

Anna didn't even look.

Donny was annoyed with her. He started to answer, "Yeah, that'd be really good ..." when Anna interrupted. "Don't bother. It's House Meeting on Fridays. We have to go. It's in our Care Plans."

She said it like a slap.

Maggi stared a moment then got busy checking her texts. Xanthe pulled a battered looking book from her bag, stretched her long legs far beneath the seat in front and read with complete concentration for the rest of the journey. Donny just sat there.

As soon as the bus pulled up, Anna grabbed her bag and pushed awkwardly past all of them.

He realised, too late, that she was in a hurry because she needed to find somewhere to cry.

"Donny-man, we need to talk. I'll meet you outside the DT block at the end of morning lessons. Okay?"

Donny nodded. Xanthe wasn't offering No as an option.

"I'll be there too," said Maggi, gathering up her bags.

The fat policeman was in the school office, waiting for Donny. Some kid had reported a lost mobile and they'd been on Donny's bus the morning before.

The policeman persuaded the school administrator that Donny should be searched. He made it sound as if Donny had come from a really bad home, full of gangs and criminals. The Welfare Officer was there too, smirking.

They took his map – which didn't really matter because he hadn't done a lot of work on it – and they didn't bother looking inside *Swallows and Amazons* which was where he'd put Great Aunt Ellen's telegram.

They didn't find a mobile of course. Donny hadn't ever had a mobile in his life. It was just humiliating and dirty and made him late for his first lesson and then he had to explain what had happened to Mr McMullen who had been sent for by the subject teacher when he didn't turn up.

And there was everyone in the class listening.

When he met Xanthe and Maggi at lunchtime he couldn't see he had much more to lose. So he told them everything. About Granny, about Skye, about Great Aunt Ellen, about the fat policeman and the welfare officer. About being a scrounger and a fantasist. And now a thief.

The sisters were silent for a moment after he'd finished. Then both spoke at once.

"Count us right in, Donny-man!" said Xanthe. "Mum's a magistrate. She'll get you off the full custodial sentence … Only joking," she added quickly as Maggi turned on her.

"Our dad's a doctor. Maybe he could help? Is Anna's mum in hospital too?"

"I don't know. I don't think so. She said some things last night … I can't repeat them. But I feel really sorry for her. Like, I don't think she's even got a Rescue Myth …"

"Especially one that might arrive in less than a couple of weeks! All we have to do is get you to Shotley. How easy is that! I feel seriously undervalued."

"Well …" started Donny.

But Maggi was on a different tack.

"Maybe when your great aunt arrives, we should work out

what we can do to help Anna? She doesn't exactly give the impression that she'd welcome anyone getting involved right now."

"But Great Aunt Ellen doesn't even know that *we* need rescuing. I don't know what she knows. I never heard of her before. She might take one look at me and Skye and go straight back to China. And *that's* if I even manage to get to meet her in the first place."

He'd made up his mind.

"There's one thing I know I want. It's my big ask."

"Try us –"

"That first day on the bus – you said that you go sailing?"

"It's our life!"

"Well I've done it once and I *totally* want to do it again. It was like … magic. I wondered whether maybe you could give me some lessons? I have to convince Great Aunt Ellen that I'm not a landlubber. Maybe a scrounger and a fantasist and a … thief. Just not a landlubber. It's all I can do."

Xanthe and Maggi looked at each other.

"Sure."

"But how?"

"He could watch us train."

"That's not learning. He needs to do it for himself."

"But he couldn't sail the *Lasers,* not yet. Not on the river."

"And we're going to Weymouth on Sunday."

Donny almost wished he hadn't asked.

Except he didn't. He wanted this so badly.

"Got it, Maggi-baby – the *Mirror*! I saw her in the corner of the dinghy park a while ago. If we were to get ahead of ourselves tonight – chores, homework, music practice, goody-goody, blah-blah – we could take him for a spin tomorrow before we start training."

"On the river?"

"He'd have to. Anyway *Lady's* a bath toy – even you never managed to sink her completely – okay, okay, don't hit me, *please* …! How's your swimming, Donny-man?"

"I've never done much. I did get my 25 metres at primary school."

Their smiles faded. "The parentals aren't going to like that. You've got to promise that you'll always wear a buoyancy aid. All dinghy sailors do."

"And that, whenever you're not practising your sailing, you'll practise your swimming. We can lend you a wetsuit so you don't totally freeze."

How was he going to get any of this past Gerald and Wendy?

"If your mum does ring my foster-carers, could she … not say too much?

They understood completely. "Adults! Health and safety! They do so wind each other up. We'll get her focused on including Anna. That'll give her a challenge."

"I'm in the same sets as Anna," said Maggi. "We could form an alliance."

"Defensive *and* offensive!" said her sister. "Pipes and drums! Death to Adult Oppressors. *Vive* la Rescue Myth!"

CHAPTER EIGHT
Lively Lady

Friday, September 15th, later

Donny didn't talk at all to Anna on the bus journey home. He didn't even sit with her. Instead he got on board so fast that he got right down to the seats at the back: the seats where the Year Elevens expected to sit. He got a corner seat and slumped down so it was hard for her to see him when she climbed on.

A big lad stared at him in slow surprise. "These seats are took," he said. "Hoof it."

Round the edge of the seat he could see her at the driver's end, hesitating. He slumped down further and pointed to the front, shaking his head mutely.

"Avoidin' someone?" asked the big lad. "Wot, that bit? Well, okay then, seein' as it's Friday."

He wondered whether she'd check the whole bus or tell the driver that he wasn't there. She was meant to be responsible for him. She'd get into trouble if she didn't.

The bus moved off with no delay   and no checking.

Did that mean she wasn't bothered or was she covering, assuming that he'd bunked again? Donny wasn't at all sure that he'd read Anna right but he was guessing that it might be the second one. That's what he hoped.

"Anna," he whispered urgently, tapping softly on her bedroom door, soon after they'd got back to the vicarage. "Could you let me in? I need to talk to you."

Nothing.

"Anna, I know you're in there and none of these doors have locks anyway but I want you to open it so I can ask you something …"

Still nothing.

"And if you don't answer I'm going straight downstairs to tell Gerald … um … that you didn't check the bus when you thought I wasn't on it!"

She'd never be his friend after this.

"I've got us some fruit from the kitchen …oh *please*, Anna, be nice."

"Okay, you finally used the proper word." She'd opened the door a crack and stood glaring at him from inside. "So what do you want? I suppose you had some reason for that bus stuff – or were you just being a *boy*?"

"I want you to come to the river with me and Maggi and Xanthe tomorrow and I didn't want to sit with you on the bus because I didn't want to talk to you."

"Why bother now, then?" She didn't even sound offended. There was no expression in her voice. If he hadn't seen her nearly cry this morning he'd believe that this was what she was like.

"Because I want to tell you things I don't want anyone else to hear … and I also hid because I wanted to see what you'd do."

"To check if you could trust me?"

"Mmm … possibly."

"That's what I might have done." She sounded marginally

more interested. "What fruit have you got? If it's an apple it's completely predictable and I'm saying no."

He'd been due a piece of luck.

"It's plums."

She still wouldn't let him in her room so they found a place in the garden round the back of a shed where she said Luke and Liam wouldn't come. She'd told Liam there was a spider's nest there and Liam was scared of spiders

"Who are Luke and Liam?"

"My step-brothers. I hate them. If you want to talk about them I'm going straight back indoors and I can tell you now that there's no way you'll be allowed to go out with those two girls – unless I help you."

"Okay, okay. No need to get stressy. Have a plum. They look good. They're from some old lady in the parish, Gerald said."

It was like getting her to take the King's shilling. The plums were really ripe and incredibly messy to eat. Once they were both sucking and munching and getting juice all over their hands and wiping them on the first of the fallen leaves, she calmed down and Donny was able to tell her everything. All the stuff he'd told Maggi and Xanthe and a bit more because he actually showed her Great Aunt Ellen's telegram, which he hadn't done earlier. He'd left it shut tight in his book.

Anna dried her hands on her school skirt and read it carefully. "Have you googled 'Strong Winds'?" she asked. "If it's a famous sculpture or something it might show up."

"That's a really good idea. I bet there'll be thousands of hits though – weather forecasts and stuff. It'll take ages going through them. Even if I spend all break and lunch in the library every day. But thanks, I will try."

"I might help." It definitely wasn't a promise but there was a bit more warmth in her voice, a few degrees above freezing. "Don't leave this in your room if you don't want them to see it and don't say too much in the meeting either. They twist things. You could find you get completely banned from seeing those girls. They'll think it's sex."

"Sex!" Donny was shocked. Sex was the last thing on his mind in his new friendships. When Anna had come into his bedroom last night it was like she was his sister or something. And Xanthe and Maggi – well, they were his allies and fun to be with. Not sex! If that's what Gerald and Wendy thought, they were completely disgusting.

"But will you come with us tomorrow?" he asked her.

"I might … if you're allowed. Which I wouldn't be putting money on. I suppose that means you won't want to make dream-catchers."

He'd forgotten already. "Of course I do. If we're going to a river we might find reeds and things. Really small feathers are good too."

"So if I help you get permission, you'll definitely show me how to make one."

"Yes. I promise. I've got a few nightmares of my own to block out – if you remember."

The House Meeting took place after supper. Vicky had been put to bed and Wendy led the way into the living room where they had to arrange the chairs into a circle.

"This Circle symbolises our togetherness and trust," Wendy

explained to Donny. "It gives us a space to share our concerns and offer each other support and guidance as well as care. Sometimes we have to ask people to stand outside our Circle for a little while but we make it very clear to them that their place is waiting when they have made the necessary changes."

Donny thought of the conversation which he'd overheard between her and Gerald when they'd dismissed him as a fantasist – some trust they'd been showing!

He supposed it was possible that they meant well in their gloomy way. He decided to give them another chance.

"I'm worried about my mother," he said, when it was his turn. "No-one's told me her address and anyway sending letters isn't nearly enough. I'd like to go and see her."

Sandra had already told him that it wasn't considered 'appropriate' for him to visit Skye and sure enough all he got from Gerald and Wendy was stuff about accepting the things we cannot change. Then everyone held hands to symbolise their support for him.

"I'm worried about two of the girls at school," said Anna, lying expertly. "The two black girls whose mother brought Donny, sorry, I mean John, home the other night. I'm in the same maths set as one of them and she keeps asking me to go round to her house. She's asked John too. I know he doesn't want to go because he'd be the only boy … but I'm worried about our different cultures. I don't know any black people and I might do the wrong thing. I've said no but she keeps on asking. She said her mother might even phone up …"

For a moment Donny gaped at her. Then he realised what she was doing. She was playing opposite-day.

It worked brilliantly. If Anna truly had any worries about doing the wrong thing in a different household they were ignored. She got completely yelled at for using the word 'black' and had to stand up and move outside the Circle until she was ready to promise to behave with more understanding towards people who were Different from herself.

Wendy nodded across to Gerald who got up and went to the study. When he came back and Anna had been Forgiven and allowed to sit down, Gerald had cleared his throat and announced that they had received a generous invitation from Mr and Mrs Ribiero to have John and Anna for the whole day tomorrow. He'd accepted on their behalf and the two of them were to be ready for collection at nine o'clock, wearing outdoor clothes.

Then they all held hands again and the meeting was over.

Saturday, September 16th
"So what happened at yours last night?" asked Xanthe, when they were all four in the dinghy park that Saturday morning. "Mum rang at about six to invite and it was a complete NO-NO not even a no - ta. Then, about an hour or two later, that Gerald guy rang back saying yes to the whole day without wanting to know anything else at all. Not a whiff of a Risk Assessment. You must have done some world-class persuading. Whatever did you say?"

"I said that you're black so I was worried about your different culture and that Donny didn't want to come because you're girls," said Anna.

Maggi gasped and Xanthe spun round.

Donny's heart stopped.

Then Xanthe burst out laughing. "And it worked!"

"Anna was completely brilliant," said Donny. "Mind you, she had to be chucked out of the Circle of Trust while Gerald sneaked off to make his phone call …"

That gave them all the giggles and Anna went quite pink.

"Well, they're totally asking for anything we might do," said Xanthe. "I'd have 'em on double watches right around the Horn, up in the icy rigging with the wind gusting hurricane force and their bare hands freezing to the shrouds so the skin peels off in ribbons …"

"Yeah, yeah, terror of the seas. Come on, Xanth, they want to go sailing, not listen to you rant."

Xanthe and Maggi's *Mirror* dinghy, *Lively Lady*, was made of wood. She was painted a glossy bright yellow outside, golden varnish within. Her bows and stern were blunt but she was much more boat-shaped then the little white tub Donny had sailed on the Gitche Gumee reservoir. Maggi said that had probably been an *Optimist*.

"Good name," said Donny, remembering how blithely he'd got in and set off, knowing nothing.

Except what he'd read – and how he'd felt.

The moment *Lively Lady* slipped off her launching trolley and floated, Donny got that same sensation of certainty and happiness. He loved her sudden lightness and the way her shaking sail seemed to express her eagerness to be off. She had been a pretty object in the dinghy park. On the water she came alive.

"Do you swear you haven't done this before?" asked Xanthe,

as he motioned her to drop the daggerboard and sit amidships.

"Only that one time on Gitche Gumee – but lots in my book," he answered, looking intently at *Lively Lady*'s mainsail.

"What book? Not *Hiawatha*?"

Donny laughed and *Lively Lady* seemed to chuckle too as she gathered speed and the salt water bubbled up either side of her bows and rippled along her painted side.

"No way! *Swallows and Amazons* – the one my mum made us buy. You know, I told you."

"Oh well, *Swallows and Amazons,* no wonder …But there's one thing you don't know," she commented a few moments later. "That's about tides. They were sailing on a lake in *Swallows and Amazons* so they didn't have tides. Haven't you felt how she's being pushed sideways all the time when you're trying to sail straight across?"

"I thought that was just something I was doing wrong."

So Xanthe explained to him about flood and ebb tides and how he could usually tell from the way moored boats were lying, or, better still, from checking the flow of the water against channel buoys.

Then, "Count to ten, Donny-man! Take a pill!"

Donny had yelled at her to duck. The mainsail smashed across as he gybed *Lively Lady* 180 degrees so they were heading directly for the shore again.

"What was that about, for fathom's sake?" she asked, sitting up and rolling her eyes in pretend horror.

Donny didn't want to look back, not even for a moment.

But he did. "See that black motor boat behind us. Big one with the pointed bow. Looks like a shark."

"Ye-es …"

"The man in it. He's the fat policeman. The one who was waiting at the vicarage. And at school. Don't look round till you're sure he's not watching."

But Xanthe didn't do sneaky peeks. She stared. "Scar-*ee*! He even looks like a cop when he's in a boat. His boat's revolting. I've seen it before. It's completely bling. But he can't be official. Proper river police have marked launches and special moorings. He's been keeping that thing on a club pontoon – our club, the Royal Orwell & Ancient. I can't think why they let him."

The sight of the policeman took the sunshine from Donny's day. He sailed *Lively Lady* back to the scrap of beach and changed over with Maggi and Anna.

He guessed that Anna was dead nervous but Maggi obviously knew what she was doing. She took the helm and stayed close to the shore, managing everything herself. Then, after a while, they saw her passing Anna the jib sheet and pointing further out towards the middle of the river.

Donny saw Anna nodding. That was good. He wanted her to like it. She'd been amazingly quick in the dinghy park; understanding the way it should all work. Aerodynamic forces and stuff.

Then the fat man in the powerboat drove directly at them.

It was a collision course but there was plenty of space and Maggi knew she had right of way. She carried on sailing straight and steady, expecting the powerboat to change direction.

Nothing happened.

Maggi waved. She probably shouted.

Xanthe shouted as well but she and Donny knew they were much too far away and the powerboat's engines were too noisy. They could only watch.

The thrusting shark-bow was about twenty-five metres from the dinghy and accelerating fast when Maggi pushed her tiller down and tacked. As if it were a game of chicken and he'd been waiting for Maggi to give in, the fat man spun his wheel and swerved off. The violent surge from his twin propellers left *Lively Lady* rocking in his wake.The driver looked back and flapped a pudgy hand as he and his shiny boat sped smugly down the river.

Maggi sailed back to shore immediately. Anna was ashen-faced and shaking.

"Did you see that?" stormed Maggi. "Tossers like him shouldn't be allowed on the river. There was no way he didn't hear me when I shouted for water – but he kept coming like he thought he owned the river."

She put her arm round Anna and gave her a warm, impulsive hug. "Don't let it put you off sailing. Please. He was just a pig."

Anna straightened up and moved slightly away. She had got herself under control again. "I know," she said. "Except that's insulting to pigs. I know him. Lots of the looked-after children know him. He likes to bully people. Weaker people. He saw us – me and you, in a dinghy – and he couldn't resist."

Her bleak analysis puzzled Maggi. "But I'm a sailor. I'm not a – what did you call it? – a looked-after child …"

"As far as he's concerned you're just another low life-form."

"Because I'm a child?"

"That as well."

Anna saw that Maggi didn't get it. "Sorry Maggi, but didn't you notice how he treated your mother that night she brought Donny home?"

Maggi was shocked. "You mean …?"

"Yes. I do."

"The nasty word that Anna's avoiding, little sis, is racist."

Donny hadn't heard Xanthe drawl like that since she faced off the boy in the bus the first time he met her.

"He keeps turning up. They say he's an Inspector. He's the one who thinks my Great Aunt Ellen is an illegal immigrant because she's coming from Shanghai and he can't find her name on his lists. He wants to search the containers for her."

"Huh? At the same time that he says *you're* a fantastist and she's a Rescue Myth?"

"No, that's the other one, Denise Tune, laughingly titled the Welfare Officer. He just says I'm a liar and a thief. He says he doesn't believe Great Aunt Ellen exists but at the same time he's threatening to arrest her. I don't think he exactly does logic."

Donny was ready to talk about the fat man now, maybe try and laugh at him a bit. Anna wasn't.

"I wasn't frightened of the boat out there," she said to Maggi. "I was frightened of him. I can't cope with him at all. I physically shake. Can we try forgetting him now, please?"

Then the Ribiero parents arrived, reminding Xanthe and Maggi that it was time for their training session.

They too had seen the near-collision.

"That man should never have been in that area in a powerboat," said Joshua Ribiero. "Breaking the river speed limit and apparently with no idea of the rule of the road. I'm told he's applied to join the R.O. & A. I'm not at all sure that we want him."

"Dad's on the Yacht Club committee," said Xanthe. "A Flag Officer! *Such* a Pillar of Society!" She grinned at her father. Their likeness was startling. "What's his name, my Daddy? Can I slash his mooring lines? Do let me, please …!"

Her father stopped frowning and smiled back. "No you can't, you wrecker. But you'll like his name – he's called Flint. Inspector Jake Flint! Off to your dinghies, now. We'll look after your friends."

But Xanthe and Maggi didn't move immediately. They looked at Donny and he at them.

"Confusion to our enemies!" said Xanthe, quoting.

"And Death to Captain Flint!" replied Maggi and Donny, quoting back.

"You're so going to have to read *Swallows and Amazons* when Donny's finished," Maggi told Anna.

"Or *Treasure Island*," said Xanthe. "Fifteen men on a dead man's chest! Yo ho ho and a bottle of rum …"

The two sisters turned and jogged back towards the dinghy park, chanting, "Drink and the devil had done for the rest / Yo ho ho and a bottle of rum…"

Donny and Anna, left alone with the Ribiero parents, felt suddenly shy.

CHAPTER NINE
Snow Goose

Saturday, September 16th, later

They were going down the River Orwell in style. Sailing. In the Ribieros' classic yacht. They were heading downstream in the same direction as the shark-boat but this experience was so good – and the adults so astonishingly kind – that even Anna seemed to have forgotten Inspector Jake Flint.

Joshua and June Ribiero had decided that they didn't want Donny and Anna out on the river alone with what Joshua called 'that level of stupidity' about. So they'd wheeled *Lively Lady* back to the dinghy park and ushered the children down the sloping lawn to the club's private pontoons where their yacht, *Snow Goose*, was moored.

Snow Goose was completely beautiful. Creamy-white and elegant. Her wooden masts and spars were reddish-gold; she had a long tapering bowsprit, narrow decks and a slim stern rather like a canoe. Donny fell in love with her from the moment he stepped on board and felt the scarcely perceptible movement with which she accepted his weight. The Ribiero parents had evidently been using her cockpit as a peaceful place to drink coffee and read the newspapers but *Snow Goose* was tossing very slightly as if such inactivity made her restless.

As soon as Donny had recovered from his shyness, he bombarded Joshua Ribiero with questions and was soon following him round the deck as the girls' father gave lucid explanations of the yacht's yawl rig, her variety of sails, sheets and halyards. Anna, who had hardly spoken, stayed close to June and only her bright eyes and air of intentness revealed that she too found the boat and her functions fascinating.

Snow Goose was really old. She'd been built long before the Second World War from a design by a famous artist. "Out of the mind of God," said Joshua Ribiero, as if he was joking.

Donny knew he wasn't. He could see from the way the tall man touched and talked about the yacht that he was in love with her as well.

"So," said Joshua, "Shall we let her take us down the river? We could show you Harwich Harbour – it's exciting if you've not visited by boat before."

"It's exciting when you've been a hundred times!" said June. "Watching ships get ready for sea – "

The wind had freshened a little and *Snow Goose* heeled lazily as she reached down river, her sails towering about them, bright against the clear sky.

They soon passed Pin Mill – a picturesque jumble of boats and cottages with a pub almost in the water. Beyond the pub was a line of houseboats: some freshly painted with washing lines and geraniums on pots; others looking ramshackle and slightly crazed. What a place to live, Donny thought. Skye could surely be happy in a place like that.

Then Joshua called him to come and harden in the sheets as the river changed direction. He was allowed to take the helm and warned that he needed to keep a sharp lookout for ships going up and down to Ipswich.

"Don't only look ahead of you – keep checking behind as well. They'll blast you with their hooter if they think you're in their way."

"Aren't there rules about all that?" Anna asked. "When Maggi and I were in the dinghy she said that the man in the motorboat should give way to us. But he didn't."

"Plenty of rules – which some ignorant people don't know and a few idiots decide to ignore … Donny, she's all yours!"

This was a big responsibility – but it was exhilarating too, feeling the weight and the surging movement of *Snow Goose* as she responded to the wind and the tide and to his hands on the tiller.

"Could *Lively Lady* sail right down the river like this?"

"Certainly she could. We had a talk at the club last year by a man who'd crossed the English Channel in a *Mirror*. Then he got into the European canal system and ended up somewhere in the Black Sea."

"But you don't have to go quite that far to have a good time," said June. "You can have an adventure on any river. And there's a lot to see. I'll bring the binoculars up."

"Don't they look like a herd of dinosaurs?" she smiled, as they caught their first glimpse of the Port of Felixstowe cranes.

As *Snow Goose* carried them closer, it became increasingly obvious that this was a large and hungry herd. There was constant clanging of metal and rumbling of engines on the quayside while, high above, rectangular containers slid backwards and forwards on gantries to supply the gigantic vessels moored below. The water space had widened out dramatically,

So this was Harwich Harbour. Donny couldn't yet see the sea but he could guess where it was.

"Those ships are so big it's hard to get them in perspective." said June. "When you think that each one of those containers, being stacked up there like blocks of Lego, is a whole lorry-load ... They travel right across the world. Mainly to and from the Far East. Why don't you go sit on the foredeck with the binoculars so you can both have a really good look? We'll have to bring her round in a moment. You'll be wanting some lunch."

As they picked their way carefully forward along the narrow deck, Anna said quietly to Donny. "Do you realise that's where 'Strong Winds' will arrive – in a container on one of those enormous ships."

"I wish I knew what 'Strong Winds' is," sighed Donny. "And why Great Aunt Ellen wants us to meet her at Shotley, when Shotley's somewhere over there ... She'll have to get it across the river."

"That's her problem," said Anna. "She must know what she's planning to do. Maybe there's a ferry. But from your point of view Shotley's good. It's on the right side of the river for the vicarage. I've been looking. You can get there even if you have to walk."

"Or sail," said Donny.

"Yes," agreed Anna. "You could sail."

They took turns using the binoculars, both of them scanning the activity around the containers with the unspoken hope that they might discover some clue as to the identity of 'Strong Winds'.

"We could be looking at it right now," said Donny.

"Probably not," said Anna, sensibly. "ETA means Estimated Time of Arrival and she said ETA late September. That's still another fortnight."

"But we don't know how often these ships come and go or how long they take to unload or anything … What is it? What's the matter?"

For Anna, who had been using the binoculars, was gripping Donny's arm so tightly that it hurt. With her other hand she was shoving the binoculars at him.

"Over there," she whispered urgently. "Right at the very end of the quay. Where those steps go down."

They were good binoculars. Once he had located the steps, he could see, very clearly, the gleaming black shark-boat moored at their base and, when he focussed on the area of quay at the top of the steps, there was the hulking figure of its owner. Flint was standing with two other men. One was small and dressed in blue overalls.

Was there something fleetingly familiar about him?

Nah, the impression was gone.

The small man was standing next to Flint as if they were both talking to the third man. He was wearing a hardhat and big boots. A dock-worker of some kind?

Flint had his palm pad out, the small man was gesturing towards a pile of containers. As if they were explaining something maybe technical to the man in the hardhat.

Then they did something that Donny couldn't quite believe.

What he saw first was a bright blue bird.

The small man had it. Took it from his pocket? Donny

thought it was maybe on a short leash because, although he could see it fluttering, it couldn't get away.

"It's a bird!" he whispered to Anna. "A budgie or something. They're showing it to the other bloke. Now Flint's got it. Oh my god! No. I can't believe it. He's … pulled its …"

"Let me have a look then," she hissed, grabbing the binoculars back from him. "Oh yuck! Oh no! … That is minging!!"

She let the binoculars drop: she looked as if she might be sick. "He stamped …" she began, white-faced.

"Ready about, you two. Come aft please. Quickly!"

They'd almost reached the Shotley Spit buoy and Joshua Ribiero was preparing to bring *Snow Goose* into the wind, change tack and ease her sheets so they were heading up river again. It could have been managed with them still sitting on the foredeck but it was safer this way.

The heavy main boom swung across, its sheets running sweetly through a system of wooden blocks. The jib and foresail sheets had to be released one side then winched in on the other. Donny and Anna did what they could to help, dazedly attempting to obey Joshua's instructions. By the time Donny looked round again, *Snow Goose* was already well on her way back up the river and there was no time to refocus the binoculars on the quayside. Even if he'd wanted to.

"If you look to port now," said Joshua. "That means look over her left-hand side – away from Felixstowe – you can just see the entrance to Shotley Marina. See the line of national flags and the tops of the masts behind those breakwaters?"

Donny and Anna looked.

It had been such a blissful Saturday sail … Donny thought he'd better try and say something. He didn't think Anna could.

"So, er, how do the boats get into the marina?" he asked.

"Through a lock. It's a short distance up the River Stour. Look between that three-masted schooner and the green slope with the tall white flagpole at the top. Use the binoculars. Can you see two pillars in the river a little way off from the shore? Yes? Well that's the beginning of the entrance. Those pillars, and an indicator on the marina wall, are part of a system to help boats find the channel and keep straight as they enter the lock – even in the dark. Twenty-four hour access."

"Oh!" Donny was startled into real interest. "Like leading lights?"

Joshua Ribiero looked surprised too. Then he smiled. "Yes. I forgot – you're reading *Swallows and Amazons* aren't you? We have the full set at home. Do ask my daughters if there are further volumes that you'd like to borrow; you'll pick up all sorts of pieces of knowledge that way. Though, from what I saw earlier, your sailing skill's instinctive. Quite remarkable, actually."

For a moment Donny felt warmed by this praise: then the image of what he and Anna had just witnessed flashed back into his head. The little bird … terrified. Flint's big hand … twisting its neck. The sudden pull … He clamped his hand over his mouth. He couldn't be sick here: not in front of Mr Ribiero, not on *Snow Goose*'s scrubbed teak deck.

"Never mind," said Xanthe's father kindly, "Even Nelson suffered seasickness."

Donny couldn't answer him. Beautiful *Snow Goose* was creaming back up the river now. Wind and tide were with her and they were leaving the cranes and containers far behind. It seemed utterly disloyal to the graceful yacht to suggest her movement was anything other than exhilarating but … he couldn't even try to explain. He must have seen wrong.

"Time you took a turn, Anna, isn't it?" said June Ribiero, who'd noticed how adeptly Anna shrank into the background, particularly when Joshua was talking. "Come and stand with me and we'll see if we can cut a few corners. There won't be any food left at the club if we're very much longer."

Flint's powerboat sped past before they reached Pin Mill. By the time they'd moored *Snow Goose* and were walking up to the Royal Orwell & Ancient Yacht Club, the fat man was ensconced at a table for one with a large lobster salad, a bottle of white wine, a deep bowl of mayonnaise and an entire loaf of garlic bread.

Anna took herself off instantly to the other side of the room where Xanthe and Maggi were sharing sandwiches and a plate of chips. Donny was tempted to go with her but when Joshua and June walked across to speak to the policeman he followed them. He wasn't going to show that he was scared.

Joshua wasted little time introducing himself. "I was on board my yacht this morning when you almost ran down my daughter and her friend – I wondered whether it was an accident or whether you have something to learn about nautical rules of the road?"

Flint wiped his mouth. "Nothing that I care to be taught by

someone of your … type," he answered after a pause.

Joshua showed no reaction. "Of course not. I'm a flag officer of this club. I don't take lower level competency classes. If you give your name to the training secretary he can enrol you on some suitable course. They're open to non-members."

An angry flush crept up from where Flint's neck would have been if his jowls didn't sag straight into the collar of his shirt.

"My membership application has been in front of the committee for a month," he snarled. "The chief constable's my proposer. I've no expectation of being … black-balled." He glowered towards the table where the girls had gathered. "Your daughters and their charity playmates have a very distinctive dinghy. I'll keep a special lookout for it in the future."

Then he tore a front pincer off his lobster and crushed it between his fleshy fingers.

June almost had the last word. She turned to Joshua. "It's no good, darling. The RYA …" She looked down at Flint. "That's the R-o-y-a-l Y-a-c-h-t-i-n-g A-s-s-o-c-i-a-t-i-o-n to you," she said, apparently kindly, "could probably teach him some rules of the road and basic boat-handling but not the simple concept of politeness. The idea of 'sorry' for instance – it's going to be beyond him. Let's not ask them to waste their time."

It would have been such a dignified exit line – if Donny hadn't happened to glance downwards at that moment and noticed something … feathery … sticking to the policeman's heavy boot.

CHAPTER TEN
Family Activity

Saturday, September 16th, later still

The grey stone walls of Erewhon Parva vicarage looked dusty and unwelcoming when the Ribieros dropped Donny and Anna back later that afternoon. There'd been some talk of swimming after lunch but they'd mainly mooched about, helping Maggi and Xanthe take down the masts of their *Lasers* and pack for their trip to Weymouth the following day. They hadn't wanted to talk about Flint and the small man and the dead bird on the quayside.

"We didn't get anything, did we?" said Anna, when they had thanked all the family for the final time and were going reluctantly into the bleak house.

"Whatever do you mean?" Donny was astonished.

"For the dream-catchers. You said we were going to collect grasses and feathers and make one for each other and one for your mum. But we didn't get anything at all." She spoke in her old flat, expressionless voice.

For a moment Donny felt annoyed that she should be bothering about what they hadn't done when so much else had happened. Then, as the loveless atmosphere of the foster-home closed over them like a stagnant pond, he realised she was right: thistledown and beads, dried grass and supple twigs were exactly what they needed to block the nightmares out.

But not feathers. Definitely not small, downy feathers.

"I'm sorry," he said. "I forgot. Tomorrow's Sunday. I'll do it tomorrow. I promise. You forgot too, didn't you?"

"You shouldn't do promises," she said. "You promised before."

"I did promise. I know I did. But I didn't say definitely when. Now I'm saying that it's going to be tomorrow. Okay? Look, it's almost been a great day. Don't spoil it. Please?"

It had evidently not been a great day at the vicarage. Wendy was out and Vicky was crying in her playpen while Gerald tried to get something together for supper. Liam, the younger boy, had already been sent up to his bedroom where he was bouncing a football hard on the floor directly over Gerald's head. His brother, Luke, was sitting sullenly on the living-room sofa refusing to take any interest in the pile of old books and puzzle pads that had been placed next to him. The TV was turned off.

Anna vanished as effectively as usual but Donny hesitated a moment between kitchen and living room. He felt tired but full of fresh air and friendliness – even towards Gerald.

"Er, can I help?" he asked.

Gerald looked as if he was almost too distracted to answer. There was a Radio Four programme failing to compete with Vicky's yells and he was trying to follow a recommended recipe for gluten-free bread mix. He looked at Donny as if his arrival was the last straw and turned the radio off with a sigh.

"There's Luke," he said. "You could spend quality time with Luke."

Donny looked back into the sitting room. Luke finger-swore. Whether at him or at Gerald wasn't entirely clear.

"Okay," said Donny, wishing that he hadn't offered. The football thudded above them: Vicky's yells got even louder. It seemed extraordinary that so much noise could come from someone so small. Without really thinking, Donny went over to her pen. Maybe she was plugged into an amplifier…?

As he looked down he saw that her little face was scarlet and slubbered. Her toys had been hurled out and bits of half chewed carrot stick lay strewn angrily around the wipe-able mat. Her eyes were squeezed shut with the effort of her bellowing and he didn't know whether she'd noticed him or not. She was sort of drowning in her own rage.

"Shall I pick the baby up? I'll wash my hands," he added hastily.

Gerald must have been near the end of his tether. Otherwise there'd have been some spiel about Vicky's tantrum being part of her developmental process blah-blah. As it was, he nodded mutely and pointed to the anti-bacterial hand cleanser beside the sink.

As soon as she felt herself being lifted up, Vicky's sobs ceased. Donny worried that he was holding her rather tightly. He wasn't used to babies and was frightened he might drop her if she wriggled. He was glad he was still in his river clothes. She was not a hygienic sight and, close up, she was smelly.

"Um, she's a bit smelly," he said to Gerald.

"She can't be. I only changed her nappy half an hour ago and she's had nothing since." He had a sniff. "Oh. Yes. Well, I can't deal with that now. I'm trying to cook supper."

Donny supposed he could put up with it. Vicky's small body felt surprisingly warm and solid in his arms. He ignored the reek and hugged her protectively. It was nice to be touching another person.

"Does Luke know where her nappies are?" They'd done a bit of baby care in sex ed at school. He could give it a go.

"I'll come in a minute. Now, please, just let me do one thing at a time. All of you."

Donny took the hint and shut the kitchen door behind him as he left. A moment later he heard Radio Four come quietly back on again.

He looked into the sitting room. Luke started guiltily. He'd turned on the TV and was watching a game show without any sound. Donny grinned at him, pointed at the closed door of the kitchen and left the room again carrying Vicky upstairs.

He tried Anna's door but it was shut and there was no answer when he knocked. He hadn't realised she was that offended with him. So then he tried the adults' bathroom.

"Don't tell," he said to Vicky, quiet and cosy and niffy in his arms.

He'd guessed that this was where her things might be and he was right. What lost him completely was that he couldn't see any nappies. A changing mat, hypo-allergenic baby wipes, a bucket and a neat pile of folded white towels. It was only when he'd decided he'd best clean her bottom anyway, that he realised the white towels were what she was supposed to wear. She had one on already, fixed with a fearsome-looking safety pin. Not at all like the neat, disposable nappy that they'd practised putting onto the life size doll at school.

Liam came in then. He didn't say anything and he wasn't much help.

At least he didn't bring his football.

Vicky had begun to kick as soon as Donny took the towel off. He'd managed to get most of the poo down the toilet but there was still some on her bottom and a big smear across the changing mat as she rolled over and started to crawl away.

Liam seemed to think this was funny and started urging her on, "Go Vicky!"

Donny tried to keep calm but the floor was soon littered with used wipes and rumpled towels as Vicky did laps and Liam made everything worse. There was no way he was ever going to work out how to get the towel back on so he gave up and began running a bath. At least he could get her clean. He got a few more of her clothes off, then Liam splashed her. Not hard and she didn't mind but all the rest of her clothes got wet.

They must have been making a lot of noise though none of them were exactly speaking to each other.

Anna came in.

"Out," she said to Liam who had soaked a pile of cotton wool balls and was trying to get Vicky to watch him as he flicked them at a goal he'd drawn with toothpaste on the mirror.

"Sorry," said Donny.

He'd not seen Anna do anything with the baby before. She was good, very good.

And Vicky was good too, sitting on Anna's lap while she was dried, accepting the dry vest and clean baby-gro without a struggle, then lying quite contented on the mat while Anna fixed the nappy. If babies could show feelings it was obvious that Vicky liked Anna.

"Sorry," he said again. "I did try. I wasn't used to those sort of nappies."

"Environmental," she answered briefly. "Don't tell them I changed it or they'll make me do it all the time."

"Oh, okay," he said, smiling at Vicky. "You'll have to show me. I don't mind. I think she's cute."

"She's my half-sister," said Anna. "As far as I'm concerned she's caused a lot of trouble."

"But she's a baby!"

"She lost us our mum," said Anna shortly.

Donny was shocked. "You can't blame her. I mean, of course I don't know anything about what happened but, whatever it was, you still can't blame a baby."

They didn't look much like each other. Anna had washed Vicky's hair and rubbed it dry and Donny could see the feathery curls were pale red, far finer and softer than down. He stretched out cautiously and twisted one round his finger. It was so light he could hardly feel it. Her eyes were maybe like Anna's. They were grey.

"Logically I don't," said Anna. "But, also logically, the way she's most useful at the moment is for keeping people like Gerald and Wendy occupied – changing her nappies and getting up to her in the night and all that."

Donny blinked at her. What was she talking about?

"So, if you actually want to be helpful, you can take her downstairs again and make sure she gets right under Gerald's feet while Wendy's out. Slow him up. Then I can stay in my room till supper. The later the better."

Obediently he picked Vicky up and headed for the stairs. But when Vicky saw she was being parted from her sister, she began to cry again, the same high, abandoned wailing that Donny had heard in the night. So he took her into his own room and played peek-bo and tickling games. He even tried signing to her and telling her poems.

Being with Vicky made him long to be with Skye.

Sunday, September 17th

"A Family Service is part of a Family Sunday," said Gerald wearily. The children were all around the breakfast table. Rev. Wendy had already taken an early service somewhere and was back for a cup of coffee before she moved on to her next parish. "So if you expect to be part of our Family Activity in the afternoon, it's only reasonable you should attend church in the morning."

"What do you do in the afternoons?" asked Donny. His head felt heavy and his eyes hurt. The nights here were terrible. He'd spent ages last night making a new map and drawing a set of detailed pictures of *Snow Goose* for Skye. He'd have to find somewhere to hide them. Inside his pillow, for now.

Then he'd read *Swallows and Amazons* so that he could fall asleep in a tent with those other kids – John and Susan, Titty and Roger.

But it hadn't worked. His dream had been confused and terrifying: container ships and fog and little Vicky needing him. Some book he didn't know and couldn't find.

He'd got to get those dream-catchers sorted.

"Those who attend the Family Service have their say in choosing the Family Activity," Gerald replied.

"And those who don't …?"

"Have freely chosen to exclude themselves so spend the afternoon in their bedrooms," Wendy snapped, spreading some over-boiled jam on a piece of Ryvita.

"My choice would be to go and see my mum."

No response from either adult. No surprises there.

"But if I'm still not allowed I'd like to go for a walk. We could maybe go down to Pin Mill and explore the woods beside the river – ?"

The Ribieros had said something about a footpath and Anna had thought he could even walk to Shotley.

"Then you can come to the 10.30 at Harkstead with me," said Gerald. "Anna, Liam, Luke – what do you choose?"

Anna shook her head and didn't answer.

Gerald sighed.

"Wanna play football," said Liam.

"Don't care," said Luke.

This was sufficient for Gerald to decide that they would all – except Anna – be attending the Family Service in the morning and going for a walk in the afternoon. He brushed Liam's football pleas aside by saying he could bring his ball on the walk with them and told Anna sternly that she should remember that the Circle was always Open to her when she had learned to take a more Positive Attitude. She should consider that either he or Wendy would have to remain at home to supervise her.

"Doesn't bother me," she told Donny. "Whichever one stays

behind goes on about my negativity for a while then sends me upstairs so that they can snooze on the sofa with the papers. I *love* Sunday afternoons. Keep them out for as long as you can."

Donny's spirits lifted as they left the vicarage and set out down the single-track road to Pin Mill and the river. It wasn't far and when they got there it was just as good as it had looked from *Snow Goose*. The foreshore was cluttered with boats. There were boats that had become houses, boats that were being built or repaired, boats that had been abandoned and were slowly rotting back to their skeletons. Out in the river, there were more boats of all sizes, sailing, motoring, rowing boats; dozens and dozens of boats tugging and swinging at their moorings.

He yearned for one of them to be his own.

"Get real!" he told himself.

The other boys weren't enjoying themselves much. Luke was silent and Liam was sulky because there was nowhere that he could kick his football without it splatting into water. Donny felt guilty that he'd made them come.

Gerald, however – away from his kitchen and possibly also away from his wife – became rather skittish and demanded they play tracking games as he'd used to do on boy scout summer camps. He had Vicky in a sort of canvas chair on his back and seemed keen to go galloping about making funny noises. He and Liam would lay a trail through the woods, he announced: something very simple using twigs and stones to indicate changes of direction. Donny and Luke could prove they'd followed it correctly by collecting the ten different leaves that he'd place at turning points along the way. He lent Donny a watch and said they would meet back at Pin Mill Hard no later than four o'clock if they hadn't caught up with each other earlier.

This sounded all right.

Donny wasn't planning to spend too long in the woods, though. Okay, he wanted to find nuts and stuff for the dream-catchers but he also wanted to check along the strip of sandy beach that seemed to run behind the houseboats. See whether it really led to a footpath that might take him down along the riverbank for however many miles it was to Shotley.

As long as he could get Luke to co-operate they could always scoop up a few random leaves before they got back.

He must have seemed a bit too cheerful because Gerald suddenly became ponderous about the importance of Sticking Together, Playing the Game and Not Speaking to Strangers.

After which he cheered up again and galumphed off into the woods with Vicky bouncing on his back and Liam looking marginally happier at the prospect of being the one who might choose the pathways and confuse the other two.

Donny was left with Luke.

They hadn't been alone together before and were awkwardly silent while they waited to give the others their agreed start.

The tide was rising and there were several empty dinghies rocking and jiggling near the top of the Hard. Presumably their owners had come ashore to walk up to the shops or go to the pub. Donny couldn't resist wandering across to have a look. Some had outboard motors; others had oars and rowlocks.

He leaned over to touch the smooth wooden handle of an oar, fitted it experimentally into a rowlock … He was sure he could do this. Rowing was something people did a lot in his book. This dinghy was clinker-built – like *Swallow* – but not varnished. It had been painted a delicate pale green outside, a workmanlike grey within. *Margery*. Someone had painted a cluster of flowers beside the name.

Margery was tied to a chain, quite safely – Donny admired the knot – but there was enough water in the runnel beside the Hard to keep her floating. It wouldn't do any harm, would it, if he climbed in …?

Luke had got bored and was throwing stones at a coke can. One of them, rather a large one, missed the can, ricocheted off a mooring post and hit the pale green dinghy with a sharp crack, removing several fragments of paint.

"I say!" shouted an untidy-looking lady with a big nose who was drinking beer in the pub.

But the boys didn't wait to hear what the lady was going to say. They turned and legged it up the path behind the pub, disappearing as quickly as they could into the trees. They didn't dare stick to the main path for long in case she came after them. There was obviously no chance of them pausing to look for twig arrows or whatever Liam and Gerald had left to mark their trail. As the main path curved upwards they took a downhill track that soon had them pushing through dense rhododendron bushes and jumping across the damp bed of a stream.

They were at the edge of the wood before they knew it. There was a straight drop of two or three metres to the beach. Luke was about to hurl himself over when Donny pulled him back.

"Stop a minute. We need to look around. Once we're down there, we maybe can't get up again."

A few paces to the right an oak tree spread low branches out across the sand. Donny wriggled out to a broad fork where a burst of thick leaves screened them from view. He noticed some startlingly pale acorns still in their cups, and dropped a few in his pocket for Anna. They were about the same colour as the dinghy they'd damaged.

Then he took a look at his companion. Luke had followed a little way out onto the branch, then stopped. He was sheet-white and trembling. Not at all the hard man who'd been finger-swearing in front of the TV or kicking his brother in the vicarage garden.

"I didn't mean to …" he said, to himself rather than to Donny.

"I know you didn't. You'd have had to be a snooker-champ to get an angle like that on purpose!"

Luke didn't seem to be listening.

Donny tried again. "It was me she must've been watching. I was about to climb into that boat. Like I was in a dream or something. I don't know what I was thinking. Let's hide here for a bit and see whether we see her go out onto the river."

Luke still didn't speak. He looked cold with fright. Donny checked the watch.

"We've got about an hour before we have to go back. She'll have got fed up by then. Maybe the dinghy wasn't even hers."

113

"Will it break?"

"Of course not. You only chipped the paint."

"This … tree?"

"No Luke, it won't." Donny scrambled back along the branch. "It's been here ages. You can see. The cliff's eroding but the tree's still here. Its roots go right into the sand. Look down here, you'll see what I mean."

"Can't."

Luke sounded as if he might throw up.

"Okay, okay, so you don't like heights. Tell you what. That lady's not going to come. Let's get ourselves down onto the beach. You don't have to look. I'll go first. You turn round onto your tummy and slide. I'll catch you."

But even as Luke slid, Donny heard the sound of rowing and he guessed their luck was out. The big-nosed lady was rowing *Margery* steadily along the beach, quite close in. She had her back to them so Donny dragged Luke into the only possible shelter, a sort of cave, made by the tree roots, where the cliff had worn away.

"Sit as small as you can. Wrap your arms round your knees. And don't move."

CHAPTER ELEVEN
A Wicked Plan

Sunday, September 17th, continued

There were two people in *Margery*. The lady who'd seen them was doing the rowing but there was an old lady sitting in the stern, facing forward. She looked quite short and dumpy and was wearing something green on her head.

Donny didn't hardly dare breathe and Luke kept his eyes tight shut.

When *Margery* was just metres away the old lady said something that made the other one look right across the river. To the far side. She kept on about it all the time the dinghy edged past. It seemed to take ages until, finally, they were gone.

Still he knew they mustn't come out yet. The lady who was rowing would be looking their way for a long while if she carried on parallel to the shore like that. Maybe he should get Luke talking. Relax him a bit. Take his mind off it. Those oars had been quite noisy. She wouldn't be able to hear them.

"Don't suppose this is exactly what Gerald had in mind for a Family Sunday – !"

Luke looked up, shook his head. Almost smiled.

"What do you do normally do then?"

"Usually football for Liam or sometimes we go to Ipswich when it's my turn."

"What do you do there?"

"Bowling or the cinema." Luke didn't sound as if these were exactly highlights.

"Is that what you like doing?"

"Not really. Makes a change from football though. Or sitting on our rooms."

"I suppose it does. Er, do you ever … you know, like go and see your parents or anything?"

Luke shrugged and looked depressed.

Donny probably shouldn't have asked. Except he badly wanted to know. He felt as if Skye had been blotted from his life. He wondered if it was the same for the others.

"Our mum's dead. Liam and I can't hardly remember her. Anna's mum had us for a bit. Then she went too. After that baby was born." He sighed. "They take us to see Dad sometimes."

"Does he live near here?"

"Don't think so. We have to go in the car and it takes ages. Liam gets sick and I don't like it 'cos there's dogs."

"Don't you like dogs?"

"Not those ones. They sniff you."

"Oh." Donny didn't understand. "I suppose if we had sniffer dogs we could give them a bit of the others' clothes to smell and they could take us along the trail really quick without us having to bother looking for twigs and stones at all. They wouldn't ever know we hadn't done it properly."

Luke brightened up. "Yeah. And when they found the others they could like knock them over and stand on them and growl if they moved. And bite their throats …"

"Er … maybe."

Donny inched forward in their shallow cave and poked his head out between the tree roots.

Not so good.

Margery had been pulled up on the sand at the far end of the beach. Fifty, one hundred metres away? The two ladies were gone, he didn't know where, and the tide was ebbing fast. Already there was a distinct gap between *Margery* and the river's edge.

She was quite a heavy dinghy. They wouldn't be able to move her in a hurry.

Donny looked both ways. There was nobody else about.

"I reckon we need to start getting back. How about we crawl out of here, as close under the cliff as we can. Opposite direction to that dinghy. Then, soon as there's a chance, we get up into the wood again ..."

"And start sniffing after Li! His trainers get well stinky!"

"Oh okay. If you want. But remember, dogs can't talk. All this stays between you and me."

Luke put his head on one side and yapped, really quietly.

Even when they were safely up into the trees again Donny didn't dare explore any further towards the Shotley end of the wood. *Margery*'s owner and the old lady must be around there somewhere. He couldn't think what they'd be doing.

A distant glimpse of the shark-boat nosing down towards Felixstowe made him glad they'd left the beach.

Luke had become a big and extremely fierce dog, panting and snuffling and cocking his leg against the larger trees. Donny soon got fed up with having his ankle bitten and being jumped on. Then he realised that the best way to cope was by appointing himself Luke's official handler so he could give commands and get him trotting to heel carrying things.

This suited them both. Luke bounded about energetically, dropping and retrieving fantasy thigh-bones, while Donny collected smooth, supple, alder twigs for the outer rim of the dream-catchers and some fibrous bark which they might shred and use for weaving. They even found a few of the leaves along Gerald's trail before it was time to give up and return to the Hard.

Gerald, Vicky and Liam arrived about five minutes later.

"That was cool fun!" shouted Liam. "We got stuck in a place where the water had come in and we had to take our shoes off and he got his trousers all wet!"

Vicky was clutching the bar of her easy-rider, looking pink and bright-eyed as if she'd had cool fun too.

Gerald was puffing and muddy. He took Vicky and her pack off his back and sat down heavily on a bench outside the pub to clean his shoes with profligate quantities of baby-wipes.

"Tell you what, Gerald mate," said Liam, who had got his football out and was doing keepi-uppies with undiminished energy, "an ice-cream all round and we don't tell Rev. Wendy the word you used when you wet your trousers. Is that a deal?"

Luke put his paws together, hung his tongue out and dribbled. He was embarrassing. Donny didn't really know where to look.

Nor, it seemed, did Gerald who was clearly troubled by the wipe-disposal question. If he took them home he could perhaps shred them for compost. But there were so many and so muddy...

He shut his eyes and pushed them in the public bin to augment the county's landfill. Then he began searching, distractedly, for the watch that he'd lent to Donny.

Maybe it had been Wendy's?

He was so relieved when Donny handed it back, that he bought the ice-creams without another word. He wiped everyone's faces before they were allowed to touch the packaging, pushed those wipes into his pocket and ignored the untidy bundles of bark, nuts, old man's beard and alder twig that Donny carried up the road and through the vicarage front door.

No one came out to greet them.

"They was in your room yesterday," said Luke, turning back into a boy again. "Checking through your stuff. But I don't think they found nothing."

"That's because there's nothing to find," snapped Donny, his good mood gone.

Monday, September 18th

"*Vive* la Rescue Myth, Donny-man!" Xanthe and Maggi swung themselves, their bags and Long John into some empty seats opposite Donny and Anna. "How was Sunday in the boot camp?"

"Could have been worse," said Donny. Pin Mill had basically been all right even if the night had been bad again

"Could have been better," muttered Anna.

Somehow Anna's Sunday afternoon hadn't worked out. All Donny had managed to discover was that Wendy hadn't dozed on the sofa with the newspapers as expected; she'd spent the time in her study re-writing a sermon. This, according to Anna, meant that she'd had to do her homework instead.

"Instead of what?"

But she didn't answer.

When he'd asked her if she wanted to make dream-catchers with him after supper she'd said no, she was busy. That left him to do his own homework.

He was beginning to worry about Great Aunt Ellen. She must be very old – in her seventies? Eighties, even? What if Flint did try to arrest her or intimidate her or something? If he could be that offensive to someone like Joshua Ribiero never mind what he had done to that bird on the quay   it would sort of be Donny's fault, wouldn't it? He'd be responsible.

Then there'd been another of those sweat-drenched nightmares.

"Better make the catchers tonight," said Anna as they had waited for the bus on Monday morning. He must have shouted out again. She must have heard him.

"Yes … if you're not too busy."

She ignored him. "What do we need?"

"Scissors, but I suppose they'll have some back there." He wasn't going to use the word 'home' when he meant the vicarage. Not ever.

"All the sharp ones are locked up. And they'll ask why we want them. Leave it to me. Anything else?"

"Well, really big needles would be good. You know, the sort they call bodkins. And, ideally, something sharp to make holes. Then those acorns I collected could be our beads. It's not how the Native Americans make them, obviously – or Mum – and they won't last very long. But, well, I don't want any of this to last very long. They can't keep me away from my own mother for ever."

"You wish," said Anna. Then she had pressed her lips together and looked pinched and thin again.

"The parentals have got a wicked plan." Xanthe told them, as soon as they'd sat down. "We were talking about you on the way home and Dad said, 'why don't we lend them *Lively Lady*?' As if he'd just that moment thought of it."

"And Mum agreed with him so fast it was obvious they'd already had the discussion and made up their minds," said Maggi. "They often operate like that. They think we don't notice."

"We play along," Xanthe agreed. "In four-part family harm-on-ee."

She stopped, awkwardly.

"It's not just the dinghy-lending that impressed us. It's the way they've thought it through," she carried on, accepting Maggi's elbow-jab with uncharacteristic meekness. "They are deeply under-whelmed by that porker policeman and they don't want him harassing you while you're on the river."

"So they think you should disguise *Lively Lady*!" Maggi dropped her voice dramatically. "Though, obviously they didn't put it quite so straight," she added, more normally. "Said that it was time *LL* had a new coat of paint and maybe something a bit less conspicuous would be a good idea …"

"Dark grey," said Donny immediately.

Xanthe looked at him sharply.

"Yeah, go for it. If it's hot, you need to paint wooden boats a light colour to reflect the heat away. But it's autumn now and, if you're thinking what I think you're thinking, charcoal could be the new white. We'll change her sails too. Use the Kevlar set. Classy but drab."

"And they want you to keep her somewhere different. Maybe the reservoir, Gitche Gumee?"

"No, we'll keep her at Pin Mill … if that'd be okay …"

He hadn't even said thank you. This was so amazing!

"But why?" asked Anna. "Why are they doing this? And why include me? I can't sail like Donny."

"Well, Mum says that you're incredibly … what was it Xanth?"

"Mature and clear-headed," supplied her sister. "And clever with your fingers too."

"Oh," said Anna, flushing slightly. She thought for a moment. "I'm not sure. I might be the fingers but I'm definitely not clear-headed. Not about Flint, anyway. I wish I was."

"He is a tad scary," Maggi agreed. "That's why they want you and the boat out of his way. You may be the muppet to end all muppets which you're not but you're our friend and we've got an Alliance. So you're in. Okay?"

The bus was at school now. There was no time for more.

"Okay," said Anna, sounding rather dazed as the four of them clambered out of the bus and joined the jostling Monday morning crowd. "Er … confusion to our enemies then."

As Xanthe had predicted, Mr McMullen told Donny that, as it was the start of a new week, he could consider himself off report. "Not that I haven't enjoyed seeing your fresh face but … somehow I've gained the impression that you'd rather spend your break and lunchtimes elsewhere. Correct me if I'm wrong?"

Donny couldn't quite think how to answer.

"Please make sure that elsewhere is somewhere that you're officially allowed to be … and, Donny – you prefer that to John don't you? – please also remember that I am your tutor and you know where to find me if there are things you want to discuss." He paused, stroked his beard and sighed, "Anything troubling you in particular?"

The question was totally casual; the teacher already turning away. This helped Donny give him a try.

"I want to go and see my mother, sir. She'll be worried about me – and I worry about her." Suddenly he felt a bit choky. He was glad Mr McMullen wasn't looking at him.

"Of course. Do you know why you're not allowed to visit?"

"No sir."

"Neither do I. I'll try to find out for you. I expect Welfare will ring me for a report sometime. It's been almost a week. I might even ring her."

Donny said nothing. Anything he said would obviously get passed back.

"She'll probably want a meeting too. The SS love meetings. But I'll let you know if that's going to happen and you can tell me what you'd like me to say. Better still, you'll insist on your own right to be there."

"Am I allowed?"

"Sometimes. But sometimes they restrict their meetings to Professionals – which implies that you and your mother have only an amateur's interest in the business of managing your lives. In that you'll need to brief me thoroughly and I'll need to be able to go. They have an unhelpful way of timing their meetings for mid-morning in Ipswich – or probably Colchester in your case. Then the school has to find cover for me and I miss half a day's session with my students." He sounded fed up. "You see my problem."

Donny did. And why should this man give a toss about his troubles anyway? Let alone care about Skye who he'd never met.

"So I'll only go to one of their Professional meetings if I think I've a chance of making a difference," the teacher continued. "That's why I wish you'd open up a bit. I won't keep your secrets if they're going to put you at real risk but I do try to assume that you have the best knowledge of your own situation." He picked up some papers as if to show the interview was at an end. "Unfortunately it's a minority view. Keep in touch."

Donny turned to go. Then, on an impulse, he turned back. "Sir, are there any after-school clubs I can join?"

Mr McMullen looked surprised. "You'll find lists in the library or on the school website. I keep this department open late two nights a week for project and exam work and there are still a few of my colleagues who do the same. Your problem will be transport. Talk to me about it when you've decided what you want to do."

"Oh … er … thanks. Thanks very much." Donny hurried away to his first lesson, his mind busy.

He saw Anna at morning break, in the ICT area, but she wasn't speaking to him.

Google found him half a million hits for 'Strong Winds' – nearly all weather reports. There was a song he liked: "Four strong winds that blow lonely / Seven seas that run high," but nothing that he could imagine even the most eccentric great aunt putting into a crate.

He gave up and looked instead at the list of After School clubs. He'd join anything: madrigal-making, earwig appreciation, litter management – anything to earn time away from the vicarage.

This was Monday.

His next free day was Saturday, the twenty-third of September. Great Aunt Ellen could be here by then! He urgently needed to talk boat.

He saw Maggi at lunchtime but she was hanging out with a crowd of people he didn't know so he didn't go up to her. Then he spotted Xanthe heading towards the music block. He abandoned his place in the food queue.

"Hi, Xanthe, can I talk to you? Your parents … *Lively Lady* … it's so totally brilliant. I don't know how to … Totally. But … you said we could repaint her. When can we do it? Where? And how can I not tell Wendy and Gerald?"

"Yeah," Xanthe was in a rush but she'd obviously taken it all in. "We need tactics. Can you and Anna stay after school tomorrow? Fake something. We'll check it in the morning. Okay?"

"Okay."

Donny dropped back. As Xanthe pushed through the double doors of the music block he felt as if he'd been caught in the wind shadow of an ocean racer.

He stood, staring after her, as the doors swung shut.

"Yer won't do no good there, mate. Her and her sister. Stuck-up tarts. Oughta get sent back where they came from."

Donny hit out, wildly. But the older boy felled him with a contemptuous swing of his sports bag. Caught him neatly below the knees and landed him hard on the tarmac. It felt like a well-practised manoeuvre.

"Bit of a girl yerself, aren't yer? – mate."

CHAPTER TWELVE

Answers and Questions

Monday, September 18th

"*Strong Winds*'s a Chinese junk – had you realised?" Anna said as they sat in his room after supper making inauthentic dream-catchers.

"A what?" Donny gaped at her.

"A Chinese junk – they're a type of boat. Thought you knew about that sort of thing." Anna's tone was light. She was obviously rather pleased with herself. "Or, rather, the term junk may be used to cover many different types of boat – ocean-going, cargo-carrying, pleasure boats, live-aboards. They vary greatly in size and there are significant regional variations in the type of rig. To Western eyes, however, they all appear to resemble one another due to their most significant shared feature, their fully-battened sails." She sounded as if she was reciting. "I've been researching them."

"How? Where? Why?"

"On the web. Once I was sure that that was what she was, I thought I'd find out a little more about them. I can show you a picture. She's a three-master, wooden, not very big. Painted but I can't tell you what colours as I've only seen a black and white drawing. I think she's at least sixty years old, probably more."

"Anna, you're amazing! When did you do it? Google gave

me half a million hits this morning – all to do with weather. I couldn't begin to sort them out."

"Oh I'm quite good with search engines. And actually it was easy once I refined the initial search by using 'Chinese'. I guessed it must be something from out there as your great aunt lives in Shanghai. Loads of typhoons of course but in the end I found a boat. That seemed to fit."

"You're brilliant."

Anna's pale, slightly freckled face flushed slightly, as it had when Maggi and Xanthe had repeated their mother's praise.

"But there's a problem. *Strong Winds* belonged to some sort of female warlord. More Malaysia than actual China. I tried to cross-check with the atlas but it was all really political with independence and stuff. Lots of islands changed their names, changed sides even. I'm not normally a history geek but it looked quite interesting – "

Donny wasn't listening. "How can you bring a boat on a boat? It sounds peculiar."

"Not really. I researched that too. If a boat can't fit into one of the containers they can be carried as deck cargo. They'd have to take its masts down and put a protective framework round it. That's what your great aunt must have meant by crating. And a Bill of Lading's just the paperwork."

" 'Her masts' – a boat's a lady. You mustn't say 'it'. It's not right." Donny was surprised how much he minded Anna using the wrong word.

Anna looked a bit surprised too. "Oh, okay," she said. "Even for those gigantic container ships?"

"Even them."

(Though maybe not Flint's foul shark-boat, thought Donny, meanly.)

"Because I've been watching them," said Anna. "The Port of Felixstowe site has a webcam. But I can't usually tell one from another except by their colour. About ten or twelve come in every day – and during the night. Loads of them are from China. If I had a container number I could work out which one *Strong Winds* should be coming on. But I haven't. Anyway it might be a different numbering system for deck cargo. The webcam doesn't get close enough to scan individual ships."

She looked disappointed with herself. It reminded Donny of the way she'd looked last night.

"Was that what you were doing yesterday? Did Rev. Wendy let you use the computer in her study?"

Anna flared up. "No, she certainly did not!" She hissed at him, always remembering not to shout. "And don't you ever mention computers around here. Or the Internet or even let them know I've heard of it. Or … I'll dob you in!"

"Okay, okay. Keep your hair on. Of course I won't if you don't want me to. I hardly talk to Wendy anyway."

He felt a bit hurt.

"Sorry. I forgot. I'm not used … Let's get on with the dream-catchers. I want to make at least two. My little sister probably has nightmares."

It was the first kind thing he'd heard her say about Vicky. He decided he wouldn't risk upsetting her again by showing that he'd noticed that the scissors, bradawls and hand drills they were using were all labelled 'Gallister High. DT department. DO NOT REMOVE.'

Tuesday September 19th

The boy who'd knocked him down and called him a 'girl' was on the same bus. There were about three of them. Year Tens, he thought, but they could have been Elevens. He sat with Anna anyway and tried not to feel self-conscious.

They were going home with Xanthe and Maggi after school to start re-painting *Lively Lady*. Donny had told Gerald that he wanted to join the swimming club – it was true that he *wanted* to – and he'd been given permission to buy a pair of shorts from the uniform cupboard.

"Age appropriate activity … social services sure to agree. Put it on the EX2 form …" they heard him muttering.

Gerald signed their late-stay permission slips distractedly while Liam had a tantrum about a Man U shirt and Luke stubbornly refused to eat his egg because he hadn't been allowed to kill it himself. Vicky was strapped in her high chair but Donny had sat next to her this morning and fed her pieces of hi-fibre rusk and played incy-wincy spider up her arm and round the back of her neck. He reckoned he liked babies.

Would that mean he was … gay or something?

Denise Tune arrived unannounced in Mr McMullen's afternoon registration session and told the teacher she was taking Donny out of school.

"So he'll be missing lessons, will he?"

"But Aim authorising the absence so that'll be alright," replied the Welfare Officer with a smile that only moved her mouth.

"I was thinking more about his education than about which

code to put in the register," said Mr McMullen who hadn't smiled back. "Donny's only joined us recently and I don't want him to get behind at this early stage."

"And Ai don't want any more complaints – from Someone – that he's been prevented from seeing his poor sick mummy." She bared her teeth a little more and spoke quietly but very clearly so all the other students could hear her if they wanted. "So Aim taking him to the *psy-chiatric* unit. Mummy had to be moved to a more secure ward … for her own … *saifty*," she added, apparently speaking confidentially. It was a great way of getting everyone's attention.

"Obviously I want to see my mum wherever you've dumped her." Donny turned to Mr McMullen. "Maybe you could write my foster-carers a note, sir, explaining that I might have to stay behind for a couple of nights later in the week to catch up?"

"Hmmm …" said the teacher. "Now is there anyone else who wants their private family business trumpeted around the classroom or do some of you people perhaps have work to get on with?"

A14, A12 – China Shipping, Cosco, White Star, Norfolk Line, Han-Jin, Maersk. Donny'd never realised how many container lorries were lumbering up the main road. A train overtook them where the road ran parallel with the railway line and he tried counting the containers that had been loaded onto the flat wagons. He'd got to about forty before the train pulled out of view.

He was going to see his mum!

Surely Skye would be able to tell him a bit more about Great

Aunt Ellen – and he could ask her about Granny. Find out if she'd known about those other brothers and sisters. Ask her why she'd called *Swallows and Amazons* Granny's 'secret' book? Even if disgusting Denise stayed in the room it wouldn't matter because they'd be signing.

He didn't care if Skye didn't have any family information. At least they'd have seen each other. He could maybe talk to her doctors. Help them understand her, convince them that she wasn't mad. Just different … and frightened, sometimes.

It was hot in the car and full of the Welfare Officer's syrupy perfume. Her dress today was a short white frock patterned with clusters of flowers that had holes in them. It looked more like she was going to play tennis than visit a hospital. She kept asking questions but Donny didn't bother answering. He was sure anything he said would get twisted somehow. It wasn't worth the risk.

The Welfare Officer had a Bluetooth appliance fixed above one ear. She made a brief call as they turned off the main road into the outskirts of a town.

Chelmsford. He'd remember the name for his map. There were roundabouts and traffic lights; people were coming out of schools and going to the supermarkets.

What if the hospital had set visiting times and they were too late?

After a few more miles they came to a halt in an un-surfaced car park tucked out of sight behind massive buildings. There were some construction vehicles in a corner but otherwise it was completely empty.

Except for a police car.

"Aim able to understand that it's a challenge for a juvenile with your past history to communicate with a Professional. Research confirms that your unsupported background will have left you seriously deficient in social integration skills."

Donny had been staring out of the window but now he stared at her.

Huh? His past history? His unsupported background?

"So Ai've brought in one of my male colleagues." That gruesome smile again. "I must explain that you will need to answer all his questions before Aim able to take you to see your mother."

Her threat was unmistakable – no answers: no visit.

Why was he not surprised?

The Welfare Officer didn't have a large car: it was a sporty soft top in electric blue with light-sensitive glass and a special edition logo. There wasn't room for Inspector Flint so Donny had to get out and walk across the empty space towards Flint's big official Range Rover. Denise walked with him looking casual, her glued blond ringlets bobbing slightly as she swayed across the pot-holed surface in her wedge heels. Donny longed desperately to run but had no idea which way to go.

There was no evidence of coercion. And Flint didn't lay a finger on Donny.

Instead he made him squash down onto the floor in front of the passenger seat. The Welfare Officer got into the back of the Range Rover and pushed the passenger seat as far forward as it would go. So that she had plenty of room to stretch out her fake-tanned legs and tap away at a laptop – certifying that the interim assessment interview was being conducted by

Inspector Jake Flint on hospital premises with herself in attendance as duty care worker.

Flint pressed the catch that activated the car's automatic locking system.

There was a loud metallic clunk.

The car windows were already closed.

Donny was shaking when they finally let him out. Shaking from the discomfort; from his anger, shame and fear. Who were these people that they could treat him like this? How pathetic was he that he let them?

He had been so cramped that he stumbled and fell onto the sharp chippings. Flint's boot was straight onto his hand.

"One word out of turn, young man, and this'll be the last time you visit your poor sick mother." He eased a little more of his weight downwards. "Do you understand me?"

"Yes." Donny was struggling not to cry.

"Yes, SIR! You need to learn Respect." Flint put his full weight on his foot and swivelled slightly.

"Yes … *s-s-s-ir!*" He couldn't not cry now. Couldn't help himself.

Flint stepped back.

The Welfare Officer was giggling as if she was drunk or something. "Yes sir, yes sir, three bags full. Go on, little boy. Say three bags full or I won't take you in to your mummy."

Donny managed a deep shuddering breath. Gulped back the tears. Felt hatred boost him like a caffeine shot. "Three bags full, then," he said and followed her like Bo-Peep's lamb, swinging his injured hand. Whatever.

The unit was called the Cedars. Flint didn't bother coming in. He was back to his car and away to pick on someone else.

The first thing Denise Tune did – before Donny realised the trick they'd played – was to send him into the gents to wash his hand and face. Gerald had given him a comb to keep in his blazer and Donny ran it through his hair as eagerly as if this were Granny he was about to visit. His heart was beating really fast and he could think of nothing except the hug he wanted to give and receive.

Suddenly he was in too much of a rush to use the hot-air dryer. He hurried out into the reception area, damp and pink and trembling. With happiness now. All the stuff in the car-park was forgotten. He was here. About to see Skye.

He looked around and read notices, fidgeting, trying to discover what sort of a place this was. It seemed all right.

There were two wards in the Cedars: Avalon and Ennisfree. Ennisfree had people walking around and sitting, though they didn't seem to be doing much. There were tables and vending machines and one or two other people who might be visitors. No-one Donny's age, though.

Avalon was completely quiet. Single rooms with reinforced glass all round at waist height and dim spaces inside where people slept. The beds had high sides and places to hang drips and monitoring equipment. Donny had a horrible conviction that they also included restraints. He didn't want to look too closely.

Avalon was a closed ward.

Skye was in Avalon.

The male nurse who came to meet them didn't think Donny

should be allowed in The Cedars at all. He wasn't unkind and Donny could sort of see his point. This wasn't a good place for children.

It wasn't a good place for his mum either.

"Denise Tune, multi-authority leader worker, S.L.A.G., School Liaison and Guidance," she said flashing an official identity card and a synthetic smile. "John has been giving cause for concern. My colleague identified a reality check as a possible positive pathway."

The nurse didn't smile back. Instead he turned to Donny and began to explain, quite kindly, about medication and reducing doses and the plans they had for transferring Skye to Ennisfree. He couldn't say exactly when, but he could confirm that it would happen quite soon and then there would be therapy and classes: a structured rehabilitation programme.

Donny didn't have to worry about signing any of the unfamiliar language to Skye because he never got closer to her than looking through the glass.

There were other people in Avalon and there were Rules.

"Did she get my letters? They were pictures, mainly. I gave them to my carers to send. The first was 'wawa', sorry, geese. And then there were drawings of a boat."

The nurse didn't know so he went to find out.

He was gone quite a long time. Denise Tune studied her fingernails and read messages on her mobile even though there was a sign asking people to switch off because of hospital equipment. She looked annoyed. That was good. Donny got hold of a leaflet that had the unit's address and postcode. He could send his letters himself now.

The pictures had arrived, the nurse reported, but they hadn't yet shown them to his mother. They needed to be certain that they wouldn't cause any further distress.

"Do you have children?" Donny asked. He was angry.

The nurse nodded. "Two wee boys. Footballers," he added.

"You'd want to know they were all right wouldn't you? Even if you were in … *prison?*"

"I would." From the way he spoke it was obvious that he'd got the point. "I don't make all the decisions, you understand. But I hear what you're saying and I'll talk to my team-leader. They're grand pictures. I'm sure your mum'll like them."

"If she gets the chance."

Donny could see Denise Tune hitching up her handbag. He decided to trust the nurse.

"I made her something else," He dug into his rucksack. "It's called a dream-catcher. You hang it on her bed. Please. It's not infectious or anything."

"Aye," said the nurse, "And why not." He took the circle of alder twig and looked at it curiously. Donny had made the net by unravelling some wool from the jersey he'd been wearing on their journey down. Then he'd added three of the pale green acorns and a single curl of Vicky's red hair. "That hand of yours looks sore, laddie. If you'll bide a moment longer I'll fetch some arnica. Boys and bruises, eh!"

CHAPTER THIRTEEN
If Not Duffers

September 19th – 20th
"So what did they want to know?"

"Haven't a clue. Which was good. Because if I did, I'd have told it. I was 100% ... gutless."

"Join the club then," Anna didn't waste time being sympathetic. "Try to think about *what* they were asking. Never mind that you didn't know the answers."

"Money. Flint went on and on about money. Did Granny give me things – you know, X- boxes, Wiis, PSPs that sort of stuff. Electronic, imported stuff. I'd have laughed except I couldn't hardly breathe. We didn't even have a TV! He turned his car heater on part of the way through. Blowing downwards."

It sounded nothing when he said it – but even the memory made him sick inside. He'd been so helpless, scrunched there on the floor, sweating and trying to answer their questions so they'd let him see Skye.

Who wasn't there at all. Only her body. And they'd known it all along. He'd been completely suckered.

But why? Why had they spent their whole afternoon on him?

"Describe our house, describe our holidays. We must have had a proper car. Not just the camper. Were there any other grandchildren? I wish there were." If Great Aunt Ellen rejected them there'd only be Skye and him left, a family of just two people. "It was like he was obsessed with finding out that we were rich …"

"Well, are you?" Anna, unusually, had not vanished to her room as soon as supper was over. She had followed him into the sitting room where he was looking at an old *AA Book of the Road.*

"I wish! Otherwise Granny wouldn't have got benefits for Skye. There was something – when I was listening to Gerald and Wendy that night – about spending everything she had on lawyers so Skye could keep me? I dunno. I feel like I don't know anything any more."

"In our situation," said Anna, "you have to grow up a bit."

"Thanks a *lot*," said Donny. "Anyway – I reckon he was only asking about Granny so he could find out about Great Aunt Ellen. That was who he wanted the presents to come from. Parcels from abroad? In our house? Chinese visitors? What planet is he on?"

Flint had had to believe that Donny didn't know the answers to these questions because he completely didn't. Even when the fat policeman had revved the engine and started to drive away from the hospital Donny couldn't tell him anything more. He had nothing to tell.

If there had been something – between Granny and her sister – she could maybe have thought she was protecting him and Skye by making sure they didn't know? Like she had hidden the maps on their journeys …

So what had Granny done to give them a clue?

Told Skye to buy him a book!

As it happened *Swallows and Amazons* was seriously annoying Donny just now because he'd reached a chapter where John had had to apologise to his mother for going night-sailing. Everyone said it was dangerous! Donny was totally with John. He'd go night-*flying* if it would get him out of here.

This *Book of the Road* was well old. Tomorrow he was going to go on the Internet at school and type in the postcode for The Cedars. See if he could reach Skye by water. Day or night. Now that he nearly had a dinghy …

Xanthe, Maggi and Anna had got together after school without Donny. They'd helped June Ribiero collect *Lively Lady* from the club and tow her on a trailer to Pin Mill where they'd begged some space in a builder's shed and painted her hull a dark, sludgy grey. They'd had to take the mast down and she didn't have her red sails anymore. She was going to have beigy ones. Apparently they were good.

"We could have sailed her there if their mum had known Flint was safely persecuting you. The others wanted to but she'd said they weren't allowed until we'd changed the colour and everything. Their dad's put in a complaint against Flint. And he's going to tell his committee that they shouldn't let Flint join their club. So she wants to make sure he's got no chance of taking it out on us. Especially me, she said. She was really nice …"

Anna's voice was full of longing. She sounded tired too.

"I've never hated anyone before like I hate Flint," said Donny. "And she's *foul*."

140

"Who? Not Mrs Ribiero …! Oh, her …Toxic Tune. Yes, she is. She gets off on watching him. I hate her even more than I hate him."

"Toxic? Yeah. Great name!"

The first thing the Welfare Officer had done when she'd brought him home was gripe at Wendy and Gerald for posting his pictures to the hospital without checking with her first.

"Quaite inappropriate. Medical staff most inconvenienced."

Then she'd told them he'd hurt his hand pushing his way out of the car.

It wasn't only the little lies. Donny knew now that she and Flint had been lying all the way through. Ever since he first met them in that stuffy room. They'd known that Great Aunt Ellen was for real. And there was some reason they wanted to get to her. But they didn't want anyone else to know.

"What are they *about*?" he asked Anna. "Why are they doing this?"

"I don't know," said Anna bitterly. "There's a system and they've got into it. Like malware."

Donny wasn't totally sure what she meant but he reckoned he got the gist. "You mean bugs. Gross, disgusting, evil bugs. Only thing is that Flint's not so clever as her. Sometimes he goes too far – like on the river when he thought he could scare you and Maggi simply because he felt like it. He forgot she might have parents watching. Anyway, I reckon he said more than he meant about Great Aunt Ellen. Okay he can't quite put his pudgy fingers on her but he does know she's for real. And that she's coming for us. That's why he wants her to be rich. Or illegal. Preferably both."

"She might be rich. If she's bringing an antique Chinese junk all the way home with her?"

"But he doesn't know about *Strong Winds*. I was terrified he was going to ask me but he didn't … Anna, do you think Flint and Toxic might be running some sort of protection racket? Not Child Protection. Ha Ha. The intimidation and extortion sort. 'Cos then they'd want her to be rich so they could make her shell out thousands to clasp me and Skye to her lonely bosom. Fat chance, obviously, when she's never sent us as much as a Christmas card!"

Anna didn't say anything but she looked as if she was really listening. As if this was making some sense?

Luke and Liam were fighting on the sofa. So Donny went on. "And the reason they'd like her to be illegal is so they could properly put the squeezers on. Like if she's actually Mrs Big in some Chinese smuggling ring – then she'll have loads of money to pay him off."

Anna almost giggled. "Why? Why would even a hog like Flint think that your great aunt's a Mrs Big?"

'Pirate?' thought Donny. "Because he's insane, obviously. Probably watches too much TV. Or plays 18+ video games. He's got a message she sent to our old address in Leeds, a couple of weeks after Skye and I had left. I don't get how he's getting info from up there but he is."

Donny paused. This was the good bit. This was where Flint had given away more than he meant. "He was on about Chinese Triads and dragons and tigers and stuff. And extreme penalties for anyone involved – even juveniles. It was after the bit where he'd threatened to drive away. So he was really angry that I hadn't said anything – because I couldn't. So he pulled out this piece of paper and sort of waved it about. I think it was meant to be his clinching proof to make me spill all."

"Can you remember what it said?"

"Course I can! It was another of her crazy telegrams. It said 'GONGS FOR GOLD DRAGON MONDAY SEPT 25th. KEEP SHARP LOOKOUT. ELLEN.'"

They looked at one another. The room had gone quiet. But not because of Great Aunt Ellen's cryptic message.

Luke and Liam had spotted Rev. Wendy looking thunderous in the doorway. "There has been Deceit in this House," she said. "Anna. I have something serious to discuss with you. Please come into my study."

Anna, always pale, went white. She stood up and, as she did, Donny noticed her push a small plastic bag out of the sleeve of her tracksuit. She didn't look at him but he moved anyway. He stretched across, still holding the AA guidebook, and hid Anna's package underneath it.

Gerald was waiting behind Rev. Wendy in the hall. The two adults and Anna went into the study together, shutting the door behind them.

"She's in trouble," said Liam to Luke, unnecessarily.

"Dead meat!" agreed Luke.

The little boys gripped fists with one another and took themselves upstairs. Donny followed, pausing only to replace the guidebook on the shelf and push Anna's contraband deep into his trouser pocket.

Once he was in his bedroom he took it out and looked at it, puzzled. There was nothing in the plastic bag except a very long piece of telephone cable with different sized jack-plugs at either end. Huh? The door of her room was open. Maybe the tools from the school DT department had been found?

Later he heard footsteps coming up the stairs and the dull nag-nagging of adult voices. Things were being moved around in Anna's room and he wondered whether he ought to go and grab his share of the blame. He didn't want to make matters worse if it wasn't the tools.

Once the sounds had stopped Donny gave it a couple of minutes then opened his own door very quietly.

He could see across the corridor: Anna's door was open, her room was empty, her mattress had been removed.

For a moment he felt pure, rudderless, panic. Then he heard Wendy and Gerald's voices from downstairs. He'd confront them. Shout, if he had to. Couldn't lose Anna.

Vicky began to cry. Then, unexpectedly, stopped. No one came up. The voices carried on.

Donny tiptoed to Vicky's door. Sure enough Anna's mattress had been moved in there and she was kneeling beside Vicky's cot, reluctantly settling her little sister. She pointed to the baby and mimed sleep. Then she held out one hand, palm upwards and blew something towards him.

It wasn't a kiss; it was a dream.

Donny knew what she wanted. He crept silently back to his room and fetched the dream-catcher that she'd made for Vicky and the one he'd made for her. He added a pencil and a piece of paper as well. She looked pleased.

Vicky didn't cry any more that night – but even if she had, Donny would not have heard her. He had dreamed himself onto a Chinese junk, off an island in an unknown sea. He and Xanthe were in the bows and there were other children in the stern. It wasn't clear to him who all of them were.

The situation was dangerous.

It was black night and they were caught in a powerful current that was sweeping the junk through a deep gorge. There were rocks to either side. Splashes of water leapt and dropped. They had no lights, no compass and there was a whirlpool ahead. They could see nothing but already they could hear the enormous swirling of the water.

He didn't know who was steering but they were skilful and he was not afraid.

The ship had steadied and was answering her helm. She danced light and responsive through the narrows and past the jagged foam-fringed rocks and treacherous sucking eddies.

Then they hit the whirlpool.

"Lie down and hold fast!"

There was a crash that shook the ship as the mainsail gybed across. Then another as it gybed back again. A thunderous flapping.

Donny felt the boat turn 180 degrees. Then again … crash! She turned back on her original course. There was someone steely calm and silent at the tiller.

This ship knew her captain. They were going to come safely to the smooth wide channel beyond.

Wednesday, September 20th

"Anna has not been judged," announced Gerald gravely as he served their macro-biotic breakfast and told Luke that he would not be offered any more eggs until it was clear that his bad behaviour yesterday wasn't hyper-activity caused by an allergic reaction to diary products. "We are seeking an interview with her teacher to clarify the circumstances. She will remain behind this morning until an appointment has been made. If necessary we will take further advice from Educational Welfare. John, we rely on you to make the bus journey alone."

Donny had found a piece of paper in one of his school shoes.

"IMPORTANT. Please get to Mr McMullen a.s.a.p. and ask him not to tell. He knows what but he won't understand why. I think he'll do it though. Thanks, Anna."

The bus journey to school from Xanthe and Maggi's stop seemed to be getting shorter every morning; there was so much to talk about. Donny sat well to the front, away from the older boys. He didn't care if they thought he was a wuss. There were things he had to be careful not to say with other students listening. He especially didn't want to answer any questions about his trip to the hospital or spell out that Anna might have been caught stealing. So he kept the conversation focussed on plans for the dinghy.

This wasn't too tricky. Xanthe'd given him a set of tide tables and was explaining how to read them.

"And Dad's photocopied you a few pages about knots and signals and the law of the sea from some really old book in the club library," added Maggi. "He says that when you can tie at least five of the knots, and you've learned the basics of the collision regs, there's something else he wants to tell you. He says it's sort of special."

"What's the book called?"

"*Sailing*. It doesn't look special. It's a how-to-do it book. Out of the ark. Crazy language – even by our standards – and someone's dunked it sometime."

They were at the school already. Donny was first out of the bus and almost the first into registration.

"Can I have a word, sir?"

"With or without an audience today?"

"A private word please, sir – It won't take long – but it's sort of urgent … It's about Anna."

"Anna Livesey? Then I'm sure she'd want us to be discreet. Not a young lady eager to take the world into her confidence."

Mr McMullen was quite shrewd.

"Yeah, well, that's sort of what she wanted me to say. She's in trouble with our carers. I think it might be about some tools that she might've, er, borrowed from this department. If it is, then it ought really to be me in trouble. But she's asked me to ask you not to tell."

Mr McMullen looked puzzled.

"Not to tell about tools?" he asked.

"Two pairs of scissors, two bodkins, a bradawl and a hand-drill. She said you might not understand *why* you shouldn't tell but you would know *what*. We were honestly only borrowing them."

"I wonder," Mr McMullen looked doubtful. "If that is what it is that I shouldn't tell. Anna Livesey knows she has permission to borrow from my department. She's one of the most promising students I've ever taught. Highly developed logical abilities and a real flair for electronics. For a Year Eight to build her own computer! As she did last year. Then refuse to let anyone see what she had done, beg me not to award her the junior prize or even mention the achievement in her report …" Mr McMullen shook his head at the recollection. "And *then* she switched to textiles! I didn't understand – and I still don't. I try to hope that she's the best judge of her own situation. You're rather keen on sailing, aren't you?"

Donny nodded, wondering why the change of subject and, anyway, how did he know?

"There's a famous message," the teacher carried on. "'Better drowned than duffers: if not duffers won't drown.' Not exactly the flavour of modern childcare but … I quite like it."

Donny had too many answers to be able to choose which one so he just sort of shrugged. Mr McMullen rubbed his beard and chuckled. "Oh don't mind me, I'm getting too old for all this. But Anna Livesey's certainly no duffer. So, if I can work out what it is she doesn't want me to tell – I'll do my best not to tell it."

Donny was almost as confused as his tutor.

"Thanks sir. I'll, er, tell her."

CHAPTER FOURTEEN

Low Water

Wednesday, September 20th

Donny didn't see Anna in school at all that day and failed to meet up again with Maggi or Xanthe. At lunchtime he checked the Port of Felixstowe website. No less than four of the twelve container ships scheduled to arrive on Monday 25th could have called at Shanghai. Or so it seemed. He didn't have Anna's confidence in cross-checking his searches. Maybe other routes linked in?

This wasn't good. Great Aunt Ellen – or Gold Dragon as he now preferred to think of her – could arrive at almost any time of that day or night. He didn't know how soon she'd be able to leave the ship. Would she wait for a crane to lift off *Strong Winds*? And would that take hours or days?

He found a list of the ships' departure dates. Some were going to stay in Felixstowe for the best part of a week, others only twenty-four hours or less. Maybe he should compile some sort of table?

Stop there.

Maybe this wasn't his problem. The point of her message was to ask them to be waiting for her on that Monday – presumably at Shotley which was where she'd said in the first place. There was a foot ferry from Felixstowe that ran three times a day via Harwich to Shotley, connecting the two sides of the harbour. She could come across on that. In her own time.

"Keep sharp lookout."

That *was* his problem. Because now there was only him, not Skye, he was going to have to bunk off school again. Maybe for the whole twenty-four hours. Nobody was going to give him permission to spend the day in Shotley because nobody, except his friends – and possibly his enemies – believed Gold Dragon was going to come. He should have wrestled Flint for that scrap of paper.

The vision made him laugh.

Seriously, what was he going to do? It wasn't only that he needed Great Aunt Ellen: she might need him. If Flint really believed that she was involved in some smuggling operation or Chinese Triad or something, he'd be the person waiting. Probably in his bloated Range Rover or foul shark-boat. Gold Dragon was old. Being bullied by the fat policeman might make her have a stroke or something – like Granny had.

"Keep sharp lookout."

He must get there first and warn her.

None of the Allies were around after school and there was only Vicky and Gerald in the vicarage. Gerald was in the living room trying to do paper work while Vicky was pulling herself up around the furniture. There was an atmosphere of suppressed irritation.

Donny played with Vicky for a while. He let her grab his fingers with her strong little hands and encouraged her to lean on him and take toddly steps. It was quite fun but Gerald kept sighing at the noise. Donny needed to get out.

"Could I maybe take her for a walk? In a pushchair or something?"

He wasn't sure he could manage Gerald's hearty backpack but he'd seen plenty of people pushing kids around in buggies. Gerald looked surprised; then he glanced down at his papers.

"Where would you go?"

"That place we went on Sunday? Pin Mill? It's not far. I could push along the side of the road. I'd be very careful."

Gerald looked at his papers again. "Oh all right," he said grudgingly. "But you'll have to wrap her up warmly and I don't want you to be out for long." Then he relaxed slightly. "You'd better take a bottle of sterilised water. Keep the teat covered when not in use."

"Could I have a biscuit or something?"

"No, no, they're a choking hazard ... You mean for yourself?"

"Yes."

"Well, don't make crumbs or spoil your appetite for supper. Take a banana instead. Be thoughtful about disposing of the skin."

Donny felt like running when he and Vicky were finally allowed to go. He controlled himself until they were out of sight then broke into a jog. When they reached the narrow lane leading down to Pin Mill, he ran. He swerved and whooped: Vicky screeched with delight.

A shed. That was where Anna said they'd left *Lively Lady*.

Pin Mill seemed to be almost as full of sheds today as it was of boats. When he eventually found the right one, a man was already locking up. He said that the paint wasn't dry and he hadn't expected anyone. It was obvious that he didn't want a boy and a baby hanging around. No public right of way, he said and went off taking the key with him.

Donny turned the pushchair away and headed towards the Hard. It was quiet there. The boatyards had closed and the pub hadn't opened. Even the river seemed to have left for the day. Donny stared in bewilderment at the expanse of grey mud. Flat and featureless. Like acres of playing field where no play could happen any more – after some natural disaster maybe.

He parked the pushchair near the spot where *Margery* had been floating so temptingly only two days before. Then he lifted Vicky out and went padding carefully along the stretch of Hard.

He could see why it was called that. There was mud either side and more mud beyond. Soft mud. The moment he tried putting a foot onto it his leg went slipping down and down. His trainer and sock were completely black.

Donny stared in dismay. How was he going to get his dinghy onto the water if the tide was as far out as this? The launching trolley wouldn't be much use.

It was cold and a squally breeze was beginning to get up. As he paced thoughtfully back along the Hard, he looked far to his left beyond the line of houseboats, along the thin strip of beach, to the point where the wood ended and the seawall began. He hadn't noticed there was a cottage there, tucked snugly beside the last of the trees. Perhaps that was where *Margery*'s owner lived? Another place to avoid.

"Pee-doh! Pee-doh You're a girl! Pee-doh!"

There was an ugly yelling at the top of the Hard and, before Donny realised it was directed at him, something flew past his ear. Suddenly he and Vicky were in a soggy shower as two of the boys from the bus stood there laughing and shouting and throwing gloopy handfuls of mud at them. They'd chucked the pushchair in already.

Donny had never felt more purely, blazingly angry. His shouting at the reservoir, his yelling at Flint, was nothing to the rage he felt now.

How could they do this to Vicky?

Shielding her as best he could and talking to her in a loving babble of slightly breathless nonsense – mainly from *Hiawatha*, he realised afterwards – he ran straight past the boys and towards the pub wall. He'd spotted *Margery* there, moored close in, fore and aft. She was a safe haven.

"Ewa-yea, my little owlet," he said to Vicky, as he sat her deep inside the big dinghy. "Who is this that lights the wigwam?"

"I hope you won't mind me borrowing this," he said, to no one in particular. And picking up one of *Margery*'s heavy wooden oars he charged at the two bigger boys, flailing it from side to side in wide, irresistible sweeps.

He must have looked completely berserk. Or perhaps they were gob-smacked that he'd come back at them at all.

They ran.

Even faster than he and Luke had scarpered on the Sunday.

"I'll have the law on you," called one of them, as he fled, across the green picnic area and away somewhere to the back of the builders' sheds and yards.

Donny lowered the oar and watched them go. Then he walked back to Vicky. She had used *Margery*'s centre thwart to pull herself up and was beaming as if she'd found herself on the best of all playpens. She wasn't even that muddy.

Donny, however, was plastered with gunk. And there was the question of the pushchair. It was a good fifteen metres out, half sunk in the ooze.

A pair of swans came flying in.

Donny was jumpy. The noise of their wide wings startled him and he shifted protectively close to Vicky as they stuck their strong short legs ahead of them and slid across the surface of the mud, curving their wings on either side to act as brakes. They toppled slightly as they did so, virtually tobogganing to a halt. Then they picked themselves up composedly and tucked their wings back in as they waddled across the softness on wide webbed feet. Their snowy fronts were streaked with black but, once they were up and walking, they scarcely sank in at all.

"That's what we need, papoose," said Donny to Vicky. "Feet like theirs."

"You could borrow my daughter's floorboards," said a voice behind them.

It was the old lady. She seemed to have sprung from nowhere. Short and round, wearing comfortable-looking clothes and a green felt beret. She was neither smiling nor scowling, merely considering the immediate problem from a practical perspective. *Margery*'s slatted floorboards would stop Donny sinking in.

"Would she mind?" Donny wasn't sure whether the old lady

thought the dinghy was her daughter or whether she meant the big-nosed lady who'd done the rowing and shouted "I say!"

"I've no idea. No need to enquire. As long as you put them back as they were and leave them clean. There's a tap round the corner, with a hose. You might need it yourself."

"Oh, okay," said Donny. "Thanks."

"Her name's Mrs Everson. She even had a bit of towel in the dinghy. She told me to tell Gerald she'd be sending round some more plums soon. No further message. 'What the eye doesn't see, the heart won't grieve over,' she said."

"Must have been Looked-After," commented Anna, automatically.

There was a new ban on spending time in bedrooms so, while Gerald was enduring the nightly struggle to get Luke and Liam to bed, Anna and Donny had taken their homework into the living room. Wendy was out.

If it hadn't been for Mr McMullen – and Donny apparently – Anna's situation would have been much worse. It wasn't the tools in her bedroom that had caused the storm; it was a computer, also marked 'Gallister High School DT Department, Do Not Remove'.

"Of course they assumed I'd been stealing," she told Donny. "But Mr Mac was really solid and said it was only borrowing and he'd allowed it anyway. The computer's sort of mine. I assembled it last term, in Year Eight. I used an old casing that they were going to throw out from the DT department and re-built the inside during Mr Mac's electronics club. It's not high-tech but it works. I downloaded a whole lot of freeware for it. Too old to be wireless, obviously. But Wendy's equipment isn't exactly state of the art either."

Donny stared at her. "You made a computer …? That's completely brilliant! Why didn't you let Mr McMullen tell anyone? He said he'd wanted to give you a prize or something."

"No way! That's why I had to give up going to his club. I really liked it but he was getting too keen. He was going to make people notice me. You can't operate like that in our situation."

"But didn't you want to keep it? If they'd known it was yours surely even Gerald and Wendy would've been okay?"

"Course I wanted to keep it. But, logically, it was better to let them waste time making a fuss about returning it than risk them taking it into their heads to have a look at what's on it. They did ask me what it was for. So I showed them a few discs and he said I'd been doing a project. And he managed *not* to say that it was the computer that was the project – which was good of him."

She hesitated, glanced at the door and bent her head close to her homework. "Because he probably still thinks that the computer *is* the project. But it isn't."

"Well, what is?" asked Donny. He felt sorry for Mr McMullen trying to keep up with Anna's complicated mental manoeuvres with Gerald and Wendy sitting opposite, listening suspiciously.

"Finding my mother," she whispered, not looking at him. "She can't have gone for ever. Not unless … something terrible's happened. She loved me ... and them."

Anna paused to steady herself. "I decided to use the Internet to look for her. I can't do much at school because there's never enough time and most of the sites I need to use are filtered out. They have a checking system too. So I've been doing it here. In my room at night. Or when I'm completely sure they're out. Or busy."

"And they don't know," Donny whispered back, in awe. "That's why you needed me to hide that long cable. You've been linking your computer to the computer in Rev. Wendy's study."

"Not to her computer, just to her phone socket. I couldn't risk my websites showing up on her activity list. I copied the ISP address one time when I was allowed to go on it for homework but I've fixed myself a separate user name and everything. The only way they'd find out is if they really, really checked their phone bills."

She looked defiant. "It's only the local access charge for logging on. I'm not taking much. If they were decent they'd let us use it anyway. They get paid for looking after us."

"But if anyone looked in your computer's memory they'd know straightaway."

"Yes, they would."

He could see why she'd been worried. "I heard them talk about Education Welfare. They'd didn't get Toxic in, did they?"

"No. I was scared about that. She'd have guessed that I wasn't using the computer just to write essays. She's such a hag."

Anna fell silent for a while, skimming through her maths. Then she sighed, "This homework's way too easy. I'd better make a few mistakes … Donny, if you get to your Great Aunt Ellen and she lets you and your mum live with her, do you think I could keep my computer at your house? Otherwise I think I'm going to have to wipe its hard disc. The operating system's too old to let me use a memory stick. I've saved some of my searches onto floppies so I've kept them separate but there's so much more. So much work. I don't feel safe – even leaving it with Mr Mac. It's not only me … "

He could hardly hear her now, her voice was so quiet. "I'm worried. If the wrong people see it – it might even be dangerous for my mother."

"Some time Anna, you're going to have to tell me …"

"No way. Think about it. You said you're gutless. What if you get done over by Flint again? I can't take that risk."

"And *you* said …"

"That he gives me the total shakes. My problem. Not yours. My mother. My secrets."

He shut up then and carried on struggling with the maths. She'd said it was so simple; it didn't feel that way to him. Gallister High started some GCSE courses well early.

And his hand still hurt.

"Use logic, Donny. If you're out of here – if you're living with your great aunt and your mum's not in hospital, then they've got no hold on you. You're not in the system any more. Then you could hide my computer for me – and I might decide to tell you stuff because they won't be able to get to you. You'll be like my personal safe house. That's all."

Now it was Donny's turn to sigh. "Yeah, sorry. Of course I will. If it ever happens. Gold Dragon wants a lookout on the

25th, which is a Monday, and I know I've got to warn her about Flint and I can't see how to do it. With school and everything. I can't get to her at Felixstowe – everything's too big and complicated – and I don't see how I'm going to manage to be waiting at Shotley all the time. I can't send her a text or an email, like anyone else would, and there's only four days to go. *And* I can't get out at night with the alarm system."

"I can fix that."

"Thanks …"

There was another depressed silence. Donny got back to his maths; Anna flicked effortlessly through some science.

"I might have an idea," she said after a while. "But I don't know enough. We need to ask the others."

CHAPTER FIFTEEN

T.E.A.M.

Thursday, September 21st, morning

"I need to stay for textile club this evening," said Anna at breakfast. "Maggi Ribiero's staying as well. She says her mother will bring us home. And John's got extra work. He probably didn't tell you."

She looked pale and poisonous, just as if she were, in her language, 'dobbing him in'. Donny was getting used to Anna's method. He stared at his plate, looking as sulky as he could.

"Is this true, John?" Rev. Wendy was getting ready to go out. She and Gerald exchanged anxious looks.

"Well, I missed some when I went to the hospital that afternoon. I don't suppose it matters."

This got a reaction.

"Of course it matters," said both adults in unison. "It's your Education. If you miss lessons you have to make them up. You ought to know that by your age."

Donny shrugged and carried on looking grumpy. "It was probably boring. Anyway, how would I get back afterwards? I don't see why I should have to go with those girls. Could you maybe collect me?"

He was betting they wouldn't want to and he was right.

"If Mrs Ribiero is collecting from school anyway I'll certainly ask her if she can find a space in her car for you," said Wendy firmly. "We must think very carefully before making any unnecessary journeys. We can all put our mite towards the Environment." And she hurried off to her diocesan conference.

"Shall I ask Mrs Ribiero then," Anna persisted, looking at Gerald. "So he has to stay at school and do his work?"

"Well, er, yes, thank you, Anna. It's good to see you taking thought for someone other than yourself. T.E.A.M. remember. Together Everyone Achieves More."

Anna looked smug; Donny almost spat out his muesli.

"I think you're mean, Anna," said Luke unexpectedly. "And so does Liam."

It was obvious that Liam hadn't a clue what they were talking about but he backed up his brother anyway.

"Yeah," he said, pushing his sticker album out of sight, "And so does David Beckham. And Wayne Rooney. And Michael Owen. And …"

But Luke cut him off before he could get the whole of that summer's England squad ganging up on Anna. "And so does Vicky. Even Vicky won't like you any more if you're mean to Donny. I like Donny. He's my dog-handler."

Donny didn't know whether to laugh or be touched by the little boy's loyalty. But then he saw that Anna had flushed pink and her eyes were suddenly bright with tears.

"Actually, Luke," he said, trying to sound man-to-man, "I think Vicky might be on Anna's side. Anna moved Vicky's cot back into her room with her last night so they're sharing now. Maybe that's why she hasn't been crying so much."

"Vicky's a baby," said Luke, moody again.

"No," said Donny, with a flash of inspiration. "Vicky's a treasure. She's our treasure. Anna can take care of her at night but I'm leaving you on guard when we're not here. Except when you're at school of course," he added, catching Gerald's bewildered gaze.

"Grrrrrrrr!" said Luke obediently. Then dropped his spoon on the floor and tried finishing the rest of his breakfast without using his front paws.

"Doh … doh…." said Vicky, who had been quite silent until then.

"We'll miss the bus if we don't hurry," said Anna whose eyes, Donny was relieved to see, were back to normal. "Bye everyone."

"I can't believe I said that," she muttered as they ran down the road.

"Which?" panted Donny. "You said quite a lot."

"I spoke to those boys. I said goodbye."

"So?"

"They're *his* kids. I don't ever speak to them. I must be going soft."

"So?" said Donny again. "They're only kids and they're in the same mess that we are."

"So?" said Anna. But without quite the previous bitterness in her voice.

On the bus she showed him sketches of Chinese junks. *Strong Winds* was sturdy-looking and curvy with bamboo masts and a high stern.

"It – sorry I mean she – does look quite old fashioned

compared with modern junks. But look at her flag. It's a dragon! Double-headed! I'm so sure I'm right about her …"

"Wow … so'm I! I *know* you're right, Anna. I dreamed about that boat. And it wasn't a nightmare. I was with Xanthe. But someone else was steering. We were sailing through a whirlpool."

"Sounds nightmarish to me … Where *are* Maggi and Xanthe? We just passed their stop. Don't say they're going to be off sick … not today! I need them to ring their mum for us."

"Uh-oh. So you hadn't arranged all that stuff about going to textile club with Maggi and Mrs Ribiero picking you up afterwards?" Anna was sometimes so convincing that he forgot how much she was capable of inventing as she went along. "We can always say it was cancelled and get the bus back. I don't want to do that walk again."

"No, of course I hadn't arranged anything. How could I? There's no such thing as textile club anyway. But it is one of Mr Mac's DT open nights and Maggi does sometimes stay and I've got an idea that involves sewing as well as designing. I just need to talk to one of them about it."

"And me … possibly?" Whose problem was this?

"Of course, you! You're the one who's going to have to do it. But you need to finish getting that dinghy ready. That's why I got you the extra time. You don't stay. You catch the bus as usual but you get off early and you go down to the river, not to the vicarage. I thought Xanthe could help you get sorted … oh where *are* they?"

That was the trouble with big schools. You could go all day

and not see someone if you weren't in the same sets and didn't know their timetable. Even Anna wasn't in the library at first break. Donny began to panic. It was Friday tomorrow. House Meeting. They'd not be allowed to stay late then. Only four more days.

But at lunchtime there were the sisters and Anna waiting, with their trays loaded and enough for him as well.

Xanthe led the way outside, to some shallow steps behind the PE changing rooms where they could sit and eat out of the wind. "Okay," she said. "It's a huddle. So what do we know, Donny-man?"

She didn't wait for him to answer but began to tick off the points, bending her long supple fingers backwards as she went. "First, we know your great aunt's not a myth. She's arriving on Monday and wants you to keep a lookout and bang gongs. Second, the bloater on the shark-boat is lying in wait to clap her in irons and march her away to Execution Dock. Unless she maybe buys him off? So, third, we've got to warn her, keep her from his greasy clutches. And fourth, if he bellyflops overboard in the process, we're not going to feel that bothered."

"Er, no … I mean, yes … both … all of them."

"Donny, how well do you know your great aunt?" Maggi was chewing the end of her baguette. She didn't look directly at him as she spoke.

"Not at all, that's my major problem."

"I mean … *could* she be a member of a Triad or something? All this Gold Dragon talk … well, it's a bit thriller-ish. And, if she is … like, a Triad member … well, they're not exactly very nice … and I know we don't rate the fat man, but he is a policeman and … maybe he might be right? Please don't be cross … it's quite an odd message?"

"Actually, that's the only bit I don't have a problem with. 'Gongs for Gold Dragon' … well, it's the sort of way that Granny and Mum and I talked sometimes – pretending to be in a story when we weren't really. Using names out of books. Her giving herself a name like that makes her sound more like family – except I don't know any stories with a gold dragon in them," he added lamely. "But there must be Chinese ones."

"You said your mum said that she might be a pirate …?" Maggi was still frowning. She wasn't convinced yet.

"Or a fighter. I'm truly not sure I got that right but, even if I did, Skye'd only have meant something else out of a story. Jack Sparrow or Captain Hook. Not a drug smuggler or a human trafficker. My mum doesn't know about things like that."

"Little sis," said Xanthe, "that's such a no-brainer. On the one hand we have Donny's Rescue Myth thundering home – because her dying sister asked her, yeah? You're okay with that? And on the other we have that racist bloater and his totally chav boat. Which is puke-making but probably cost the best part of a million. I had a look at it. It's stuffed with gear and he can't even tie his mooring ropes properly."

"Xanth … you didn't …?"

"No I didn't – but I was *soooo* tempted. That man's as crooked as a fine-net fisherman. What's he doing trying to join a sailing club? Even you can't think the best of him because there isn't any best to be thought."

She took a long swig of her apple juice and began to eat.

Maggi looked a bit crushed.

"I might know why Donny's great aunt calls herself Gold Dragon," said Anna. "It's because she's bought this very old boat called *Strong Winds*. Look, here's a picture I found on the Internet. I think that's a dragon with two heads on the flag."

"*Strong Winds!*" said Maggi, in a tone of amazement.

"*What's* your great aunt's name?" said Xanthe, swallowing her food with a gulp.

"Ellen Walker. She's my Granny's youngest sister. I think there were others but they're all dead."

"No, no, no! *Strong Winds*'s owner is POLLY LEE!!" Xanthe and Maggi looked at each other, their eyes wide, their mouths open. "Donny-man – your great aunt's not a Myth! She's a maritime Legend!!"

Then they were at him with a babble of stories about this amazing woman called Polly Lee who'd done round the world voyages single-handed in a Chinese junk. "She'd never come to England, so the British press never wrote about her. She saw her on TV once. It was such a story. She'd been born in England but she'd renounced her citizenship and gone to Australia and then to China. Everyone knew Polly Lee wasn't her real name – everyone who knew about sailing, that is. But there was some sort of mystery, something political … I didn't get that bit."

"Xanthe and I used to fight about which of us would be her. She was really famous in Canada." Maggi turned to her sister. "Polly Lee did come back to England once, Xanth. She stopped at St Mawes in Cornwall."

"That was because she was sailing in the wake of the first

Miss Lee, the real one, *Shining Moon*'s owner. *Shining Moon* was even more famous. She was *Strong Winds*'s sister ship. But Polly Lee wasn't publicity-seeking. It was a sort of homage. When the TV crew tried to come on board she threw Chinese firecrackers at them and sailed off again. They filmed it!"

No wonder Granny hadn't bought them a TV.

"But Xanth, she must be dead now ... Didn't she have some awful accident, with her hand?"

"Well, she can't be dead if she's sending ETA messages, can she, muppet?" Xanthe stood up. She hadn't finished her food or her apple juice but she had an announcement to make. "Donny-man, we are not having *either* Miss Polly Lee *or* Miss Ellen Walker given one ripple of trouble from that maritime pollutant. Tell us what we need to do. Shall we all bunk off on Monday and escort her vessel into Felixstowe with gongs and whistles?"

Donny gaped at her. Then he took a look at Anna and pulled himself together.

"Um, well, there are maybe a few things against that," he started carefully. "First, there are at least four container ships that day that might have come from Shanghai and some that have been to other places as well. Second, two of them are scheduled to arrive when it's dark. Third, those ships are so huge that, even if she was on one of the daytime ones, she probably wouldn't notice us if we were whizzing around like gnats in dinghies – or even in *Snow Goose*. Fourth, this is England so, if what you say is right, she's going to be a bit tense. If we mess up now she might just chuck a few more firecrackers and head back to China ...,"

Xanthe sat down again. She seemed to notice how much food she had left.

"Fifthly," said Anna brutally, "we have to remember her first message. We don't just need her to escape Flint, we also need her to decide that Donny and his mum aren't total landlubbers and that she wants to stay here and look after them – which sounds like something she's not going to find easy. Especially if …"

" … if the first thing she sees is you two being RYA Young Sailors of the Year in your *Laser* 4.7s and me bobbing along in *Lively Lady* trying to work out which way the tide's going. Thanks a lot, Anna."

"I'm sorry."

"No, seriously, you're right, I know you are. Didn't you have some sort of a plan?"

"Only the beginnings of one …" She faltered. They were all watching her. "There was something I noticed when I was on *Snow Goose*. I asked your mum about it. Something called the International Code of the Sea? They were pinned up by the chart table. Flags and things with different meanings."

Xanthe and Maggi nodded vigorously but didn't interrupt.

"And Shotley marina had flags at the entrance. National flags – like Holland and Belgium. I figured that was how they showed what boats were visiting. So then I wondered whether we couldn't send Great Aunt Ellen some sort of message like that … ?"

"Hoist the Chinese national flag, 'cos that's where she's come from," said Xanthe, thoughtfully, "and it's really unusual so people would look at it."

"Plus the two-headed dragon from *Strong Winds*." Maggi was holding the sketch. She looked up from it, beaming, "And a signal flag … which one, Xanth?"

"U – Uniform, 'you are standing into danger'. Anna that is such a cool idea!"

Anna looked pleased but not totally satisfied. Other students were starting to come back into school from lunchtime sports practices. There was a clatter of studs, a thud of bounced rugby balls. They needed to move.

Donny was feeling bad. Anna, Maggi and Xanthe had organised everything: his contribution had been nil. Twice he'd been called a girl as an insult. Right now he wished he was one.

"Where are we going to fly them?" Xanthe was thinking aloud as she scraped out the last of her yoghurt. "The marina people would never let us put a danger flag beside their lock gates – and anyway she's coming to Felixstowe first. That's where Flint'll lurk and that's hot security. There's a humungous flagpole up above the marina, where HMS *Ganges* was. But how do we get Donny's great aunt looking across the harbour before she's even docked?"

"Was HMS *Ganges* to do with the Navy?" asked Donny. His brain felt fogged. "I think Granny's brothers might have been in the Navy. And they would have been Gold Dragon's brothers as well. Maybe one of them was posted there? If that's right … if she's looking out when she comes into the harbour … and if it's daylight, then surely she'd glance over in that direction? It's a lot of ifs … Anyway, I might only be muddled with *Swallows and Amazons*. There's Navy in there."

Swallows and Amazons – Granny's book. He'd been reading but he still hadn't got the secret – whatever it was.

Xanthe frowned as if she was about to object but Maggi wasn't giving her any more time. She collected all their rubbish and trays.

"So, listen, are we going to do Anna's plan or not? Because there's the bell and Xanth and I've already been late once today."

"At last – the Kraken wakes! Of course we're going to do it! I'll go down with Donny to launch the dinghy after school and give him as much sailing as I can. You two start knocking up the flags – I hope you're good at drawing, Anna. Mags will struggle cutting out red and white quarters for the 'U'. And so would I," Xanthe added hastily, seeing the outraged look on her sister's face.

"Oh, CAD – Computer Aided Design. I was just planning to scan the dragon in from the sketch, plot the co-ordinates and then enlarge. They've got some good programs in textiles, you know," said Anna happily.

CHAPTER SIXTEEN
A Forgotten *Hispaniola*

Xanthe easily outran Donny down the road to Pin Mill. She and Maggi both had mobiles so she'd been able to phone ahead to the boatyard owner asking him to make sure that the shed was unlocked when they arrived. She'd rung her mother as well and checked that she was okay to pick up Maggi and Anna late from school. Then she and Donny had caught the bus and got off at the nearest set-down to the river.

After that, they'd run. There'd be less than two hours to low water, she said – and it was going to be a low one.

"What do you mean a low, low water?" puffed Donny. "What's the difference?"

"Between neaps and springs? It can be more than a metre." Xanthe answered, breathing as easily as if she was still lounging on the bus. "Springs are when the earth and moon are in line. There's sort of more pull – high tides are higher and lows are lower. That's where we're at now. It's why you couldn't get off the end of the Hard yesterday."

"We've got to do it today …"

"Too right we have. We'll luz everything into *Lady*, get her into the water however we can, then put up the mast and rig her when we're on the river. Land her on the other side where the mud's hard."

So Donny learned to row. But as he'd deep down guessed, it wasn't any problem. Dip and pull, dip and pull. He settled into the rhythm immediately. His body understood what his mind hadn't known; he could row steadily and without fuss for miles and miles if necessary.

"As you might have to one day – if you've gone too far down river and the wind dies."

"Does *Lady* have an anchor?"

"Sure – though it's not exactly the biggest in the world."

"But it would keep her safe on a beach or somewhere? If she wasn't on her trolley?"

Xanthe looked at him. "You're thinking …?"

They had reached the other side of the river now and had pulled the dinghy onto a patch of mud that was sandy and hard, quite different from the dark sticky stuff that had sucked Donny's leg down yesterday. Blazers, ties and shoes had been bundled away and Xanthe'd produced kagouls and hi-fits as well as a couple of buoyancy aids. There were rubber dinghy boots as well, though hers were a bit small and Donny's a bit big. He was impressed by her advance planning.

"Mags and I aren't total bimbos. Even dinghy sailors can die of cold and exposure. 'Specially in the winter when the water chills down."

"If not duffers …"said Donny, quoting.

Xanthe laughed. "Yeah, well … Ransome rocks! What bothers me is that I think your granny's put you onto the wrong book. There's two different ones about this area and a Chinese one as well."

"But she didn't know we'd be coming down here … Shotley

is Great Aunt Ellen's plan."

"Polly Lee!" said Xanthe. "To think we might be going to meet her! Unbelievable! Come on, Donny, let's go sailing. I'm going to tune this dinghy up a bit. See how good you really are!"

She'd stepped *Lively Lady*'s mast now and was doing complicated things with a multi-tool. Donny's confidence ebbed a bit.

"It's only my third time," he reminded her.

"Tell that to the crabs. Anyway I reckon you're much more likely to fall off the HMS *Ganges* flagpole than finish up in Davy Jones's locker. I don't see how you're going to do that last bit either. It's a long way to walk and we're away racing and I don't exactly assume that your carers are going to give you a lift ..."

"Well, yes," said Donny. "But she's your boat ... and your mum and dad have been really kind ..."

"It's okay. We've sussed that you're going to have to use her. Not the how and when. And maybe you don't want to tell because what you're thinking isn't 100 per cent health and safety-checked. Also, you possibly don't want me and Maggi having secrets from our parentals ... and you're not entirely sure how much they'd wave past?"

Donny nodded.

His only plan was to get himself down river in *Lively Lady* late at night before the 25th and find somewhere to lie in wait. Anna's flag plan was brilliant but he was the one who was going to have to put them up. And that would have to be done in the dark. There'd been a lot of adult trouble in *Swallows and Amazons* when John had gone night-sailing.

"So … let's go check it out," said Xanthe. "We've at least an hour of ebb left and the wind's good. It often dies in the evening but it feels as if it's freshening today."

"It did when I was down here with Vicky."

"You might have your hands full then. Let's head down to Shotley right now and come back with the flood. We'll be seriously late but I'll ring Mum and she can tell your lot that you're staying at ours to eat. We won't make the meal but, tough, I could do with losing the weight."

Donny looked at her tall athletic shape and didn't comment. He was hungry already.

"You're on," he said.

Xanthe made him sail as if he were in a race, pushing all the time, looking for opportunities to take advantage. Every bend in the river mattered; every change in the shoreline. The texture of every single ripple was of intense significance and, if Donny had had time to think – which he didn't – he'd have understood that this was the real Xanthe. She was a competitor. *Lively Lady* felt different too: quicker, more urgent, less forgiving.

Once they reached the harbour the full force of the wind hit them. It was coming straight in from the sea and there were white wave tips among the harsh, grey-brown expanse.

"Bear away towards those navigation posts and get ready to sit right out. If you think she's going to capsize, luff or spill your wind. My mobile's in my pocket, I don't fancy getting it soaked."

"Do you want to take over?" *Lively Lady* was rushing along at a startling angle. Not even both their weights could keep her flat. He had to shout to make himself heard.

"No, you're good," Xanthe shouted back. "Go for that red schooner. We'll get under her lee."

They'd left the River Orwell and were heading up the Stour towards the marina entrance. Harwich town was to port with pilot boats bustling to and fro and a North Sea ferry setting out from Harwich International.

The Shotley side, in contrast, was bleak and still. No one was queuing to enter the marina this evening and almost the only vessel moored nearby was the three-masted sailing ship that Donny had vaguely noticed on the previous Saturday.

"I need a breather. Bring us alongside. We'll find something to grab hold of."

Donny obeyed. *She* needed a breather!

Suddenly *Lively Lady* was in calm water, the wind banished from her sails as the sheltering side of the red schooner rose above them. Xanthe was clinging to the protruding edge of the bottom row of portholes. She gestured towards a rope which was dangling further for'ard and they edged along until she could reach it.

"What is this boat?" asked Donny.

He couldn't see a name. She was like something out of a history book, with three masts and a long bowsprit and things that looked like … yardarms? But they were maybe only wide cross-trees and Donny could see no sails. Close up the schooner looked sad, almost derelict.

"Sounds dumb but I don't actually know," said Xanthe. "She's been here for ages. Maybe she was something to do with the Navy as well?"

"If that's right," said Donny, "if she was … What do you reckon about me flying Anna's flags on her – if there's no-one about – then I wouldn't need to land and go up the hill to that mast. It looks much further away now we're here …"

Okay, so he was gutless. He just knew he didn't want to have to go ashore and risk running into fences and security men and that kind of trouble. Afloat was his best place.

"That could well be cool. Even if this boat's nothing to do with the Navy, she's plumb in the eye-line. And she's so … bizarre. How would you get on board?"

"There's the mooring chain … I could maybe scramble up? Then onto her bowsprit?"

"Like Jim Hawkins in *Treasure Island*! Go, Donny!"

That was okay then.

"I could bring the flags already fixed on a line. Your dad sent me knot instructions. As long as she's not lit up …"

"I've never noticed that she is. I don't think she even has a riding light. But don't totally trust me – I've only ever seen her as an obstruction that might take my dinghy's wind." Xanthe glanced at her big sports wristwatch. "We're out of time. Look up her masts to see if she's got any signal halyards. Though they'll probably be rotten."

Donny was getting used to walking into an atmosphere of suppressed disapproval every time he returned to the vicarage.

This time was no different. It was only just after half past seven when Joshua Ribiero dropped Donny (neatly in his school uniform) and Anna (wearing her most withdrawn expression) back to Erewhon Parva, but they were made to feel

176

that their unplanned absence from the supper table had inconvenienced everyone.

"I'll finish anything you've got left," offered Donny, trying not to look as ravenous as he felt.

This was not acceptable. He knew he was supposed to have been eating supper at the Ribiero's – not storming back up the River Orwell with the beginnings of a spring flood under them and a force five wind astern. Donny had had no idea that a small dinghy could travel so fast. When Xanthe had set the spinnaker as well, he'd wondered whether *Lively Lady* could stand it.

"This is nothing," she'd said. "I'd be planing if I was in my *Laser*. The wind's behind us which makes it okay to crowd on. And we've got racing sails. They're much stronger. Her rigging's good too. I checked."

Donny let himself thrill to the power of *Lively Lady*'s surge forward. Would she take off? There was a tight adrenaline knot in his belly that had stopped him thinking of food. Only when he'd changed back into his uniform and sunk onto the back seat of Joshua's car had the feeling of tension and excitement begun to disperse.

"Good sail?" Xanthe's father had enquired.

"Unbelievable!" He'd found he was trembling slightly. It must be a reaction.

"How're you doing with those knots?"

"I'm only reliable on about four. I've got parcel string to practise with but, for the splices, I think it would be better if I used something thicker. I meant to look around the boatyard today and see if there was any old stuff thrown away."

"And the Laws of the Sea?" Joshua had been kind but implacable.

Somehow Donny hadn't wanted to make excuses even though he'd only been given the photocopied pages two days ago.

"Um, well, I've read what you gave me but I found it pretty complicated. There were some bits that weren't quite the same as what I thought Maggi and Xanthe said. It'll be me being dim of course – "

"Do you remember which they were?"

"Yes, because it was about who gives way and … that was what I sort of read the hardest."

"Carry on …"

"Well, there's loads of detailed instructions for ships and fishing boats and what noises to make in fog … but the bit I noticed being different was about sailing boats. The pages say that running-free gives way to close-hauled but I thought Maggi said it depended which side the wind was coming from – not what angle you were at."

"That's right," said Joshua. "You're doing well. There's a lot of history there and I'd like to talk about it with you. I hope we'll see you soon. Keep studying."

"I guarded and guarded our Treasure. But you didn't never come."

Vicarage atmospheres were no big deal but the disappointment in Luke's voice was something else. The younger boys' lives must feel so endless and empty. Luke and Liam had no adventures to keep them looking ahead, as far as he knew. No Rescue Myths that had sent them telegrams.

"I'm really sorry, Luke. Would you like me to …" (What could he offer? What would Granny or Skye have done for him?)"Tell you a story before you go to sleep? Something exciting?"

Even Gerald looked more agreeable.

"I'll come right now," he said, trying to avoid Anna's gaze. She probably wanted to talk about the flags, show him what she and Maggi had done. Get a bit of thanks even.

She waved casually in his direction before heading upstairs to her bedroom where Vicky's cot was now permanently installed.

CHAPTER SEVENTEEN

The Black Spot

Thursday, September 21st, after supper (none)

"Once upon a time," Donny began, desperately trying to remember how *Treasure Island* started, "there was a boy, probably about my age, called Jim Hawkins, who lived with his mother in an old pub. His father had died and Jim and his mother were pretty sad about that. And they were worried about how they were going to manage the pub and carry on earning their livings. If they couldn't earn any money, they'd go hungry."

Donny's stomach rumbled loudly.

"Jim and his mother had a problem. An old sea captain called Billy Bones had come to live in their pub. At first they'd been quite pleased but now he'd stopped paying his bills. He got drunk a lot and sang loud songs and frightened the other customers. They didn't know how they could get rid of him."

What had Anna said? Was it Luke and Liam's dad who used to get drunk a lot? Donny hurried on.

"Jim's mum's pub was on a lonely stretch of road near the coast. Not near here – somewhere else. Billy Bones had asked Jim to keep a lookout and tell him straightaway if he ever saw any other seafaring men, especially an old blind man with a stick called Pew or a one-legged man called Long John Silver. 'They'll be after my chest,' he said.

"One day an unknown seaman did arrive. But it wasn't Blind Pew and it wasn't Long John Silver, it was a man called Black Dog."

Granny had always made a big thing reading these names. You could even sign them like they were dramatic.

"Jim couldn't stop Black Dog meeting Billy Bones. But Black Dog didn't say a word to the old sea captain. He just pressed something into his hand and went away. 'The Black Spot! They've tipped me the Black Spot!' Billy's eyes were rolling and he was foaming at the mouth."

Donny tried acting up a bit. Luke and Liam had gone completely quiet. He was worried they were getting bored.

"Then Billy Bones died and Jim prised open his dead hand. In his dead fingers he was clutching a scrap of paper called the Black Spot. On the back it said 'We're Coming Tonight'. Soon, it was the middle of the night and everything was quiet."

Donny paused. The vicarage was very quiet.

So were Liam and Luke.

"Jim heard a noise getting nearer and nearer. Tap, tap, tap. Tap, tap, tap. It was Blind Pew and he was getting closer. 'Mum, we've got to go,' said Jim. His mum had been at Billy Bones's chest counting out the exact money that the old sea captain owed her. Jim was dragging at her to make her come. Then he grabbed another old piece of paper that was in there.

"Jim and his mother hid under a bridge. They'd only just got out in time. Blind Pew was almost there and a gang of bad men. They broke into the pub and crashed about inside. It was as if they were looking for something and were angry because they couldn't find it.

"Then at last some soldiers came and chased the men away. Blind Pew was killed and it was safe for Jim and his mother to come out. Jim was holding a very old map. A map of an island. There was a cross on the map. 'The treasure is here,' it said."

Donny stopped. Luke was completely motionless and he couldn't see Liam at all. Just a lump under the duvet. Maybe *Treasure Island* didn't really work for them. Wrong generation?

He was so hungry. Xanthe'd given them both some mint cake and a swig of water from the emergency box that she and Maggi had stowed in *Lively Lady*. She hadn't wanted them to eat much and at the time he hadn't minded.

"Is that the end?" Luke asked.

"Not really," said Donny. "But it's the end for tonight. I could tell you more tomorrow. If you wanted …"

"*Yessssss!*"

Still nothing from Liam. Donny guessed he might have fallen asleep. "Night then," he said to Luke.

As he reached the door, the duvet was heaved further over the lump and a weepy voice came muffled, "Don't like Blind Pew … he gives me bad feelings!"

What had he done? thought Donny. They were only little kids. "Hey, Liam," he said, re-crossing the room. "It's okay, honest. Blind Pew's gone. He got killed. And all the other bad men ran away. And Jim went and found the doctor at an important man's house where they were eating a really big supper. And he had supper. And his mum went to her friends in the village and she probably had supper too."

"Our mum's dead," said Luke. "We don't usually think about her much."

"Shit!" thought Donny. He didn't usually swear but he was so angry with himself. "I don't know what happened to Jim's mum but I'm sure she was okay. Then Jim sailed off on a ship called the *Hispaniola* and he had such adventures."

"Did Jim like football?" Liam's head peeped cautiously out.

This sounded more promising. "Well, I didn't ever meet him, so I don't know. I expect he would have liked football except he never got much chance. First he was on the *Hispaniola* so there wasn't space, and then he was on Treasure Island and there were mountains and jungles and things."

Liam was not convinced. "I've still got bad feelings. They're not in my feet or my tummy any more but there's still some in my head ..."

"I've got something in my room," said Donny, improvising desperately. "Something special. Stay still and I'll fetch it for you." He hurried to grab the dream-catcher Anna had made him. The younger boys lay still and silent. Only their eyes following him.

"This is a magic thing that Anna made. My mum used to make lots. You have it in your room and if bad dreams fly in they get tangled up in the net so they can't get to you. The good dreams can slip through the holes. Vicky's got one and that's why she's not crying at night any more. You have mine for now and tomorrow we'll make special ones of your own. You can think about how you'd like them to be."

"Do they sell Man U ones?"

"Dunno. We could try and make a Man U one. What about you, Luke?"

"Mmmmm thinking…"

The voice sounded pretty sleepy. Donny didn't reckon Luke'd be thinking for long. He turned to go again.

"Vicky only cried at night because Anna woked her up."

Huh?

"I've hung the catcher between your beds. It'll stop anything bad getting in. Sleep well. See you in the morning."

"Promise?"

"Promise."

Donny knew Luke was telling the truth. Anna's pale figure on the landing. The feeling he'd been watched.

Poor little Vicky! Woken. Then left on her own to cry until Gerald came lumbering up.

So that was how Anna got her Internet time.

But Anna was his friend. Vicky's sister. She couldn't have …

Anna was desperate. Anna was ruthless.

Of course she could.

Donny was *so* hungry. Okay, he wasn't going to get any supper but if he could just have a hunk of bread and a glass of milk, or some of those bananas Gerald was always dishing out, he'd be asleep in seconds. He started downstairs again to ask.

Rev. Wendy was coming out of her study. "That was Mrs Ribiero on the telephone," she called loudly. "She wants us to take John out of school on the 25th. All day!" Her voice was outraged, as if June had suggested they take Donny to a strip club.

"Why on earth would she want us to do something like that?" Gerald sounded bewildered. "She seemed such a sensible woman. She's a JP you know."

184

"I know. It's extraordinary. Her daughters have got some idea that this mythical great aunt of John's is actually going to arrive! The boy *is* very plausible …"

"I was beginning to think he was rather a nice lad," said Gerald, sadly.

"Yes. Although there's been a complaint at school about fighting. We must always remember him in our prayers. Denise Tune's arranged a meeting for Tuesday morning to finalise the legal arrangements. They can't extend the emergency order any further. He'll have to go."

"They're quite sure?"

"Oh yes, they've checked everywhere. Inspector Flint took personal charge."

"And you told Mrs Ribiero this?"

"Of course … She just said that if the boy is convinced, we should listen to him."

"And when no-one arrives … " Gerald cut in, sounding angry. "Hasn't Mrs Ribiero considered the trauma for the lad?"

"She agreed it would be a deep disappointment and he'd need a lot of support. She even offered to rearrange her own diary so she could spend Monday with him. At Shotley!"

"Ridiculous," snapped Gerald. "Who asked her to interfere? He's much better off keeping busy at school. Poor boy. He'll need quite enough support when they tell him what's been arranged at next Tuesday's meeting."

"Yes," agreed Wendy. "Sandra's going to take him out and explain what's going to be decided. He certainly doesn't need emotional disturbance on Monday as well."

Donny legs seemed to buckle. He sat on the stairs not caring whether anyone saw him or not. The hall lights were on. This felt like another act of the same bad play. Who needed nightmares when the adults behaved like this?

"Denise isn't inviting him to attend the meeting then? I wouldn't mind taking him into Colchester with me …"

"No. I did ask her, but she's assessed John as having a severe attitude problem towards authority. She doesn't think he'd react well. And there's no need for you to come, dear, I can represent us both."

"Oh," said Gerald, sounding disappointed. "By the way, dear, I've noticed that the boy prefers to be called Donny, not John."

"Oh," said Wendy. "Well, it's not for much longer is it? Were you planning to watch the News?"

Donny took several deep breaths. Got up from the stairs and marched into the kitchen.

He found the cling-filmed remains of the wholemeal pasta they'd had for supper and ate all of that. Then he made some thick slices of toast, opened a can of baked beans to tip over them and fried himself two large eggs. He had a mug of tea as well. With sugar. Research had showed that hot sweet drinks were particularly damaging to dental hygiene – so Gerald said.

He'd finished everything and was wondering about taking an apple and biscuits upstairs, when Wendy came into the kitchen carrying a tray. She was so startled she almost dropped it.

"John! I mean … Donny. Whatever are you doing?"

"I'm eating. What does it look like?" He spoke rudely. His voice had got a bit deeper.

"But what? Why?"

"Whatever I could find and because I was hungry. Is that a problem?"

She backed out and he heard her calling to Gerald. "Did you give permission for John to be in the kitchen helping himself to food, dear?"

Donny stood up and dumped his mug and plate in the sink with the pans he'd dirtied.

"No, he didn't. And I didn't ask. I'm tired now so I'll leave the washing-up. I don't suppose you'll do it. You've got too much to pray about."

He lifted the protective cover from the fruit bowl on the clean Formica table and chose two apples to take with him up to bed. Plus a banana that he didn't really want and a whole handful of biscuits. The SS were coming to tip him the Black Spot but he wasn't going to drop dead like Billy Bones. He was well-hard now.

He saw Gerald coming blearily out of the living room so he chucked the banana at him. Good shot.

"Choke on that then!"

He got Wendy a direct hit with the spare apple and went to bed feeling considerably better. Granny had always told him that it was wrong to waste food and he knew that he hadn't.

CHAPTER EIGHTEEN
Going AWOL

Friday, September 22nd

He wondered in the night whether they'd call Flint or Toxic to take him away. He wondered about legging it back down to *Lively Lady*. But there was the alarm system and his promise to Luke. He heaved an empty chest of drawers across the door instead. Then he went to sleep.

It was stand-off time at breakfast the next morning. Gerald and Wendy were evidently uncertain how much Donny had overheard and he wasn't planning to tell them.

Everyone else was rather cheery. Liam and Luke alternately said "tap, tap, *tap*," to one another in their most sinister voices, then fell off their chairs and rolled around on the floor with their soya milk substitute frothing out of their mouths. Vicky banged her spoon and said "doh … doh" while Anna, who had pulled the high chair up close to the table, and was sitting next to her sister, tried to encourage her to turn doh into Donny.

Hypocrite, thought Donny.

He felt fed up with Anna as well. A bit.

"It's not me she's looking at," he said eventually. "It's Luke. She started saying that when he was pretending to be a dog. She thinks he's funny and he's going to help look after her when I'm not here, aren't you, Lukey?"

"Our Treasure," said Luke.

Anna didn't say anything but she didn't totally freeze Luke out. And, when Liam started asking her about making Man U dream nets, she managed a muttered "maybe" before leaving the table to collect her school bag. Vicky began to yell when she saw Anna going but Luke pretended he had fleas under his collar so she laughed instead.

He was going to miss them.

Even Anna. Even now he knew what she'd been doing to Vicky to get Wendy and Gerald out of her way at night. He understood how living in the system began to change you. Made you hard and angry.

Okay, be honest. Donny was going to miss Anna most of everyone. Whatever she'd done.

He didn't know where he'd be if Gold Dragon didn't show up on Monday but it wasn't going to be here and it wasn't going to be anywhere arranged by anyone else's meeting. He'd rather live rough. Camp out behind The Cedars maybe?

"I'd like to speak with you before you leave, John." Rev. Wendy was standing near the kitchen door, finishing her coffee.

"No," said Donny. He stood up and realised that he was almost as tall as she was. Gerald was much taller but he wasn't scared of Gerald.

Rev. Wendy was blocking his exit. "You have school to attend and it's important that you go forth in peace," she said. "We forgive you your behaviour last night."

"Nope." It was all he could think of to say.

Anna was on the other side of Wendy, waiting for him. She held his rucksack up to show she had it. But he couldn't quite bring himself to push past. Not with the younger ones watching.

"I need to go," he said, "or I'll miss the bus. I'm posting another picture to my mum. I don't want your forgiveness but I'll take a stamp." Wendy didn't move. She didn't look as if she understood. "If you don't give me one – two or three would be even better – I'll either steal or send it without and then the hospital will have to pay."

"Hrrrrrp …" Gerald was trying to catch his wife's attention. He pointed to Anna. Anna had opened the study door – threatening to go in.

Wendy turned to defend her sanctum. And Donny ran.

He and Anna both ran. But only as far as the road. Their carers weren't the types to come hammering after them all the way to the bus stop.

"Did you get any stamps?"

"No, sorry. You were too quick."

"I'll have to nick one later. Seems I'm set for a life of crime."

"Like I said, join the club. What were you being forgiven for anyway?"

She took it really badly. He told her all he'd heard last night: how Flint and Toxic were still lying to the carers; how Rev. Wendy wouldn't let the Ribieros help; about the meeting that had been fixed for Tuesday; the decisions that had already been made.

"So if your great aunt doesn't come on Monday …"

"Or she doesn't like me …"

"You're going to steal the Ribieros' dinghy and go AWOL?"

"What's AWOL?"

"Absent Without Leave. It's what they say about deserters."

"That is so unfair! Think about it! What else can I do? Whatever Toxic's got worked out for me will be foul. I'm not allowed to go to the meeting because of my attitude problem and the only other person who might be on my side is Mr Mac and he says he only goes if he has a chance of making a difference. And if he doesn't and I haven't, it's too late, they've got me."

"But that is thieving. Taking a dinghy's not like taking a stamp. And they trust you. The Ribieros. They're kind people."

"Okay," he snapped at her. The bus was coming. "I'll go without *Lady* if that'll make you feel better. I just won't have any shelter or anywhere to keep things and I'll get caught much quicker. But if that's what you want . . ."

They didn't speak again or sit together. The bus was quite crowded and when Xanthe got on with her cello the driver made everyone stay in their places while he got out, unlocked the luggage compartment and stowed it in there. Muttering about regulations and abusing the contract. He grumbled about its weight as well.

Maggi was carrying a small sail bag, which she passed to Donny.

"It's a bosun's bag. It's from Dad. Loads of bits of rope and different sized cod-line, and pulleys and shackles and whipping twine and a sailmaker's needle. I don't reckon he thinks you've got anything else to do except practise splicing and Fisherman's Bends."

"I've put the flags in there too," she told Anna, once the bus had arrived at the school, and they were waiting for the driver to finish complaining and give Xanthe back her cello. "They're not totally finished. The parentals are picking us up from here to drive straight to Rutland Water. We're racing tomorrow and we'll be back late. I mean, we'll be around at the club on Sunday. Dad's got some meeting but we weren't sure if we could get them to you in time."

"Believe me I did try to help but I sew like a squid on a slab," said Xanthe, joining them. "So I added about twenty metres of cod line to the bosun's bag and a knife with a marlinspike. The *Hispaniola's* signal halyards looked okay but I couldn't properly see. If they're not, you need to tie something heavy to the end of the line and heave it over her lower cross-trees."

"Like John did with the lantern and the lookout pine," said Donny. "Xanthe, Maggi, your mother rang Rev. Wendy last night. How much do your parents know?"

The sisters looked at each other. "Don't blow us out, Donny-man," said Xanthe. "We though it was worth a try. Mum and Dad like you – they like both of you – they want to help."

"Mum saw the flags, you see," explained Maggi. "Not 'U', luckily – just the two-headed dragon and the Chinese national – so she thinks they're welcoming, not warning. They can't understand why you're not being allowed to wait down at Shotley on Monday. They got quite wound-up about it."

"They're worried you might do something silly," said Xanthe who seemed to be breathing heavily as she hefted her cello case across to the music block. "So we asked how they would define silly…"

"And Dad said it was driving up the A1 on a Friday evening towing a couple of over-canvassed daughters plus two chattering dinghies. He was in a bad mood. He's put in that special book he wants Donny to have. Anna, wait!"

But Anna was already through the swing doors and lost in the crowd.

"Is something wrong?" Maggi's expressive face was troubled.

"Mmmm, sort of … tactical. She thinks I might be going to … do something silly. Um … deceiving. She's worried about your parents."

"Ah …" said Maggi.

"Since you mention it," said Xanthe, "you might want to meet me and Long John in one of the practice rooms this lunch time. Maggi might or might not."

"And Anna very likely won't," said Maggi. "Lend me back that bosun's bag, Donny. She and I might go and be girly in textiles."

Xanthe hadn't been offering him a music recital. Long John had stayed at home. Instead there was a torch with spare batteries, a sleeping bag, waterproof cover, wetsuit, tiny camping stove, billycan and tins. There was also another, larger, sail bag for Donny to transport them to the dinghy. She'd used the case to get everything out of the house without questions.

"But, Xanthe, you don't do things without telling your parents."

"Yeah, yeah – that's what Maggi said, but sometimes it's for their own good. None of us wants you to be a duffer, none of us wants you to drown but my view is that exposure's your most likely danger. Should you just *happen* to be caught out late at night in an open dinghy trying to do the right thing by your incredibly brilliant but unfortunately aged relative. Much less dufferish to lay in a few supplies. I'm sure they'd be pleased if they knew."

He wished Xanthe'd been on the bus after school. The mud-slinging boys from the Hard had the third member of their gang with them and kept up a barrage of abuse, mainly of the 'pee-doh' variety.

Donny didn't care that much but he felt sorry for Anna. She'd been a bit more cheerful after her session with Maggi but now she was white and tense and withdrawn again. She was sitting next to him and the insults meant she was getting noticed. Xanthe would have found the words to face them off. Maggi would have got people round to their side with her tact and charm. He just wanted to hit them. And he couldn't.

"What was all that about?" she asked, when they finally reached their stop.

"You don't need to know, believe me."

"Gits."

"Too right."

"How were you planning to get those bags indoors without Gerald seeing?" she asked, pulling herself together as the bus trundled away. "I suppose we could put them in the shed with the jumble sale stuff …"

"Nah, I'm taking them straight down to *Lively Lady*. She's beyond the far end of the beach now. Xanthe showed me a good place. Though nowhere's that good when the tide's right out."

"But ... It's Friday ... House Meeting?"

"Oh, stuff it." Donny had completely forgotten. "And stuff the Care Plan too. Now that my attitude problem's been Professionally assessed I might as well get value from it. Set a good example to Luke and Liam ..."

She'd gone a bit quiet.

"Er, will they take it out on you if I don't show?"

"It's okay. I'm not too bothered. I thought I might pretend I was still worrying about Deceit. I could start with my computer and the tools – ask them whether it would have been okay if I'd told them in the beginning that Mr McMullen had lent them to me ... That'll give them the chance to lecture me about Trust and Openness etc. Then I'll look all enlightened and say that I realise now that I should always tell people things – even if it might upset or worry them – because it's better that they have a chance to express their opinions first than find out when it's too late."

Anna opened her eyes very wide, tilted her head slightly and mimicked herself looking enlightened. Donny couldn't help laughing.

"Then, before they get us all holding hands on it, I'll ask if the rule applies to adults too?" She snapped back to her usual sharp-faced self. "Whether it'll be alright for me to do really mean things behind people's backs when I'm an adult, if I think it might upset them to know in advance. Like fixing meetings and deciding people's futures without even asking them or hinting what's going to happen."

Donny wasn't sure. "I dunno that they'll get it. Seems to me they just assume they're right all the time. Rev. Wendy does anyway and Gerald follows her. Or they both trot along in blinkers believing whatever Toxic Tune decides to tell them."

But Anna was not going to be knocked back.

"Well, it'll be quite of a shock for them when your Gold Dragon turns up on Monday, won't it?" She handed him the bosun's bag she'd been carrying, with the completed flags inside. "Perhaps I should simply ask whether they think we should be planning a tea party for Great Aunt Ellen to Welcome her into our Family Circle or whether it would be more sensitive if we gave you both Time Alone. See what they say to that."

Donny laughed. "Tell them I've gone for a walk, okay? You don't know where."

Time alone with *Lively Lady* – him and his boat and the river. It was a calm, grey end to the afternoon, with an overcast sky and very little breeze, quite unlike the blustery conditions of yesterday when they'd come roistering up with the flood.

He had a lot of gear and it was hard to decide where he could put it all. He and Xanthe had taken all the sails off and stowed them in the aft locker with the waterproof clothes and boots. There was a bit of space under the deck in front of the mast. He shoved as much as he could there and then worried that it might unbalance her.

"I wish we were going now," he said softly to the little boat. "Two whole days to wait. I'll come down tomorrow though. Just to check you're okay."

"My daughter thinks it's a mistake to leave oars in a dinghy if you're not remaining close at hand. I expect she'd apply the same rule to a rudder and a daggerboard if they're detatchable."

That old lady again in her green beret. Was she some sort of leprechaun?

"It puts temptation in people's way, she thinks. Even this far along the beach. Not only by the Hard."

"Is she here? Your daughter?"

Margery wasn't on the beach. Hadn't been here the previous night either. Or he'd have told Xanthe they needed to find somewhere else.

"Gone away again. She comes quite regularly to check up on me. A good-hearted girl, if hasty. You can leave your equipment behind my boathouse. I might not notice what you're up to."

He didn't believe that, but what choice did he have? So he mumbled some thanks and checked *Lively Lady*'s anchor one final time before picking up the oars, daggerboard and rudder to follow his benefactor to the cottage by the wood. He had already taken a few pieces of codline out from the bosun's bag so he could carry on practising those knots. Plus a stiff rectangular package addressed to him in what must be Joshua Ribiero's handwriting.

Donny placed it carefully in his rucksack. Something special, the girls had said.

CHAPTER NINETEEN
The Salt-Stained Book

Friday 22nd – Saturday 23rd September

"Hide those plums! Hang them out of the window or something."

"Why?"

The old lady had given him a bag and shown him the tree with the wonderful plums. She'd told him to take as many as he liked and share them with his friends. Then she'd explained how he could get back to the vicarage by a field path, which meant he didn't have to use the road at all, except the very last bit. He'd vaguely thought he could use the plums to sort of cover for his absence. Divert attention.

"You're still such an idiot! Do you want them to know exactly where you've been?" Anna was totally exasperated. "Never tell them *anything*. Because, when you bunk off, that'll be the first place they look. Even better, lie to them."

He used some of Joshua's codline and did as she said. It was a good thing that his second-floor room was at the back of the house as it could have looked odd. Maybe he'd haul them in later and share them with the others. Have a feast.

"Won't Mrs Everson wonder what's happened? When Gerald or Wendy don't thank her?"

"Too bad. You haven't got long anyway. Toxic's been here."

"What!"

"She was here when I got back from the bus. Didn't exactly lap up my 'he's gone for a walk but I don't know where' line. Ripped off at Gerald for letting you out with Vicky. You've been terrorising the local youngsters apparently."

"Huh?"

"You're grounded all weekend and not allowed on the bus any more. Too disruptive. She's taking you to school on Monday and you'll be on report again. For your own *saif-ty*!"

"So's I can't go down to Shotley and wait for Gold Dragon, more like. Where's everybody now?"

"Walking down to Pin Mill looking for you. Not her of course. She swung her Jimmy Choos into her flash car and drove away purring."

"Jimmy Choos?"

"Her shoes. Surely even you've noticed? They cost hundreds and you never see her in the same pair twice. There's no way a normal Welfare person could afford them."

It was so weird. Why didn't the adults see it?

Donny gave up. "I'll go and pinch a couple of stamps then. I've got a letter ready for mum. I suppose I could write to Mrs Everson to thank her…"

"If you must."

Supper was late, burnt and congealed. Everyone was bad tempered. Wendy and Gerald kept on at Donny, asking where he'd been on his walk. But by then, he could say, quite truthfully, that he'd been out looking for a postbox.

When he announced that he wasn't coming to House Meeting neither of the carers objected. Gerald possibly looked relieved? Then when Anna said she'd like to use the opportunity to plan a Welcome for the New Arrival in Our Midst, Rev. Wendy decided it was too late to have a meeting at all.

"Luke and Liam have an early start in the morning. Third Saturday in the month. Time to visit your father."

The two boys looked at each other. Liam stopped eating.

"I feel sick," he said.

"But you're not even in the car yet!" said Gerald. It almost came out as a wail.

"Have your bath," said Donny. "And I could tell you more of the story."

Gerald looked at him. "That's … kind of you. Er, what sort of story?"

"Organised crime, extreme violence and strong language," Donny longed to answer. But not this evening. "*Treasure Island* by R.L. Stevenson. It's a classic."

"I think we read it in school," said Gerald. "Those little red books. Do you remember, dear?"

"Not in my school," said Wendy shortly. Donny looked at his plate to stop himself laughing.

"We expect that you older two will lend a hand with the baby while I'm away with the boys. There's still an Order preventing me from taking her …"

"Take her over my dead body," muttered Anna.

"And Wendy's so busy preparing for the Harvest Festival," Gerald continued as if he hadn't heard. "Though of course she'll always Be There. So we thought, Anna, and, um, Donny, that you two might …"

"Save Social Services the expense of a baby-minder?" enquired Anna, sweetly.

"Well, yes . . ." began Gerald.

"No," snapped Wendy. "We are offering you an additional opportunity for quality-time bonding with your own sister. John is confined to the house in my absence but you may both bring her with you to the village hall for the afternoon and help with the preparations for the Parish Supper. It's a way of putting something Back into the Community."

"Where is it Luke and Liam go to see their father?" Donny asked Anna, much later, when he had given the younger boys their second instalment and reassured Liam that he hadn't forgotten that he needed a Man U dream-catcher of his own to keep the bad feelings away. Liam had pleaded for it to be ready by the time he and Luke came back with Gerald in the car tomorrow evening. "I can't make any sense of what they're saying. A big place with lots of other men and dogs and keys."

"Prison." She almost spat. "It's where he belongs." And she stepped instantly into her and Vicky's bedroom and shut the door in his face.

Joshua's package contained a slim blue book, *Sailing* by E.F. Knight. The book was obviously old but not antique. It hadn't come off the Armada or anything. It was just an inexpensive, well-used handbook with its covers buckled by damp and disfigured by a dry white stain.

Donny worked out that it was the source of the photocopied pages that were teaching him about knots and the laws of the sea. But was that it? Maggi or Xanthe had said that their father had borrowed it from the yacht club library. So it wasn't even his book.

It had belonged to a Gregory Palmer. His brothers and sisters had given it to him for his fourteenth birthday. They addressed him as 'Captain John' as if it was a family joke and gave themselves the same names (in brackets) as the Walker family in *Swallows and Amazons*: Edith Palmer had been 'Mate Susan', Eirene Palmer 'Able Seaman Titty', Ned Palmer had been 'Ship's Boy Roger' and Ellen Palmer 'the Ship's Baby', though she couldn't actually write.

Donny decided to read Joshua's letter.

"My Dear Donny,"

"Xanthe and Maggi have told us that you are hoping to meet your great aunt on her arrival at Shotley on Monday. This is good news and we are all delighted for you."

They do believe me!

"We are, however, concerned that there appears to be little expectation among the authorities that this happy event will actually take place. June has just had a telephone conversation with your carers that has left her anxious for your well-being in the immediate future.

"Of course it may be that you decide that the wisest course of action is to attend school as usual on Monday hoping that your great aunt will find her own way to make contact with you. In which case you are not at any physical risk and I cannot criticise such a decision."

Joshua had crossed out the next bit but Donny could still read it.

"(Though I must say that if I had travelled halfway across the world in response to a dying sister's wish I would be a little disappointed to

find no-one at all to greet me.)

"June will spend time at Shotley marina on Monday. This may or may not be the location your great aunt has in mind but we feel it offers the most promising vantage point, being at the tip of the peninsula. I wish I could offer to take a watch myself but I have a full operating schedule, which I cannot rearrange.

"Meanwhile, you have Lively Lady which you may continue to consider as your own and use as you find most helpful. You must however remember that you are very new to sailing. Please be aware of your own ignorance. I am not saying Don't – but I am saying THINK.

"I am sending this book as your companion. Its first owner was the captain of a destroyer in the Arctic convoys of the Second World War. He was lost at sea – a good captain and a brave man. The circumstances were tragic. He had witnessed, at close quarters, the utter destruction of a ship commanded by his younger brother. It had been his duty first to search for survivors and then to abandon the search. The subsequent Enquiry concluded that he had acted in every way properly. He handed over command and, suicidally, threw himself into the sea as his vessel, obeying his own final orders, steamed away from the area. This book fell from his pocket at that moment.

"It was retrieved by a fellow-officer who presented it to our club library on his own retirement from the Service. He once told me that he had received an extraordinary impression that the book had chosen to remain with its ship. As in any other circumstance Captain Palmer himself would certainly have done. 'A Captain's Duty is to his Ship' – as every seafarer knows.

"An unspoken understanding has grown up in the club that members may borrow this book when they are embarking on some more than usually lengthy or hazardous voyage. I feel that I am extending the rules *only slightly by borrowing it on your behalf.*

"I frighten myself when I think of the foolish things you may do left unsupported in possession of a dinghy. However I am going to trust you not to do them. You have a boat and a book to look after and there are people who care what becomes of you. I expect this volume to be returned safely.

"There is absolutely no need for rashness, even if you are disappointed on Monday.

With best wishes,

Joshua Ribiero."

Donny sat still, breathing deeply. It was as if a weight of worry was being lifted off him. This was a permission letter. It didn't remove any of the things ahead which frightened him but it took away the guilt that he'd be abusing the Ribiero parents' kindness if he used their dinghy to reach Gold Dragon.

It wasn't exactly a charter to do a runner afterwards if she didn't show up – he'd need to think about that.

Gregory Palmer had obviously taken *Sailing* wherever he went. So had the fellow-officer who'd kept it all those years after his death. Its binding was becoming loose and the edges of the cover were frayed with wear. Donny could almost sense the imprint of the other hands who had picked up the book and opened it, either idly or urgently, needing information. He turned it over in his own hands. It felt as comfortable as a long lost friend.

The birthday dedication was on the first page. On the reverse side Gregory Palmer, 'Captain John', had written a list of ships in which he'd served. He had careful handwriting that began childish and matured with every entry: *Corky, Ceres, Snowdrop, Barnacle Goose, Sea Thrift, Oystercatcher* ... The list had only reached halfway down the page when the writer had made his final entry: HMS *Sparrow* (1945).

He couldn't have been very old when he died, thought Donny. He ran his finger over the dry white watermark that the sea had left. He felt the swollen and buckled boards. This book was disfigured, permanently scarred by that event.

Suddenly he didn't want to read any more.

Saturday, September 23rd
The vicarage felt really peaceful with only him and Anna and little Vicky there.

They ate plums and made dream-catchers. The silky material Anna'd blagged from the textile department to make their warning flags was red and black and gold – exactly the Man U colours that Liam wanted. Anna helped him make beads by twirling long triangles of plain paper round a thin pencil then gluing and colouring them. Donny decorated them with players' initials. Wayne Rooney and David Beckham might as well do their bit towards keeping Liam's bad feelings away.

Then he began plaiting Vicky a friendship bracelet but she was so much more interested in chewing it that he had to plait longer and longer to prevent it being classed as a Choking Hazard.

"I'd like to make you something," he said to Anna. "But it seems silly when you're so much better at making things than me."

"It's no big deal," she replied firmly. "I'm not treating it like you're going off for ever. All you've got to do is get down that river, meet up with Gold Dragon and make sure she doesn't get copped by Flint. Then you just charm the sea boots off her, extract your mother and get me my Internet access back. Okay?"

"Um, yeah, okay – since you put it like that. Sounds a total doddle. But I'm not coming back to live here whatever happens. So I need to say goodbye to the other kids. I like Luke and Liam and Vicky – whatever their Dad's done."

"They can't keep secrets, you know. They're useless. They get muddled and blab it all out."

"I'll tell it in a story then. No-one'll notice if that gets muddled and they can add bits if they like."

So he finished *Treasure Island* that last Saturday night with an unscripted addition in which Jim Hawkins came back and went off and had other voyages. And came back again. Like it was *Treasure Island II* and *Treasure Island III*.

Then he presented the Man U concoction to Liam and told Luke that he was giving him his own dream-catcher that Anna had made. "Because I might need to be like Jim Hawkins and have to sail away and rescue Ben Gunn. So I could do with you taking care of this special thing for me till I come back."

"With a sea chest and a wooden leg."

"Yeah, that's about it!"

"So I have Vicky as my Treasure in the day and keep the dream-catcher safe at night?"

"And it keeps you safe as well. Like Liam's does …"

Donny said his final good night and was slipping out of the boys' room, privately congratulating himself on his child-management techniques, when Luke called after him. "But you won't really, will you, Donny, you won't really go away? I like it now you're here."

"Um, well, you see, Lukey, I might have to. I'm hoping that my great aunt's going to come but I don't know."

"What's a great aunt?"

"She's my family. That's all I've got except my mum. No brothers and sisters like you have."

"We could be your family! Even Anna likes you and she doesn't usually like anyone."

"But I don't think Gerald and Wendy and the Welfare people want that."

"Then I hate them even more."

"Mmm, me too. So I thought I might go on an adventure for a bit. That's why I need you to look after things."

"How long till I can have an adventure?" The younger boy's voice was full of yearning.

Donny wished then that he was staying. He could have taken Luke and Liam sailing. They could all have got into *Lively Lady*, like the *Swallows and Amazons* kids – or Gregory Palmer's brother and sisters with their made-up names. Okay, so they probably couldn't have camped out on an island in a lake but at least they could have gone for a picnic or rowed across the river to dig worms.

"Dunno. Sometimes adventures just happen. When Anna and I were at Xanthe and Maggi's club last weekend there was a fat man with a pointy boat that was mean like a shark. He was horrible and gross and tried to frighten Maggi and Anna. And his name was Flint, same as the pirate in the story! So we sung fifteen men on a dead man's chest."

"Yo, ho, ho and a bottle of rum!" came unexpectedly from Liam's bed.

"That's right, Li, that's how it went. Then, down the river on Thursday, Xanthe and I saw an old three-masted schooner with nobody anywhere near her. So we called her the forgotten *Hispaniola*. It's as if *Treasure Island* is happening all round us."

"But we're not in it," said Luke after a moment's thought.

"One day you will be. We all will."

"Even Vicky?"

"Yeah, why not! She's our Treasure so she'd better come along. Now you settle to sleep, both of you, and think up some plans and one day we'll all get together and do them."

"You promise?"

Donny gulped and mentally crossed his fingers. Then he mentally uncrossed them.

"Yes, I do. I just don't definitely promise when."

Once again he reached the door and once again a voice called after him.

"Um, Donny …" This time it was Liam.

"Yes, Li?" Donny tried not to sound impatient.

"I want you to have something." The little boy was sitting up looking in a shoebox beside his bed. Donny went over and waited until he'd made his choice. "I want you to have this."

'This' was a Euro 2004 fridge magnet, probably out of a cereal packet.

"It's a medal. It's well wicked. It's one of my best things."

"Wow," said Donny. "Thanks, mate. That's really awesome."

"And it still sticks," said Liam, giving his treasure one last look before handing it to Donny and snuggling down determinedly.

"Thanks," said Donny again. "Night Li, night Luke." And this time he was gone, not feeling quite so sure of himself.

He sat up late, reading both his books.

The happy ending of *Swallows and Amazons* left him depressed – all those children waving goodbye to one another and making plans for next year. He noticed that there were other books in the same series so they must have had a next year – and a year after that, probably. He couldn't even see into next week.

Their mum and the baby came strolling down the field to meet the children when they came sailing home.

Fat chance of that!

Donny sighed. Whatever Granny had been trying to explain, whatever secret she was trying to share, he hadn't got it.

Then he had another look at *Sailing*, Joshua's recommended read. What was it with adults and their special books?

He turned to a chapter on sailing theory but his brain refused to grapple with the technicalities of leeway, lateral resistance, griping and weather-helm. So he started flicking through, looking at diagrams without understanding them. Until he came to a section of miscellaneous hints and several paragraphs of instruction concerning 'the Management of Open Boats in a Heavy Sea'.

Donny read the ensuing pages with mounting horror. Even launching a rowing boat from a beach was hazardous, apparently. The author spared nothing in his description of the previously unsuspected perils of broaching to, foundering, capsizing, swamping, being thrown end over end in heavy surf. "In this way," he warned his readers, sternly, "many lives are annually lost."

Donny shut *Sailing* with a snap. "Will all this happen to me?" he wondered. Gregory Palmer – 'Captain John' – had died. His book seemed stained with blood, not salt. Dry, white blood.

The bedroom light was still on and the thin covers were actually quite warm but Donny shivered.

Down, breathless, down into darkness, crushed by the weight of the icy sea …

The room went black and Donny's chest began to hurt. There was an unbearable pressure building up at the back of his mouth and nose but he didn't dare breathe because he dreaded that first gush of freezing water filling his airways, smothering his lungs. His stomach began to hurt. There were red flashes behind his eyes. He couldn't bear it – he was waving, kicking, fighting, desperate to break back to the surface.

Donny opened his eyes, panting and bewildered. He'd been holding his breath. Stupid or what! He shoved *Sailing* away as if it carried a curse. "Well, there's one thing I can do," he thought. "If I don't go to sea, I can't drown."

But he could drown in the river too; he could have drowned on that reservoir – 'Gitche Gumee' as he'd so blithely named it. Donny's hands went clammy as he remembered how confidently he'd set out in the little *Optimist* that first day, how recklessly he'd endangered the child as well as himself. He wouldn't be doing that again! Not now he realised how perilous it was and how much knowledge he didn't know.

Granny had been quite right. He should keep away from water.

They all should.

Donny pulled the pillow over his head as he hadn't done for years. He'd get his dream-catcher back from Luke tomorrow and make the younger boy a new one. He'd have plenty of time because he wasn't going anywhere. Not by water anyway.

Lively Lady would be okay. She could sit on the beach at Pin Mill near the old lady's house until he got the Ribieros to bring their car and tow her back to the dinghy-park. He would relax, stay safe. Maybe he'd play a bit of football with the kids.

If Great Aunt Ellen turned up, she could fetch him from school.

CHAPTER TWENTY
Dinghies in the Dark

*Nancy stood up and pushed at the bottom with an oar. John put the
lantern down on the forward thwart. He wanted to use both hands and
all his strength. Swallow slid off. John got a knee to the gunwale and
gave a last kick to the shore. They were afloat. And at that moment there
was the sharp crack of a rifle away to the south, a crash and tinkle of
broken glass and the lantern toppled down from the thwart and went
out.*

(from Peter Duck *by Arthur Ransome*)

Sunday, September 24th

As the pale light of early morning crept across the bleak
vicarage bedroom, Donny's first instinct was to get up, take
both his books and go.

Go now. Leave. Before he could change his mind again.

In his emotional panic of the previous night he'd forgotten
that he wasn't taking *Lively Lady* down the river for fun. This
was a rescue mission.

His dream had sent him a message. You could know things
through dreams, Skye had said.

It had been dark and he was John Walker – the real 'John
Walker' – and he'd been rowing John Walker's dinghy, *Swallow*.
There'd been a girl called Nancy, a rifle shot, the crash and
tinkle of broken glass. They'd rescued a fat man from an
unknown shore

"Now do you understand?" said Nancy.

Not really – but he got the gist. 'Nancy' was an Amazon. Like Xanthe? Everything else was muddled – except that his Great Aunt Ellen was in danger. She needed him.

And so did Skye.

And after that he wanted to help Anna.

Donny hoped that none of his friends would ever know how close he'd come to bottling out. How could he have thought he could have faced Maggi and Xanthe if he'd just left their dinghy on the beach? Gutless or what? There was minimal risk involved in sailing a well-maintained and well-equipped dinghy, like *Lively Lady*, down the River Orwell in good conditions. He'd done it once already. This wasn't the Arctic Sea. They were not at war.

Donny stomped about the room picking things up and shoving them in his rucksack. He was going to take the new swimming shorts he'd been allowed to buy. Then he realised,, just in time, that their absence could give away that he was heading for water. Logical thinking! Anna would be proud of him.

After that he crept downstairs, filched two plastic bags from Gerald's recycling system and wrapped them carefully around his books. Even if he got completely soaked there would be no more white bloodstains.

Okay. Captain Palmer was dead. And that was very sad.

But most old books must have belonged to people who were dead. All those classics of Granny's – *Hiawatha*, *Treasure Island*, *Peter Pan* – all the kids who'd read them when they first came out: they'd all be dead by now.

Granny was dead as well. Nothing to do with water.

If he was too scared to sail *Lively Lady* down to the harbour, he'd have to stick close to the riverbank and paddle. Like Mole in *The Wind in the Willows*.

If he woke Anna, she could disable the alarm for him.

But once he'd got everything properly packed and waterproof, Donny realised that he couldn't set off immediately. If he woke Anna he'd most likely wake Vicky – which would wake everyone. Even if it didn't, leaving now would give Gerald and Wendy – or Flint and Toxic – all day to search for him. Wait until tonight and his absence mightn't be noticed until Monday morning – Monday, September 25th. The day Great Aunt Ellen had promised to arrive.

By then his warning flags would be flying.

And after that? He had no idea.

That Sunday was the slowest day. Only Liam had agreed to go to church so the Family Activity that afternoon was two hours in the village recreation ground. Even Anna was made to come. Liam soon got fed up with their lack of football skill and went off to play with a ferociously energetic group of youngsters, all wearing logo-ed team strips. Donny, Luke and Anna took turns to swing Vicky and then sat on a bench practising some of the knots and splices from *Sailing*'s photocopied pages.

Gerald, who was supervising, got quite interested. It bought out the buried Boy Scout in him and he reminisced contentedly about campfires and woggles, while Luke devised ever more fiendish bondage systems – for the man in the shark-boat, for the whole of the SS and for Blind Pew too.

Gerald never listened properly to anything Luke said. Unfortunately even he couldn't avoid making the connection when a furious Flint came hammering on the vicarage door shortly after tea to complain that his powerboat had been vandalised.

"Is that the fat man? The one who tried to frighten Anna?" Luke asked loudly, as Gerald explained that the children had been in the park with him all afternoon and under the care of a Social Service-approved home help whilst he had attended church in the morning.

"And yesterday?"

"The older two were in the village hall from lunchtime assisting my wife with the decorations and at home here during the morning looking after the baby. My wife's the vicar, you know. We take regular advice from Education Welfare."

"Where were you, sir?"

"I was … elsewhere. With two of the younger children."

"Visiting day in Her Majesty's nick, was it? In fact you've very little idea what this big lad might have been up to, either yesterday morning or today."

"I haven't been anywhere near your boat. Not since I saw you driving it last weekend."

"Is he the one with a boat like a shark? The mean one? Donny – is he?" Luke wouldn't be denied.

Donny couldn't help grinning though he guessed it would be disastrous. "Could well be – but it's not very polite to make personal comments in front of people."

Flint seemed likely to explode. "Very helpful, thank *you*. Shark-boat eh? You're coming down to the Station with me, my boy. Now, march!"

Donny turned to Gerald. "I've not done anything to his boat. I'm not going. Why should I?"

Gerald was at a loss, torn between his wish to justify the reliability of his child-minding arrangements and his in-built habit of deferring to authority. He stuttered and dithered.

Anna, who'd vanished immediately she spotted the policeman, reappeared at that moment, bringing Rev. Wendy with her.

Donny would never be more grateful for Wendy's slow carefulness and her boring adherence to procedures.

"I'm sorry, officer," she said, when Flint had repeated his angry demand, "but you haven't brought anyone with you. John's a minor and therefore it would be incorrect for you to take him to a police station unescorted. I'm on my way to Evensong and my husband has all the other children to supervise. So, until one of us is available to accompany you, or until you can provide an alternative escort, I'm afraid John must remain here. There's probably a duty social worker you could contact. I assume you have the necessary paperwork?"

Obviously Flint hadn't. He returned to his car and sat there in the drive making telephone calls.

Wendy shook her head sadly as she collected her cassock and car keys. "This is very disappointing, John. Very disappointing indeed."

Donny's gratitude imploded. He turned on her. "Sorry. Are you deaf?" That was an insult he never normally used. "I said that I've never touched his boat. I've never even been near it. You like rules. What about innocent until proved guilty, huh?"

There was more that he could have added but he didn't have the time. He turned and ran upstairs to his room, vaulting the safety-gate. A moment later he heard Wendy drive away.

His rucksack was packed and so was the bosun's bag. He'd even written a note for Anna to give Mr McMullen next morning. He dropped his bags out of the window down to the flowerbed but couldn't see how he could follow them himself. All the long bits of rope were on *Lively Lady*.

He didn't want to risk the hall with Gerald still flapping around. Couldn't think how he was going to get out of the drive with Flint parked there in his fat black car.

Except that Anna would surely organise a diversion.

He went down a floor to Luke and Liam's room. Sheets, duvet covers. That was the classic method. He could do the knots. Set the boys a good example. They'd enjoy having to haul all their bed-linen back through the window when Gerald had shooed them upstairs.

There was a carrier bag beside the stair-gate. It held a big bottle of water, some bread and bananas. He knew it was for him. She'd already got Vicky screaming in the kitchen and it sounded as if Liam and his football had broken something major.

"Shall I make the nice Inspector a cup of tea?" he heard her say – in her sweetest, most dangerous voice.

Out of the window. Down into the garden. Mud on the duvet covers. Tough. Collect the bags. There was chain-link all round the garden. No chance of getting to the field path that way. Donny crept to the corner of the house and peeped into the drive.

Flint was parked right across the entrance. He must have blocked it deliberately after Rev. Wendy had left.

There was Anna bringing Flint a cup of tea and Luke beside her with the box of the special chocolate biscuits that Wendy and Gerald kept in the study – more to look at than to eat. They were carrying their offerings to the police car as if they were in a solemn ritual. As well as the biscuits, Anna proffered a tray and a large china cup, a milk jug and a sugar bowl with tongs. She was volunteering to be allowed to count the sugar grains into the cup and virtually drip in the milk so she could be certain it was exactly as Flint liked it.

Luke waited beside her in total silence. How had she managed that?

Anyone who knew how sick with terror Anna felt whenever she had to go close to the fat policeman would have understood how brave this was. Donny knew she wouldn't be able to keep her hands from trembling. He guessed that Flint would relish her fright, would leer over her and try to make her feel more and more wobbly and nervous. He would be ready to bellow at Luke, trample anything he said, enforce what he called Respect.

Donny tiptoed a few metres from the corner of the house to the laurels on the other side of the drive. Then he got down and crawled. Up to the rear of the Range Rover and underneath. If the car moved now he'd be crushed.

He knew Anna knew he was there but he didn't dare glance at her or at Luke. Couldn't risk a flicker of distraction. Let the bloated bully dither between double-choc truffle-crunch and butterscotch-crackle cream cookie. Or savour the gourmet delights of oppressing a fantastically clever and gallant thirteen-year-old girl – and a kid on his first adventure.

Donny was on his stomach now, struggling to pull his bags along without making any noise or touching the underside of the vehicle. His rucksack was centimetres away from its carbon-encrusted exhaust.

Someone called Flint's car-phone. But by then Donny was out on the empty road. He was hidden by the evergreen hedge and running as if a fleet of 4x4s was in pursuit, while the rucksack bumped on his back and the plastic carrier and bosun's bag swung madly by his side. He didn't slow down when he reached the field path though it got harder to run on the rutted, summer-baked ground.

Donny had no idea what Flint was accusing him of doing. Maybe someone really had vandalised the shark-boat – Xanthe would have been keen enough.

Or maybe the policeman was lying in order to get Donny banged up so he couldn't reach Shotley tomorrow. Except that Toxic was already on the case – and Flint had looked genuinely furious.

All he knew for sure was that the policeman wouldn't give up easily. And it wasn't nearly dark yet.

The good outcome of his hasty exit from Erewhon Parva vicarage was that he arrived at the river about three hours earlier than planned. There was water almost up to the beach.

What wasn't so good was that *Margery* was lying there, too, hauled up onto the sand and anchored companionably close to *Lively Lady*. Which must mean that the big-nosed lady was checking up on her mother. And that mother, with her spooky habit of popping out from nowhere, would be checking up on him. He needed to get *Lively Lady*'s equipment without them seeing.

Donny walked carefully round to the back of the cottage. Maybe they were having an early supper or watching 'Songs of Praise' or something. Oars, rudder, daggerboard. It was hard to manage everything. He dropped the carrier bag.

"I say!"

With a gigantic effort Donny controlled his urge to drop everything else and run.

"I say! Did you know you've lost your water?"

He looked towards the beach. It was okay, tide-wise. No mud, yet. Not too far to push the dinghy. As long as he didn't hang around.

"Would you like me to refill it?"

So that's what she'd meant. The top had come off his plastic bottle and the precious fresh water had spilled onto the cottage path. The big-nosed lady was trying to help.

"Going far?" she asked, screwing the top firmly back onto the refilled bottle and helping carry the oars and rudder as they walked to *Lively Lady*.

He hadn't got a lie about him. Anna would have been ashamed. "Not really."

"Plenty of kit, though."

"I'm, um, checking up on someone. My great aunt."

"Ah," she said, watching him break out the dinghy's anchor and coil the warp away. She was quite wrinkled, close up, but she had big burly shoulders and he was reluctantly glad of her strength as they swung *Lively Lady* round to face the river. The wet sand was surprisingly sticky and *Lady* felt cluttered with his bags and her disorganised equipment.

"Setting your sails here?"

"Just the jib. Need to get off really."

He laid the oars straight, fixed the rowlocks and made sure *Lady*'s rudder and daggerboard were ready to be lowered. Then he pushed with all his strength. *Margery*'s owner went further forward, got a grip of the gunwale beside the mast and lifted.

Slowly the dinghy began to move.

Come on! You could see why people used launching trolleys.

The big-nosed lady lifted and pulled. Donny pushed. At last they reached the river's edge. She held *Lively Lady* steady while he fixed the rudder and scrambled in. As he went over the stern he gave one farewell kick at the shore. The river was the place to be.

"Thanks," he remembered to call back, as he let down the daggerboard. The untidy lady was already plodding up the beach to her mother's cottage.

He didn't go far at first. Just let the tide and the early evening breeze take him down and across to a shallow patch on the opposite bank – where his map told him there was no road access. There he dropped anchor again and changed his clothes. If it had occurred to Flint to look for a boat, he'd be searching for a yellow dinghy with red sails and a scruffy charity kid, not a slate-grey dinghy with Kevlar racing sails and a young helmsman dressed in all the proper gear.

Unless he decided to question the mother and daughter in their cottage. Why had he said 'great aunt'? He was going to have to kick his truth habit.

Xanthe had left everything on board: wet suit, pull-ups, rubber shoes, gloves and a buoyancy aid. He put them all on. The clothes were much more comfortable than they looked. They helped build his confidence in his ability to face the night ahead.

He rolled his old clothes into a sausage and stuffed them away with the food and the rucksack. Then he hoisted *Lively Lady*'s mainsail, pulled up her anchor and headed downstream, thinking.

There was a lot to think about. How to keep out of sight until it was dark enough to board the forgotten *Hispaniola* and raise Anna's flags? Where should he go after that? How could he hide himself while staying within full view of Felixstowe and Shotley? He'd be waiting all day to identify a woman he'd never met arriving at a time he didn't know. And surely when a Looked-After child went AWOL, all sorts of extras would join the hunt?

The rhythm of the sailing took over his body. Problems of shore started to seem far away. Soon Donny stopped thinking about anything at all – other than his next tack and the set of his sails. That magical feeling of connectedness had returned.

He stopped planning. He'd sail for as long as the tide was with him. Then, when it turned and the daylight began to fade, he too would turn and come blowing back. If the ebb took him out beyond the harbour, so much the better. He was longing for a glimpse of the sea.

This non-plan worked better than he probably deserved. There was no dramatic exit to Harwich Harbour, no traffic lights or control towers, just a widening of the horizon, a gentle increase in the motion of the waves until Donny, bearing away to starboard, assumed he must be at sea but wasn't sure exactly when he'd left the river.

The breeze was dying with the light. A steady stream of cruising yachts and motorboats passed the boy and his dinghy. They were contented weekenders making their late way home. Donny brought *Lively Lady* round and followed them, increasingly glad of their navigation lights as night closed swiftly in. The wind fell away to nothing and he got out his oars. By the time he was among the small boat moorings off the Harwich shelf it was dark.

Lively Lady seemed to have shrunk now she was no longer flying along under sail. Donny hung close to the shore as he crept past the Navyard. Every so often he rested his oars so he could twist around and check where he was.

It was a relief when he identified the quick-flashing Shotley Spit buoy. It had seemed unmissable when he sailed down earlier – imposing even. Now it was no more that a pinprick of light against the towering side of a container ship.

A pilot boat shot out of a high-walled dock and the dinghy rocked in its wake. There was a prolonged hooting from somewhere up the River Stour. Donny saw what seemed like a city of moving lights. It was a cruise ship setting off down the deepwater channel on some long, exotic voyage.

Donny took the dinghy even closer inshore and was shouted at by some men in a fishing boat who were cutting the corner to get back to their own mooring behind the Halfpenny Pier.

He realised that invisibility was not what was wanted just now. He allowed *Lady* to drift while he found Xanthe's torch and fixed it as high up the mast as he could. Then he looked around him intently and repeatedly and settled to row the half-mile across the harbour as soon as the liner had passed. That pilot boat would be on its way to meet some other mammoth vessel. Donny didn't want to be caught in the middle when it arrived.

He had no power beyond the strength of his own arms, and the confused pulling of the tide. The cruise-liner's wash had left everything rolling in her wake. Even when she was finally out of sight new turbulences continued criss-crossing the inky water. *Lively Lady* jerked and rocked as Donny struggled to keep straight.

The clang and clatter of the Felixstowe container port sounded a thousand times louder that it had during the day. Powerful arc lamps lit up the dockside area and made the night seem darker everywhere else. Where there were no reflections the water was oily black. No moon tonight.

He could see the lights of two tugs in the distance waiting to pull some new monster into position beneath the busy cranes. Then, when he glanced round at the Shotley shore, he saw nothing. His eyes weren't adjusting and every time he looked behind him his rowing went crooked.

Night work was scary. Donny thought of John in *Swallows and Amazons* dashing to and fro under sail in the darkness with rocks on either side. No wonder his mother had thrown a strop when she heard what he'd been doing. Rowing was safer but such hard work. And so slow.

In *Swallows and Amazons* they'd left a sister waiting on the island to light lamps at their harbour entrance. The sister with the odd name – Titty. Donny wished there was someone waiting for him. Then he remembered that he did have Allies. The kids at the vicarage were probably being given a hard time now he'd disappeared. Probably Xanthe and Maggi were being questioned too. He wasn't on his own, not really. They'd done all they could.

To use leading marks, or lights, you had to get both lights in line and keep them there – as he'd said so confidently to Joshua Ribiero, that day on *Snow Goose*. He supposed he might as well give it a go. Not to get into lockgates but simply to stay straight as *Lively Lady* wobbled across the vast darkness.

It was hard selecting two lights from the dazzling array on the Felixstowe side. Harder to keep them dead in line. Even harder to remember which way he needed to turn to correct his course when they moved apart. It forced him to concentrate, stopped him feeling quite so helpless.

He missed the *Hispaniola* on his first attempt and found he'd almost run ashore. That meant he was across the harbour and safe in shallow water. Donny abandoned his leading lights and rowed more calmly, searching for different densities of black.

Eventually he found himself groping along the schooner's cold dark sides, reaching for the same dangling warp that Xanthe had found. He pulled hard to check it was secure, then attached the dinghy's painter and inched forwards until he could reach the iron chain that sloped up to the schooner's bowsprit.

He wasn't feeling very *Treasure Island*-ish now but he had no choice. Donny stowed his oars, shoved the bosun's bag and the carrier into his rucksack and looked for handholds. *Lively Lady* swung away as he stepped out of her and he gripped the schooner's chain so tightly that the links dug into his palms.

Black water lapped beneath him.

One hand was already on the bowsprit. Come on – it really wasn't hard. Forget the cold dark river. Think tree – or playground even. Donny made himself look up. Brace, stretch, pull. The climb was effortful but quick. Once astride the bowsprit he had only a short distance to wriggle before he was securely on board the forgotten *Hispaniola*.

Shotley Marina wasn't far away, perhaps a hundred metres, but it lay almost completely concealed behind its breakwater. Donny could see the control tower beyond the lock and some subdued light from within but he had no fear at all that anyone there would see him. He crouched down behind the schooner's high bulwarks and knew that he was completely hidden. He ate a bit of Anna's food to celebrate then dealt with the amazing complexities of Xanthe's waterproof clothing to have a pee.

He'd asked her what was meant to happen if he needed to do anything else when he was on board *Lively Lady*. This problem hadn't been mentioned in either of his books. She'd laughed and said he could use the ship's bucket if he was really desperate but to rinse it out thoroughly afterwards. Donny'd wished he kept his mouth shut.

The *Hispaniola*'s signal halyards didn't feel rotten, and the flags went up easily: first the red flag of the People's Republic of China with its yellow stars; then Anna's masterpiece, a rampaging double-headed dragon, gorgeously gold on a black silk background, and finally the simple crimson and white quartered signal flag – U – Uniform – 'You are Standing into Danger'.

They dangled limp in the still night. He hoped there'd be enough breeze tomorrow to enable them to spell out their message when Gold Dragon – a.k.a. the legendary Polly Lee – arrived across the other side of the harbour.

How brilliant that his great aunt was a famous sailor! How extra brilliant that Flint hadn't been able to find her name on his official lists! Lubber! For the first time Donny felt real excitement at the prospect of meeting this person who Xanthe and Maggi spoke of as a heroine.

He sat on the *Hispaniola*'s broad deck to plan his next move; decided that he could think better if he was lying down – and was instantly asleep.

CHAPTER TWENTY-ONE
Strong Winds

Monday, September 25th, morning and afternoon

Donny woke confused and stiff. His rowing muscles ached and the palms of his hands were sore. His nose and ears, even his fingertips, dripped.

Everywhere was wet and white. A dream-world. The schooner's deck was glistening with moisture and he could scarcely see her bows or stern. Above him her masts vanished after only three or four clouded metres.

Fog.

It must be morning because it was light. He had no watch so he'd no idea of the time. If he listened hard, he could still hear the rattle of the gantries and a distant ship's hooter. Where were they? Donny stood up and tried turning his head to listen in different directions. Nothing made sense.

Then he looked over the side. Water. Swirling past.

But no *Lively Lady*! Donny hurtled for'ard, his rubber shoes gripping the slippery deck.

Breathe again. He hadn't thought to moor the dinghy fore and aft so when the tide turned she had swung independently from the *Hispaniola*. Her mast and shrouds had become tangled beneath the schooner's bowsprit and her stern was jammed hard up against the mooring chain. It seemed to Donny that his companion looked reproachful.

"I'm coming, *Lady*, I'm coming," he said aloud. He ran back along the half-seen deck and collected his few pieces of equipment.

Hungry but only time for a swig of water. He needed to be away from here. Couldn't see the flags but guessed they'd be hanging dark and limp as old dishcloths.

This was not going as planned.

Before he climbed into *Lively Lady* Donny worked his way cautiously along the bowsprit to check exactly where her mast was stuck. Tried to push it away without success, then realised that his own weight was making matters worse. Once he was down in the dinghy, she sank deeper and the mast sprung free. Able then to swivel her round, lean his full weight on her stern and release her from the schooner's anchor chain. Her bright varnish had been badly scraped by the rusty links but there seemed to be no worse damage.

Donny breathed a sigh of relief so immense it should have blasted a channel through the mist.

It didn't. If anything the fog seemed even thicker now. The hull of the schooner was blurred above him. Elsewhere there was nothing but the dense white vapour, curling round and over him, reducing the entire world to a ghostly capsule. Donny guessed that it must still be early. Maybe four or five o'clock? A mist like this could lift astonishingly fast when the sun rose higher or a breeze sprang up. He mustn't be caught clinging to the *Hispaniola*'s side like some stranded starfish.

There was still no wind so he'd have to row. And as soon as he left the schooner he'd be lost. His best chance of lying low for the day was on the Harwich side. But that meant re-crossing the harbour. If it was as early as he guessed, this tide was still the ebb. So if he missed the opposite shore he could be swept blindly out to sea.

What would Gregory Palmer – or 'Captain John' Walker or Joshua Ribiero – do now? Look at the blue book, maybe? That was so carefully packed. It'd take him half the morning to unearth and unwrap. He hadn't got that sort of time.

He could find the photocopied pages. They'd tell him what noises he should make to avoid being run down in this fog.

He dragged them out of his rucksack. Scanned them avidly.

No help at all. Apparently he was supposed to blow horns or ring bells every two minutes. He hadn't even got a watch – never mind bells and horns!

Donny's eye fell on the first paragraph of the next chapter, which had been included in the photocopying almost by accident: "*As soon as the amateur leaves the bay or river with whose features he is well acquainted and ventures to take his vessel along a coast unknown to him, he must provide himself with the necessary instruments for finding his way …*"

Oh, ha, ha! thought Donny.

To rub salt in his own wounds he took a look at the list of 'necessary instruments': a chart – he'd printed an Internet map of the harbour so he'd sort of got that; a compass – that's what he really needed …

They'd done something at school about compasses … an experiment … They'd rubbed needles against magnets to get all their atoms facing the right way or something. Then they'd taken the magnets away and pushed the needles through small sections of cork so they floated in saucers of water.

Donny vividly remembered his feeling of delight, almost awe, when his needle, together with most of the others, had wavered for a while then settled, pointing surely to the magnetic North. He could repeat that experiment, right now, he realised. For real. He had all that he needed. The sailmaker's needle in Joshua's bosun's bag was stuck into a cork for safety; there was no shortage of water; he could use a bucket instead of a saucer and he'd brought blessed little Liam's Euro 2004 fridge magnet with him!

Donny's hands shook as he began stroking the needle against Liam's piece of treasure. He scarcely dared breathe as he pushed it through the cork, floated it in a few centimetres of water in the bottom of the bucket and waited.

It swung, it dithered, it swung back again, it settled.

It was miraculous!

The harbour map told him that he'd need to head due south to reach the Harwich side. So, he had to be perfectly clear which end of the needle showed North and which South. Or he'd be hitting Shotley. There was a bit quite near called Bloody Point. Exactly where Flint would expect to find him!

This was Monday September 25th. This was the day.

The tide sluicing past the schooner knew where it was going – down the river and out to sea. Would that be East? South East? Maybe he should do the opposite; start by rowing as hard as he could in a westerly direction, dead against the tide, heading further up the River Stour before he swung south to cross the harbour.

Donny remembered stories where you turned to stone if you were caught above ground when the sun came up. He'd got to get hidden. Soon. One more look at his makeshift compass, bobbing in its centimetres of salt water; then he untied *Lively Lady*'s painter, set to his oars again and rowed with all his strength.

It hurt.

The white walls of fog closed around him. Disorientating. The water in the bucket rippled: the compass needle shook. But if he paused to let it settle, *Lively Lady* was swept backwards, fast. He learned to row by feel. Couldn't stop for a moment. Mustn't let his attention wander. Had to sense the line of most resistance. Had to carry on forcing the dinghy to move – painfully slowly – directly against the rushing ebb tide.

Hours passed. Or it seemed as if they did. Every fibre in Donny's arms and back felt separately strained to breaking point. Was *Lively Lady* travelling anywhere at all or was he busting himself to hold her on the spot? Was there some new and cruel enchantment keeping him trapped inside this cage of fog, rowing against the tide for ever.

Except that he couldn't row much longer. His bruised hand was throbbing and fiery-hot, his lungs hurt and his strained muscles were beginning to seize.

Then the dinghy hit something. Donny un-shipped his oars and hurled himself forward, grabbing the painter as he went.

Lively Lady had collided with a metal pillar. It reared up above them into the mist, festooned with bladder wrack, encrusted with barnacles. He hung on with the strength of desperation until he finally managed to use the painter to make the dinghy fast.

Now the Ribieros' dinghy had a prang on her bows to match

the scrape on her stern but no real damage had been done. And he'd gained a few moments' rest.

Donny dipped his stinging palms into the river. Where was he? Still nothing but wispy whiteness to be seen.

The little compass was going crazy. He realised that the metal pillar had de-magnetised it. The ebb of the tide was all the directional information that he had. Donny pulled out his Harwich Harbour map and worked out the course he should have been following if he had been rowing successfully. He'd have passed the entrance to Shotley Marina and then …?

He looked upwards. Wow, there it was! A green, starboard-hand triangle on the top of the pillar. He'd hit one of the entry marks.

It was a bit depressing really. He'd only travelled about two or three hundred metres from the *Hispaniola* and it had taken him how long? Half, three-quarters of an hour? More? The good thing: he could allow himself to begin his crossing to the other side.

Donny ate a banana. He didn't want to let go: he didn't want this respite moment to end.

He ate two bananas. Maybe Gerald had his good points.

Then he forced himself to untie *Lively Lady*'s painter. The tide pushed her backwards at once. Out with his oars again. Tried to keep the pillar on his starboard quarter but he'd not taken more than twenty strokes before it was gone into the ghost world.

Afterwards, he realised that the green triangle had been sending an extra message. The fact that he'd been able to make out its colour should have been his first hint that the early morning fog was lifting.

Soon little cat's-paws of wind were ruffling the grey surface of the water and it wasn't long before there was a definite gap between the river and the mist. Then there were whole empty patches. Suddenly the sun was up, an easterly breeze was blowing and his view ahead was clear.

Lively Lady had already reached the further shore. He'd completely over-estimated the angle at which he'd needed to point the dinghy and had therefore been rowing up the river as well as across. Maybe the waking wind had pushed him that way as well. The closest thing to Donny now was a gigantic high-speed catamaran, still moored, but with its engine purring silkily. He could have rowed straight underneath. He shivered at the thought.

Donny lost no time in turning sharply into the wind. Up with *Lively Lady*'s sails and he was away, beating briskly down the river. Monday, September 25th. This was the day that would decide his future.

It was also his fourteenth birthday.

He looked across to the *Hispaniola*. Her flags were flying bravely now. They'd surely attract Polly Lee's attention as soon as she glanced towards Shotley.

The schooner slipped out of sight as he rounded the point. He eased his sheets and reached for the scatter of small boat moorings he'd noticed on the previous day. *Lively Lady* wouldn't look out of place here and he'd have a direct view of the foot ferry route.

"Keep sharp lookout," Gold Dragon had ordered.

Xanthe had included binoculars in the survival bag.

Donny chose a small, rather sea-weedy mooring buoy that probably hadn't been used for some time. He made the dinghy fast then fixed Xanthe's groundsheet over the boom like a tent. This, he figured, would make *Lady* look as if her owner was away. He'd hide underneath and stay completely still, so as not to rock a supposedly empty boat.

This, it turned out, wasn't such a problem. Once the business of the harbour got underway, there was so much wash from passing motor vessels, even those that seemed to be away on the far side, that all the small boats in Donny's area were repeatedly set lurching wildly. He was glad to discover that he didn't get seasick.

He'd brought Xanthe's tidetable as well as his Internet list of ship arrivals and ferry times. Even without a watch he could work out what time it was when the tide turned once more and *Lively Lady* swung to the incoming flood.

The first of the four container ships that could have come from Shanghai should already have arrived. The last wouldn't dock until late that night. Donny was pinning his hopes on Great Aunt Ellen being forced to use the foot ferry to Shotley. The ferry was open, easy to see everyone on board and Donny could also watch the patch of beach where travellers from the Felixstowe side waited to embark.

The hours crawled by and Donny had ticked off three of his four possible container ships; two of his three possible ferry crossings. The ferry hadn't had many passengers. There'd been four or five cyclists, an elderly couple who Donny actually saw locking up their parked car before walking to the beach and a small man in overalls with something heavy in a wheelbarrow. He sort of looked familiar, but he couldn't be Gold Dragon.

It got worse. On the second running of the ferry, the shark-boat came nosing down the river, circling suspiciously. Donny scarcely dared peep from under his groundsheet.

Evidently Flint too was disappointed. He turned away and moored against the far end of the container terminal, where there were those steps giving direct access to the quay. Donny managed to make out some odd-looking marks around the shark-boat's bows but whatever the vandalism had been, it had evidently failed to put it out of action. Donny wished now that he had been the perpetrator: he'd have wreaked some proper damage.

The only passengers waiting for the last scheduled ferry were a young woman with a double buggy and a man in some sort of uniform. No Gold Dragon.

What to do next?

Sail back to Shotley Marina in the slim hope that somehow it would be Great Aunt Ellen that he'd find there – not Gerald and Wendy or Toxic Tune? Or should he put out to sea? Around the coast to Essex and then via inland waterways to Chelmsford. To Skye?

He knew he did not have permission and his friends would feel badly let down. He'd have properly gone AWOL.

His mother was the person who truly loved him. Had loved him all his life. If he believed he could help her by going he'd be out to sea like a hungry gull.

Lively Lady swung again. Another six hours had passed.

But she didn't swing round completely. The wind had freshened during the day and shifted towards the south. For a moment she was broadside on to the harbour entrance, held indecisive between wind and tide. Time to go? Donny wondered, lifting the edge of his waterproof sheet and gazing towards the wide horizon.

Then he saw her. Running before the wind with her extraordinary sails spread either side, wing and wing, catching the gold of the afternoon sun.

Strong Winds!

She wasn't arriving as an item of deck cargo to be heaved up by a crane and dumped on the concrete quay. She was arriving as a living thing, waves gurgling beneath her and a flurry of white water being sliced aside by her gilded bow.

The shock of her beauty and the glorious relief of knowing that Great Aunt Ellen was almost here! It made Donny want to leap up, punch the air and shout his heart out.

Instead he tore off the waterproof cover, bundled it up and stuffed it for'ard. Pushed the rest of the day's clutter higgledy-piggledy under the centre thwart. His hands were trembling as he set the jib and he couldn't undo the knot to slip the painter. Oh never mind, he'd cut it.

Donny rummaged for the knife Xanthe had lent him. Was it in the bosun's bag? Had he left it on the *Hispaniola*? No, he'd used its marlinspike when he was fixing the cover.

Muttered swear words. Grew sweaty with frustration.

Then he remembered. This wasn't how sailors behaved. Great Aunt Ellen – the famous Polly Lee – the person at this very moment coming over the horizon towards him   didn't want a landlubber for her great nephew. She'd said so. He had to make a good impression.

Donny took a deep breath, deliberately willing 'Captain John' Walker, Gregory Palmer and all his siblings, the entire Ribiero family – every old salt since the Norsemen crossed the Atlantic to America – to come to his assistance now.

Perhaps they did.

Juddering with suppressed haste, he folded the waterproof cover so that it didn't impede access to the anchor, stowed everything else quickly and neatly – and found Xanthe's knife.

Then he understood something extra. You didn't do things right in order to make a good impression: you did them because that was the right thing to do.

So Donny didn't use the knife to cut the painter. He opened its other end, the end with the marlinspike and worked methodically to loosen the knot. It almost fell apart.

Up with the mainsail and he was away.

It was lucky for his moment of level-headedness that he hadn't noticed the black powerboat cruising smoothly down river to check the last running of the foot ferry.

Strong Winds was coming closer every moment.

Donny didn't glance behind at all as he headed arrow-straight towards her, sailing as close to the wind as *Lively Lady* could be persuaded to go.

The shark-boat turned away. Then back. A momentary hesitation, as if its owner's brain had been slow to register the Chinese-ness of the approaching vessel and to make the obvious connection to Shanghai.

Now the powerboat was rearing up, hurtling towards the junk, full throttle, engines roaring.

Donny heard the noise and looked round. Flint's vessel was travelling so fast that its white underbelly was almost completely out of the water as it balanced on the thrust of its twin propellers. There was a gaping red mouth painted on its bows but Donny had no time to stare. All his effort was focussed on racing towards Great Aunt Ellen.

Lively Lady couldn't sail any closer to the wind. The junk was too far away for him to shout or wave and her billowing sails prevented him seeing the helmsman. Donny made his decision. He eased the dinghy's sheets and bore away just a few degrees. Now *Lady* was sailing more easily, picking herself up and leaping over the waves.

"Ready about…" muttered Donny to himself when he was close enough to see the gilded scrollwork on *Strong Winds*'s port bow. He tacked to bring his little dinghy onto a collision course with ten or twelve tons of antique boat.

"Please, Gold Dragon, please see me! Please know what you've got to do!"

The wind was on *Lively Lady*'s starboard side: *Strong Winds* was goose-winged.

Lady was close hauled; *Strong Winds* was running free.

By all the laws of the sea the junk must give way to the dinghy. Instantly. It was outrageous of him to have put her in such a position.

She did it, of course – Polly Lee, the round-the-world yachtswoman. The junk's foresail and mizzen were gybed across with the same distinctive crack that he'd heard in his dream. *Strong Winds* altered course away from him.

And away from the on-rushing powerboat.

Donny was ready to tack again. He was amidships of her now and could see a small figure shaking her fist from the high poop. It didn't matter if she was angry. He'd made space to reach her first and warn her.

But Flint was already there. He roared recklessly between the sailing boats and swirled round behind *Strong Winds* with a cascade of turbulence. The powerboat's wash caught *Lively Lady* broadside just as she was coming about. She capsized.

There was nothing Donny could do.

The shock left him stunned. He'd jumped out to avoid being trapped as the dinghy went over, but now he wasn't quite sure what was meant to happen.

She'd gone right over: upside down, turtle. He knew he mustn't leave her – he felt no temptation to do so – but he had no idea how to right her. So he pulled himself onto the up-turned hull and sat watching the confrontation as if on a grandstand.

It was pretty one-sided.

Flint had evidently tried to come alongside *Strong Winds* and had been rebuffed. He'd circled away and was approaching again at a more normal speed. He was standing up, wearing his official cap and shouting through a megaphone.

Polly Lee was unimpressed. She let him come close then Donny saw her arm come up and over as she threw something. There was a small rattle of explosive and a distinct burst of smoke on the powerboat's foredeck. Donny hoped it had done some damage.

Flint wheeled away once more. Then turned. His threat was unmistakable: "If you won't let me board you, I'm going after the boy …"

The shark-boat reared up again, engines roaring, hurtling towards the upturned dinghy.

Donny couldn't afterwards believe that the fat policeman had fully intended to run him down. The threat was a means of asserting himself; increasing the pressure on an elderly lady; putting the frighteners on an intractable child. Flint was foul but he wasn't totally stupid. Or a murderer. Was he?

At the time Donny didn't feel rational. He felt terrified.

Polly Lee wasn't taking any chances either. As Flint surged past, she stepped quickly to her ship's side and hurled another missile after him.

It wasn't a firecracker this time: it was a simple heaving line, a ball with a long trail of strong thin rope.

It landed beautifully between the shark-boat's whirling propellers, got caught round first one, then the other and, as Gold Dragon gleefully paid out metre after metre of increasingly weighty cable, the powerboat's engines spluttered, choked and died.

She threw the last of the coil in after him. Then, without bothering to look at Flint again, she trimmed *Strong Winds*'s sails until she hove to gracefully beside the drifting dinghy.

"Should I call you Sinbad?" asked Great Aunt Ellen.

CHAPTER TWENTY-TWO
Gongs for Gold Dragon

Monday, September 25th, evening

Great Aunt Ellen had Granny's face, almost exactly, and Granny's quick decisive way of doing things. Except that the things Granny used to do had never included lobbing firecrackers at obnoxious policemen.

Granny had kept her short iron-grey hair tucked neatly behind her ears with two matching combs: Great Aunt Ellen's hair was dark, with silver streaks. She wore it in a long thin plait running straight down her back to her waist. And, instead of a left hand, Great Aunt Ellen had a metal hook. Skye's word 'pirate' suited her.

"Why Sinbad?" was all he could think to ask.

"Because of a story long ago that my sister Eirene loved." Her voice had a lifting Australian lilt to it – quite unlike Granny's formal English manner of speaking. Donny wasn't sure he'd caught the name – Irreny?

"It had a half-drowned kitten way out to sea on a chicken coop. Needing rescue."

"Did you like the story too?" Somehow Donny felt that this answer was important.

"Yes," said Great Aunt Ellen after a thinking pause. "Yes, I did. In those days I liked pretty well everything that Eirene liked."

She paused again, then sort of shook herself as if this wasn't quite the moment for nostalgia.

She had definitely said Irreny – not Edith.

Donny was admiring the way she had adjusted *Strong Winds*'s sails so that the junk remained effortlessly still while her captain was talking. The tide, however, was pushing both boats towards the shipping channel. He badly wanted to know about this other sister. But not right now.

"I'm not sitting on a chicken coop," he pointed out.

"No," said Great Aunt Ellen. "She's a dinghy. So why don't you right her?"

"Because I don't know how. I may as well tell you that I'm only learning to sail. I've read one and a bit books but I don't think that the people who wrote them ever turned completely upside down like this."

"Possibly not," said Polly Lee. "But I have. Frequently. You need to stand up, get a hold of her daggerboard, lean back and pull like hell."

Donny did exactly as she said. It took all his weight and there was a moment when he wondered if *Lively Lady*'s mast had got stuck in the seabed. Up she came, at last, the water pouring off her as if she were a dog emerging from a swim. Donny almost expected her to give herself a shake.

"Pass your painter over, Sinbad, and I'll tow her while you bale."

"Er, what about him?" said Donny, pointing at Flint who seemed to be drifting rather faster than they were.

"He'll have radioed for help by now. Hobos like him prefer getting other people to sort out their mess. The high-speed cat's due in about ten minutes. I rather hope she'll slice straight through him."

She'd made his painter fast using her hook almost as naturally as her hand. "Get the water out and come on board. I suppose you've got a bucket?"

"Er, yes," said Donny who'd learned to be profoundly grateful for that particular piece of equipment. He'd stowed it in her for'ard locker when he was tidying up and there it was still. *Lively Lady* wallowed as he moved cautiously to reach it. Weighed down by all the water sloshing inside her. She looked sorry for herself.

"Tosser!" he muttered, furious with Flint. Then he chuckled. Gold Dragon had given the policeman a well bad time. Maybe he'd steer clear of little old ladies after today.

It didn't take him long to bale out *Lively Lady*. His great aunt tossed him a rope ladder when he'd finished and he scrambled up to join her on *Strong Winds*'s spectacular high stern.

The beauty of the boat wasn't the first thing to catch his eye, however. It was a Harwich Harbour Authority motor launch approaching on their port bow. Two other official motorboats were close behind.

A VHF radio crackled. The junk's equipment must be a lot more modern that she was. The HHA were calling up the junk and Polly Lee responded, giving *Strong Winds*'s name and call sign and confirming her home port as Shanghai.

Donny looked up. There was an aerial on the top of the mainmast where he'd expected to see the dragon pennant. The gold dragon streamed out from the mizzen and, on the foremast, he glimpsed a navy blue flag with white stars, which looked somehow familiar. There was a small red ensign too and a yellow flag whose function he didn't know.

"That yellow flag's an old style request for customs clearance," said Polly Lee who'd finished her radio conversation and was continuing to sail *Strong Winds* towards the outer reaches of the harbour. "It's not strictly necessary now Britain's in the E.U. I radioed as soon as I was inside territorial waters."

"Have you sailed all the way from China?" Donny was grappling with his emotions; relief, admiration, amazement – and a niggle of discomfort at his crazy display of ignorance.

"Too old. Both of us. And not enough time. So much to settle when Edith's letter arrived – fifty years of my life – I couldn't get ready for sea as well. So we shipped to Rotterdam and unloaded there. I'm not sentimental but I couldn't finally face arriving back in England on one of those things." She gestured towards the container ships, now visible under their skeletal line of cranes as *Strong Winds* made her way steadily into the harbour. "I hadn't expected a reception quite like this. They asked me if I had a John Walker on board. I answered affirmative."

"But I'm Donny – John's in a book."

"I know that. I'm family, remember. They also said you'd run away from some foster home. That's why we have the extra company."

The police boat was close on their starboard side. The two officers on board appeared to be armed. The customs boat was to port and the Harbour Authority launch was cruising steadily ahead.

It wasn't ideal but Polly Lee didn't seem all that bothered. She stood small and erect, left hook linked into small metal hoops on her gleaming curved tiller, right hand ready to adjust *Strong Winds*'s complex array of sheets and halyards.

"Was your running away connected with the redneck we met beyond the Beach End buoy?"

"Yeah, sorry. Unfortunately he's a policeman."

"Didn't look much like one with all that paint over his bows. Had you been having some kind of festival?"

"No. I don't know what that was. I didn't really notice."

"You were too busy obstructing my passage."

"Yeah, sorry," he said again. "I was trying to warn you."

She looked at him. Her eyes were bright and hard. They were not an old person's eyes.

"Against what?"

He felt stupid again. He'd been expecting a fragile eighty-year-old, not this decisive missile-slinger. "Um, well … I'm not exactly sure. Against Flint – the policeman – anyway. I thought he wanted to scare you, get money out of you."

"Why should he think he could do that?"

"Um, well … Either because he thinks you're rich and you'll pay to get to me and Skye. Don't worry," he added hastily, not understanding the way she looked, "I know you wouldn't. You probably don't want us anyway. Or because he thinks you're Mrs Big from some smuggling ring."

This time she looked as if she might laugh. "Mrs Big, eh? No one's described me like that for years; I must meet this man. But you ran away?"

" S'pose so. It wasn't just him. I mean … well, I didn't know you then and it had all got a bit complicated …"

How was he going to explain everything about Skye and the SS and the mental hospital and Gerald and Wendy? "I made some good friends though. We've got an Alliance."

The VHF crackled again before he could try explaining any more. There was another formal, slightly tetchy conversation punctuated by call-signs and repetitions.

"… and out."

She turned to Donny. "They won't let us enter Shotley unless we have two of them on board. I don't like passengers and I like invaders even less. But I've agreed. Put the fenders out, Sinbad. Starboard side. I don't want my topsides scraped."

She sounded irritated. Donny's heart sank.

It wasn't hard for him to do as she ordered. Everything was in place. A few moments later a male and a female police officer were on board *Strong Winds* asking them for identification. Great Aunt Ellen gave her name as Polly Lee but agreed that she might also be identified as Miss Ellen Walker.

"But not when I'm sailing this ship," she said fiercely and the police didn't argue with her. Instead they requested permission to go below and have a look round.

"She was searched at Rotterdam. I don't tolerate damage."

"That's all right, ma'am. We've had contact from the Dutch. And from the MCA. We just wanted a look, really. My colleague here's a fan of yours and she's read about this boat. Officially we're only required to remain in attendance and get the boy back safe."

She snorted. "I'm quite able to manage that myself. I'm his great aunt."

"You certainly are, ma'am. But the boy's subject to a CPO – that's a Child Protection Order – and our Social Services have been in a panic since he went running off yesterday. They've got someone waiting at the marina. To check all's well. We need to be seen to be returning with him. Bit of window-dressing really."

Polly Lee – or Gold Dragon – snorted once again but not quite so fiercely. She was definitely dragonish when she was dealing with people, thought Donny. Quick and clever around her ship and ready to spout flames at anyone who bothered her. It had given him a really good feeling when she asserted herself as his great aunt.

The Harbour Authority boat peeled off when they passed the Navyard: then the Shotley side of the river came into view. Great Aunt Ellen stared at the farther shore.

"It's completely different," she muttered, sounding for a moment like an elderly lady, not dragonish at all.

Then she noticed the *Hispaniola*. She pulled out a telescope and peered intently. "So they have been having a festival … No, it's a signal hoist. U – Uniform – You are standing into danger," she read. "And that looks like a remarkably good copy of my house flag. Would this be your work?" she asked Donny. Her tone gave nothing away.

"Yeah. And my friends."

"Have we had the danger?"

"Not sure … think so … probably."

He hoped it wasn't Toxic who was waiting at the marina.

"Handsome," she commented as she took *Strong Winds* close to the lonely schooner and gazed up at the three flags flying

248

just below the cross-trees, "though it should have been the Australian not the Chinese national flag. You identify the nationality of the owner, not the boat."

"Oh, er, sorry." He was a bit confused by this but relieved that she liked the flags. "My friend Anna made them. Maggi and Xanthe helped with every thing else. And their parents. And *Lively Lady*."

"Tell me later. We need to drop our sails now." And to Donny's slight surprise she pressed an inconspicuous black button. Tonk, tonk, tonk. An engine started chugging musically, deep inside *Strong Winds*. "Lister Marine, starts like a dream," she commented. "Your great uncle Ned would have loved it. Now lend a hand with that tricing clew. Stand by fore and aft."

Another relly?

Donny and the police officers did as they were told and *Strong Winds* moved slowly into Shotley lock; her sails furled, her engine gently turning over and *Lively Lady* following sweetly in her wake. The police launch went in ahead; the customs boat tied up at the small holding jetty where the foot ferry usually docked.

Donny was taken aback to see that there was a crowd of people waiting. These weren't casual lock-side spectators; these people were pointing, waving, flashing cameras. A white van marked Anglia News was parked close to the marina office. It had an immense aerial from the centre of its roof and a TV camera on a tripod.

Donny gulped and hoped Gold Dragon had run out of firecrackers. Someone cheered. Then there were more cheers and shouts of welcome as Donny and the police officers made the junk fast and fended her off as the gates behind them closed.

The sluices opened.

The water swirled in, silently. *Strong Winds* was rising steadily towards the level of the spectators.

Polly Lee didn't move. She raised her hand to acknowledge the crowd but otherwise said nothing except to give terse instructions to her uninvited crew.

Then Donny spotted Anna. She was waving frantically and there were tears streaming down her face.

He'd never seen Anna like that. Luke and Liam were brandishing England flags and Gerald was there with Vicky in her easy rider, desperately trying to persuade the boys to stay away from the edge.

"Smile Miss Lee, smile for the camera!" shouted a photographer.

Great Aunt Ellen tried, but she couldn't. Donny understood how hard she would be finding this. She was his granny's sister. Never mind that Polly Lee had been a sailing celebrity and this probably wasn't the first time she'd been greeted by crowds on arrival in a distant port; this arrival was something different. She was maybe eighty years old. She was coming home, the last of all her brothers and sisters, and nothing so far had been as she expected or remembered.

Donny guessed that she was struggling not to weep.

It was a good thing that most of the spectators were more interested in her boat than they were in her. People were pointing to *Strong Winds*'s three sturdy bamboo masts, her flags, her carved deck-fittings and ornamental scrollwork. Some of them smiled when they noticed the bedraggled *Mirror* dinghy astern. There were lots of photos.

What was strange was that the TV camera seemed to spend almost as much time focussing on him and the two police officers as it did on Polly Lee and her beautiful yacht.

A man from the marina office stepped over the protective barrier and handed her an envelope.

"Arrived for you this morning," he explained. Donny recognised the envelope he'd posted with one of his stolen stamps. She was looking at it suspiciously.

"Don't worry," he said. "It's only from me. I sent you Skye's address, in case they caught me first. She needs rescue."

"Are you responsible for … this, as well?" she indicated the crowd.

"No," he was shocked. "I certainly am not."

"Donny! Donny!" Someone was thrusting a furry microphone in his face. "How does it feel to find your auntie after all this time? And you stole a boat to meet her!"

"No! No, I didn't …" he began but the man from the marina office was shooing the reporter back behind the barriers.

A smart lady with a conciliating smile and an SS Media Relations badge came hurrying forward saying that it wasn't appropriate to speak to the child now. Perhaps a photo-call with the foster family later…

"Child? Huh, I'm fourteen today!" Donny felt like shouting. But there was no one there who cared, except himself. Then he saw Gold Dragon reaching into a cardboard box.

"Duck!" he yelled at the PR lady.

Nothing was actually thrown but the lady got the message. She hopped back smartly, gabbling that she'd be happy to explain the Local Authority's position – somewhere else. Back in the reception area maybe?

The lock gates at the far end were opening. The police launch moved forward and *Strong Winds*'s crew cast off their warps to follow her.

At that moment there was a tremendous clanging from the seaward side. Xanthe and Maggi leapt up, hammering on what appeared to be two large cymbals from the Gallister High music department, and chanting "She's a twenty-two gong tai-coon, she's a twenty two gong tai-coooon" to Gilbert and Sullivan's 'Gentlemen of Japan'. They were still in their school uniforms but they were each wearing red stocking caps with tassels – a sisterly trademark that Donny knew they'd pinched from *Swallows and Amazons*. Their dark faces were ablaze with delight and they were jumping up and down like mad things.

Even Great Aunt Ellen couldn't resist. Her weather-beaten face crinkled into helpless laughter and the TV man got a wonderful picture of her dashing back unshed tears as *Strong Winds* moved into the smooth water of the marina basin.

Donny was leaping up now and punching the air, as he'd wanted to do ever since he'd first spotted those golden sails. He shouted with happiness as he saw Anna, Luke and Liam break away from Gerald and come charging round to meet them.

Snow Goose was already there: her white hull glistening in the last light of evening and somehow Donny wasn't surprised to see June Ribiero sitting in the cockpit, chatting amicably to Mr

McMullen and Sandra, the okay social worker.

No Toxic!

Snow Goose's occupants waved, nodded and smiled, but stayed where they were.

It wasn't until *Strong Winds* was securely moored, the TV van had left, and the marina staff had closed the access pontoon to everyone except berth-holders that the three more sensible adults came on board to calm the situation down. Sandra told Donny that she'd been very worried about him but was glad that he was safe. She asked Great Aunt Ellen where Donny would be sleeping that night.

"Here, of course, where else?"

"In that case I think I can safely say that we'll be postponing tomorrow's review meeting."

"Surely you mean *cancelling* ..." said Mr McMullen. Donny remembered how much his tutor disliked meetings.

Sandra smiled ruefully. "Obviously that's what ought to happen but I've afraid the system doesn't work like that. Donny's case has to be considered in the light of the legal processes of care and adoption and I understand that there are further issues to be resolved. Our Education Welfare Officer has serious concerns about behavioural issues, safety and a pattern of unauthorised absence from school."

A quick look from Mr McMullen stopped Donny from exploding. Pattern, indeed!

"You can reassure Ms Tune that Donny's absence today was not unauthorised. Anna Livesey delivered his note of explanation this morning and the school was easily able to authorise his absence under the category of exceptional family circumstances. We'll stretch that to cover tomorrow as well – though there'll be some class-work to make up if he's continuing at Gallister High. I allocate special after-school sessions to students in his situation. As I believe he already knows …"

Mr McMullen looked again at Donny – who wondered guiltily whether his tutor guessed that he'd used one of those sessions as a cover for a trip to Pin Mill. Then the teacher stepped forward to shake Gold Dragon's hand.

"I'm delighted to meet you, Miss Lee. Did a bit of sailing myself years ago. Down channel – nothing to match your exploits. Ho hum. Registration usual time, usual place, Wednesday morning, Donny and I'll see you tomorrow, Anna. Is there anything you'd like me to say to my colleagues in the textile department?"

Anna, who was inconspicuously as near Donny as she could be, shut her lips and shook her head violently. Mr McMullen laughed and left. Sandra went too and so did the police officers – once they'd been repeatedly assured by June Ribiero that Donny had her husband's written permission to use their dinghy and therefore no conceivable offence had taken place. Clearly Rev. Wendy hadn't counted her stamps …

"The other party has decided not to press charges about the vandalism, ma'am," said the male officer.

"I'm relieved to hear it," June said, with a severe glance at Xanthe and Maggi. "Nevertheless my husband and I have no intention of withdrawing our formal complaint against Inspector Flint."

A customs officer arrived to ask Polly Lee if she had

anything to declare and then left after getting her to sign a photograph of *Strong Winds* for his collection.

At last they were all gone and Gold Dragon turned back into Granny's sister and invited everyone to come on board, whilst apologising for only having tea to offer them. "With no milk either. I've been out East too long."

She looked round at the darkening marina. "This was a playing field when I was last in England. It was part of the naval training college, HMS *Ganges*. My mother used to walk me down here when we were waiting for Father to come home. Or waiting for the older ones when they were off sailing. We were always waiting for someone ..."

"Is that why you wanted me and Skye to meet you here?"

"Yes. I thought that might make it easier. To have someone waiting for me. Perhaps I was wrong. Do come below. I've plenty of space even if there's nothing to eat."

"May I help?" This was June. "I had time on my hands today so I've made enough supper for everyone. Perhaps the older children could bring it over?"

She nodded to Xanthe and Maggi who turned back towards *Snow Goose* as if this had all been pre-arranged. Anna and Donny went with them. This gave Donny the chance he needed to ask Xanthe the burning question. "What *did* you do to Flint's boat?"

"Me?" Outraged innocence. "You accuse *me*, Donny-man? It was sweet little sis. She decided that her sewing efforts might not be enough to get the message across, so she daubed a big shark's mouth and plenty of teeth on the fat man's bling."

"You'd said his boat reminded you of *Jaws*," said Maggi who didn't seem at all ashamed of what she'd done.

"I take it back. Totally. The comparison's insulting to sharks. We were at the club on Sunday morning, after we got back from Rutland Water, and he made some of his gross comments. Mum thinks that's what upset us. But it wasn't that at all. We didn't care what he said. Mags was simply doing her bit for the Alliance."

"You've all been amazing," said Donny. "And Gold Dragon's amazing too. I just wish my mum was here."

"Ah," said Anna.

"Hmm," said Maggi.

"Mum's the word," said Xanthe, loading him with two extraordinarily heavy cool bags.

CHAPTER TWENTY-THREE
The Word is Mum

Monday, September 25th, later

Supper on board *Strong Winds* was plentiful and increasingly riotous. Rev. Wendy wasn't there and Gerald seemed happy to revert to hearty Boy Scout once again. He made one feeble protest about Vicky's bedtime but was instantly squashed by Luke who declared that they were on an Adventure and Vicky was their Treasure and they couldn't leave her behind Ever because the pirates might come and dig her up.

Great Aunt Ellen seemed immensely pleased by this and invited him and Liam to sit next to her and feel her hook. Then she promised to tell them tremendous tales of villainy from far away in the South China Sea.

"When you all come sailing on board *Strong Winds*," she said, looking round at her cabin-full of children.

"You're a twenty-two gong Tai-coon!" chanted Xanthe and Maggi at once. This was still incomprehensible to Donny and Anna but not to Gold Dragon.

"I'm honoured," she replied. "But that was the real Miss Lee. The Ransome one. The one who owned *Shining Moon*. *Strong Winds* is a sister ship, built slightly later on the same island. I took Miss Lee's name as a tribute. And Polly after my sister Eirene's parrot – for the same reason."

"I'm quite muddled," said Donny. "I didn't really know

Granny had another sister. Apart from you. And I only knew about you when Granny was dead."

"Didn't know about Eirene …? But didn't your mother …? Where *is* your mother, Donny? Didn't she want to meet me?"

"I told you in my letter. She's in Avalon. It's a closed ward in a mental hospital. I need you to get her out."

"No," said a voice from the companion way. It was Joshua Ribiero. "You would need more than that. To obtain the release of a patient for whom compulsory certification papers are in the process of being filed, you need forms abc to xyz as prescribed by the Mental Health Act. You also need a qualified doctor and a Care Plan. Oh, and in addition you need Accommodation that has been checked to the Appropriate Standard by a representative of the local Social Services Directorate. A barrack-room lawyer helps too."

He smiled at June who smiled at all three of the new arrivals.

All three …

It was true. There she was. Skye, his mum, looking terrible – pale, flabby and bewildered – and clinging improbably to Rev. Wendy.

"MUM!!" Donny signed. And he was in her arms.

"Doh … doh." But it wasn't Vicky, it was Skye. And she *did* mean him. "Your birthday. I missed you. Love you so much."

"Love you too, Mum," he signed back, twining her hand with his.

No one else spoke. Anna had turned away and was sobbing helplessly. Maggi had her arms round her and was trying to comfort her without understanding what the trouble was.

"We should go now," said Joshua. "Can you accommodate

your niece tonight, Miss Walker? June and I will be sleeping on our own yacht with the girls. We won't be far away. I signed her release papers. I am a doctor."

Great Aunt Ellen was looking stunned. "What was that you said about Appropriate Accommodation …?" she managed.

Rev. Wendy spoke for the first time. "I'm afraid I may have uttered a falsehood," she said. "The vicarage where John has been looked after is regularly inspected by Social Services because of the children. I allowed the mental health authorities to assume that his mother would be staying there."

Donny gasped. Rev. Wendy bucking procedures?

She heard him. "Yes, John … I mean … Donny, I owe you an apology. I didn't listen when I should have listened. I believed other people when I should have believed you. Can you forgive me?"

She held out her hand. This was unbelievable. Donny shook it rather nervously and did his best to smile. "I nicked your stamps," he said.

Then they were all gone.

Donny had asked whether Anna wanted to stay but she'd shaken her head. Her face was blotched with emotion.

"Thanks, Donny. I'll stick with my lot tonight. You need to be with your mum." She looked hesitantly at Skye. "We'll be round after school tomorrow though. If that's okay?"

Great Aunt Ellen didn't seem so happy now.

Maybe she was tired.

It was dark outside and quiet, though the cranes kept up their ceaseless rattle in the distance. Maybe they should all just go to bed. But they were still sitting in *Strong Wind*'s cabin, looking at each other, not saying much.

"You have to understand why I stayed away," she began at last. She'd lit a single oil lamp, which hung above the varnished table. Its light faded softly into dimness round the cabin's edge.

Donny and Skye were propped together like rescued castaways. Skye was filled with medication and Ellen was finding it hard to get used to her niece's deafness and her few inarticulate noises. Although Donny was signing to Skye as he always did, he didn't think his mum understood anything of where they were or what had happened.

"Edith and I had never got on very well." Ellen didn't look in the least like a marauding Dakotah: she looked elderly now and rather sad. "People used to say we were too alike. I couldn't see it. But we felt the same about the one important thing. We both wanted the baby. Your mother, Skye Walker. The boys were dead and Eirene was gone and we were each desperate to have her."

"But …" said Donny.

"You would have thought we could have shared, wouldn't you? Two childless women, both bereft … But we couldn't."

She was silent for a moment, as if she found her younger self almost too difficult to explain. "It must have been because of what had happened. Our brothers dying like that. Both together. Two official telegrams on the same day. Ned's ship had been torpedoed and Greg had gone after him. Into the Arctic Ocean! Abandoned his ship. He must have been out of his mind. It sent Edith temporarily out of hers. Then there was the Enquiry. Our parents were already dead. Which was probably a mercy."

The lines on her face deepened into waves of old grief. "You don't know what it's like when someone's lost at sea. You have nothing. Nothing to bury, nothing to touch, nothing to weep over. 'No roses on a sailor's grave.'"

Donny began to try to put all this together but Ellen couldn't be stopped. "And then when Eirene went ... Eirene of all people; the one with the dreams, the words – the middle child – when Eirene went, it was probably inevitable that Edith and I would split apart. Too much pain does that to people, you know. It can hold you together but it more likely breaks you.

"The publicity made it so much worse. Greg was quite well known, you see. One of the youngest officers ever to be promoted Captain. His use of asdic technology had been innovative. Possibly the key factor in our struggle against the U-boats. Which made the loss of Ned's ship – excruciating. Though everyone knew sonar was unreliable in the Arctic. Different water densities. Greg must have blamed himself – though no-one at the Enquiry did."

"I'm really sorry, Great Aunt Ellen, but I don't know what you're talking about. At least I'm almost sure I don't ..."

Maggi had fetched his rucksack from the dinghy earlier. He started digging into it. The two plastic bags crackled underneath his hand.

"The only clue Granny gave me after she was dead was this." He pulled out the paperback *Swallows and Amazons*. "But I didn't manage to solve it."

She laughed when she saw it. Not a joyful laugh.

"That book! Of course she would. Did you never wonder how you got your name? Did you never … ask your mother?"

"My mum gave me lots of names – little owlet, Hiawatha, small He-Bear, Doh-Doh – she sort of makes shapes with words. Granny called me John but she never explained why and most people call me Donny. I was quite glad she did, though. Donny Walker works much better in school than Mum's names would have done."

This made her laugh more easily.

"I'd say! Well I'm glad some good came out of it. Walker isn't our name at all. We're called Palmer – which I like much better. It feels more like a traveller's name – a far-flung traveller. Edith made us all change, by deed poll, after the publicity . . . and after the deaths. We copied from *Swallows and Amazons* because the book had meant so much to them as children. Not to me, particularly."

She misunderstood his gasp.

"I did what Edith wanted. She was my older sister. And Reeni said Edith was the person most in need of comfort. She and Greg had been so close. Such a happy childhood. All that sailing. I was too young for most of it but I loved it too. More than Edith ever understood. That was what caused our final quarrel. Eirene had gone and I wanted to take the baby – your mother – to visit a lake. Greg's first dinghy was still there somewhere and I was planning to try to find her. I didn't want to do much: show Skye the water, maybe sit with her in the dinghy. Let her feel the motion.

"But Edith wouldn't have it. She couldn't bear to be near water herself and she couldn't bear for the baby to be there either. She said we were never to take that risk. Skye was never, ever, to be taken on a boat … for as long as she lived."

Ellen glanced across at Skye, as if bewildered by the presence of this big sick woman in her cabin.

"I didn't manage it too well. Edith was having a bad day – a North Wind day – and I knew looking after the baby was difficult; it was amazing that she'd survived at all. I wouldn't have let her get chilled. I just thought she'd like the breeze on her face, maybe the rocking. Then I lost my temper. I said we would be betraying the others if we brought Skye up as a landlubber. We would betray everything that Edith herself had loved: that Greg and Ned had died for. Skye was our only descendant. I said I wouldn't do it. After that, I left."

"Granny must have known best," said Donny, loyally, though in his heart he agreed with Ellen. Baby Skye would have loved those things. "Granny was her mum. She had to make the decisions."

"Edith? Her mother? No, no, no!" said Ellen. "*Edith* wasn't her mother. She was her aunt. The same as me. Skye was Eirene's baby. Not Edith's."

Donny gaped at her. Somehow he knew that she was right.

"Well … wh … what had happened to Eirene then?"

"Oh," said Ellen, "Eirene had gone. She went as soon as the baby was born and named. She knew she could trust us to take care of her. Always. That's why I came as soon as Edith wrote. I wish it had been sooner."

Skye had fallen asleep now, still leaning against Donny and he was leaning against her. The rucksack was underneath: it was difficult to reach his second book. He'd need to tell Joshua that he wouldn't be returning *Sailing* to the club library.

The rich mahogany of *Strong Winds*'s cabin glowed deep and warm. The berths on either side were covered in dark crimson leather. They were hard but there were embroidered cushions and soft colourful blankets which Gold Dragon was tucking round his mother.

She looked peaceful now. In the half-light around the edges of the cabin Donny glimpsed curios – beads and carvings and bamboo scrolls. Though the marina was calm, *Strong Winds* was never entirely still. There was something in the action of the water on the wood that made the boat feel as if she were alive, a large quiet creature holding all of them safe.

Donny noticed bookshelves in the shadows. Tomorrow he'd ask Great Aunt Ellen to explain what she'd meant about Eirene 'going'. But this was the moment to give back her brother Gregory's most treasured possession, salt-stained as it was. He'd have to winkle out that rucksack.

And after that there would be absolutely nothing more that he needed to say or do.

From the Cabin Bookshelf

I've always loved books – and that was how this story began. On board our boat, *Peter Duck*, we have two bookshelves. One has books which almost never change – many of them have been there since my parents owned the boat: the other has newer books. *Sailing*, the book which fell from Gregory Palmer's pocket and which Donny is about to give to Great Aunt Ellen at the end of this story, has been on *Peter Duck's* shelf ever since I can remember. I didn't take much notice of it as a child but as an adult I realised that *Nancy Blackett*, another boat once owned by the writer Arthur Ransome, also had a copy in her cabin. Then I noticed that in Ransome's story *We Didn't Mean to Go to Sea* the hero, John Walker, consults this same book when he is caught in fog in Harwich Harbour. It seemed to cross from the actual world to the world of imagination.

I like the way that books (and boats) can link people together. I never met Arthur Ransome but my parents did and Ransome also knew my uncle who gave me my first copy of the book *Peter Duck*. Reading the book, *Peter Duck*, on board the boat *Peter Duck* led me to read all Ransome's other sailing adventures, beginning with *Swallows and Amazons*. Then, much later, I read some of them to my own children. The stories that were particularly in my mind when I was writing *The Salt-Stained Book* were *We Didn't Mean to Go To Sea* and *Missee Lee*. Both of them feed into Donny's dreams – as *Peter Duck* does in chapter twenty.

I hope that you don't feel that you have to have read *Swallows and Amazons* to enjoy *The Salt-Stained Book*. Think of it as any story that has meant a lot to different people in the same family. In the same way you don't have to have read Robert Louis Stevenson's *Treasure Island* yourself in order to enjoy *Swallows and Amazons* or *Peter Duck*. It's just a book that the characters have read and which gives them exciting ideas or names

– as it does to Donny and Xanthe when they are alongside the mysterious schooner.

Not so many people read *Hiawatha* nowadays though Ransome and Stevenson probably did. Its author, Henry Wadsworth Longfellow, was the most popular American poet of the 19th century and based the poem on actual research. I knew nothing about Native American culture and history when I read *Hiawatha* as a child. I simply loved the words.

There are plenty of modern adventure stories on the cabin bookshelf. A.J.MacKinnon, an Australian teacher had been teaching in Shropshire when he decided to enjoy a couple of weeks sailing in the school's *Mirror* dinghy. Four thousand miles later he and the dinghy arrived in Romania … He's the person June Ribiero mentions in chapter nine. You can read his true story in *The Unlikely Voyage of Jack de Crow*.

With no disrespect to any of the intrepid adventurers above, Richard Woodman has travelled more sea-miles than any of them – and very likely written more words as well. The detailed research that went into *Arctic Convoys 1941-1945* (the book that gave me the idea for my first scene) would be achievement enough for most people, but that, and the five-volume history of the merchant navy, and the fourteen volume 'Nathaniel Drinkwater' series and a host of other titles are merely the second career after thirty seven years at sea. And he still finds time to go scudding around Harwich harbour and off to the Northern seas in his cutter *Andromeda*.

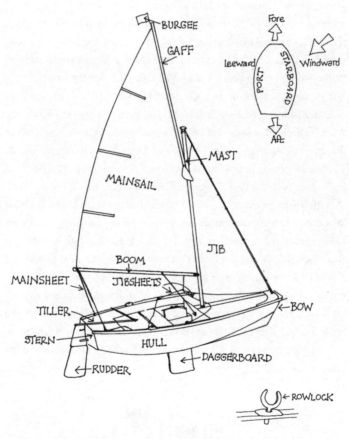

The Parts of a Dinghy.

If your sailing skill is not quite as instinctive as Donny's you'll enjoy Claudia Myatt's RYA handbook *Go Sailing*!

Fingerspelling alphabet

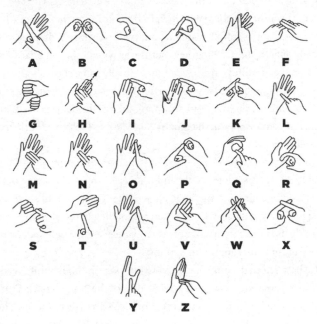

The British fingerspelling alphabet.

Image: Action on Hearing Loss.

For more information visit www.actiononhearingloss.org.uk

My Thanks

The first version of this story was written unobtrusively early one summer while I allowed my nearest and dearest to assume I was still checking footnotes for a PhD thesis. Some of the characters had begun to take shape the previous year when I'd been sitting on the edge of Alton Water reservoir in Suffolk watching our two youngest children learning to sail *Optimist* and *Taz* dinghies. But it was when I was on board *Peter Duck* on the beautiful River Deben that I finally came clean about what I'd been doing and asked my son Bertie, then aged eleven, to have a read. He read intently and without stopping, first in the quarter berth and then, less comfortably, in the dinghy *Karl Marx*, as I rowed us back up to Woodbridge.

This gave me the courage to show the manuscript to my partner, Francis. He too read it in a gulp and has never stopped believing in the story and encouraging me to keep sending it out to publishers and plugging away at the re-writes. When I admit that it has taken five years from the first draft to this final text I'm sure everyone will understand how truly grateful I am for his support.

He hasn't been the only one. David Miller was the book's third reader and then came Nicci Gerrard, Peter Willis (of the *Nancy Blackett* Trust), Richard Woodman, my mother, my brother Ned and niece Ruthie. They have been staunch allies. My son Frank managed the particularly high-risk activity of mixing encouragement and criticisms as we tramped round fields with his oldest daughter Gwenllian and various dogs.

Pippa Thistlethwaite, Anna Bentinck and Arnold Cragg read it aloud to each other beside a log fire one cold New Year and offered useful suggestions. Heidi, Olly and Aidete Carhart let me steal and distort some aspects of their lives; Ann Palmer, a former owner of *Peter Duck*, allowed me to use her family's names; my youngest son, Archie, tried hard not to fidget while I read – which was depressing but salutary. I think he knows who, in the book, he is.

Georgeanna, Ros, Miles, Rhiannon, Patricia and Alice all read and encouraged. Caz Royds, Christina Hardyment and Roger Davies offered perceptive comment and practical help. (Specifically I'm grateful to the Arthur Ransome Literary Executors for permission to quote from *Peter Duck* on page 212.) Veronica Wheen spoke lyrically of the beauty of British Sign Language. Imogen Robertson put me in touch with David Smith who saved the book when it was foundering: Peter Willis introduced me to Claudia Myatt who enhances it. Lesley Simpson stepped in when Roger Davies fell ill. Jan Needle and Maddie Masters gave me wonderful reader responses exactly when they were most needed. I'm also grateful to John Skermer, Mel Howells, Jim Sheehan, Craig Brown, Kate Saunders and Griff Rhys Jones.

Why did I ever call a halt to the re-writes? Because Angus McKinnon finally stepped in and, after three proper editorial readings, said "Full Steam Ahead, Publish and be Damned" – or words to that effect. It was a very good moment – almost as good as that first summer's reading with Bertie on the Deben. After that, I hoped, there would be absolutely nothing more that I needed to say or do.

Except that, if you have enjoyed this story, I hope you'll look out for its next instalment, *A Ravelled Flag*.

Julia Jones, Essex, 2011.

When JULIA JONES was three years old her parents bought Arthur Ransome's yacht, *Peter Duck*. Julia was give the quarter berth where Ransome had stored his typewriter. Boats and books have been part of her life ever since. She has five children, two wonderful daughters-in-law and hasn't totted up the number of grandchildren recently. She and her partner Francis Wheen own *Peter Duck*, *Goldenray* and almost as many dinghies as grandchildren.

JULIA has written and edited biographies but this is her first novel.

CLAUDIA MYATT spends most of her time drawing boats, writing about them or messing about in them – from coracles to tall ships. She has written and illustrated the popular *Go Sailing* series for the RYA and contributes regular cartoons to yachting magazines.